H. Gorlitz Scott

ISBN-10: 1975660773
ISBN-13: 978-1975660772

Cover Illustration and Design by H. Gorlitz Scott, Dragonmun Studios
Editing by Pati Geesey, Geesey Editorial Services

H. Gorlitz Scott
Dragonmun Studios
Sivoa: Sunrise

TABLE OF CONTENTS

CHAPTER ONE

For all of the stars in the sky, he couldn't sleep.

Flag had been sitting in the small antechamber to his room for what felt like an eternity. However long he had been really sitting there was completely unknown to him, for there were no windows to read the sky by and he had given up counting seconds long ago.

The only thing he knew for sure was that his wife, Ta'nia, had gone into labor fairly early into the evening and her attendants had ushered him out because it was considered bad luck to have a man in the birthing chamber – regardless of the fact that it was his room as well.

He had left his book behind in the rush to leave and he wished he had such a distraction on hand – even if he never actually read it. This sitting still, worrying about the situation on the other side of the door, was driving him mad.

At one point, he heard her screaming obscenities at one of the wet nurses and his heart leapt up into his throat. Was she okay? He knew there could be complications during childbirth that could kill the mother. What about the baby?

He ran his hands through his hair and rolled backward to lie on the rough cobblestone floor of the hallway to stare at the contrastingly smooth ceiling above. His lack of sleep must have caught up with him because the next thing he knew, a rather frantic attendant was shaking him awake.

The sorcerer mistook the fear in the way the woman carried herself and he jumped to his feet. "What happened?" he demanded, grabbing her by the shoulders.

The attendant, Ta'mika, winced at his grip, but managed to keep her resolve. "Lady Ta'nia is calling for you."

Flag released his breath for a moment. The fact that his wife had summoned him was enough for him to know she was fine. "And the baby?"

Ta'mika sighed. "You better go in."

Flag shoved past the woman and ran through the entrance to his bedchamber. He tried to stay calm, but the sight of his wife across the room crushed his chest and he fought for air. Ta'nia was only a shade of her former self, frail, and fading faster than the setting suns. In her arms was a small swaddling of cloth that was frighteningly silent.

This vision couldn't be real. He was still asleep in the hallway waiting to be woken up by the good news that preceded a life filled with a happy family. He wasn't losing everything now. It just wasn't possible!

His legs gave out just as he reached the bed and he took his wife's small and impossibly weak hand into his own. Tears that formed beyond his control started to distort her face and that frustrated him, making them form even faster. "Ta'nia..."

She slipped out of his grasp and reached up to touch his face, silencing him before he could unleash a stream of questions at her.

"I'm sorry, Flag." The blur of color that was her face looked down at the bundle lying silent in her arms and he could hear her release the most despairing sigh he had ever heard in his life. "I should have told you before."

He was confused. "Tell me what?"

She barely grazed his lips with her finger to silence him before letting her hand fall back onto the bed. "You know the power of my family lies in the women... This is why."

He was still completely lost, but at least she was becoming more visible as a slight curiosity started to take him over. He remained silent to allow her a chance to explain, but she had trouble finding the words to do so.

"You have to kill me, Flag," she blurted out.

"WHAT?" He shook his head violently against such an idea. "That doesn't make any sense!"

Ta'nia nodded. "I'm dying anyways... If you don't, she will never get the chance to live."

Panic took over again and he could feel his chest heaving with the pounding that was going on inside of it. "I can't do that! I love you!"

"That is why you must carry on my... our legacy." She grabbed his hand and placed it on her chest. "She must inherit my life energy to live."

She became a blur again and his eyes burned the worst they ever had. He wanted to respond, to protest against this, but the words were caught in his throat, forcing him to choke on his own breath. All he could do was shake his head.

He could feel her pulse under his shaking hands and it was fading fast. Everything he had ever loved was being snatched from him and he was powerless against it.

"Please..." she begged, her voice barely a whisper.

Flag shook his head even more. His mind was a reeling jumbled mess of thoughts and emotion. Just as he found his voice to argue, she clenched her hand around his wrist and invoked one of his spells through him.

He felt like someone had clapped their hands over his ears, and he was thrown backward by the transfer of forces. After a long dark moment, he realized he could hear a tiny voice crying persistently.

Flag opened his eyes and slowly focused on a figure standing above him. She was saying something, but he couldn't make it out. As the world faded back in, he realized it was the handmaiden who had woken him earlier.

"You killed her!" she screamed at him, upsetting the baby in her arms even more.

He fought his way into a sitting position to try to correct her but froze when he saw the bed. Ta'nia appeared to be sleeping, but her color was wrong and she was entirely too still. The servant's words were abrasive and he turned to snap at her, only to be greeted with another reason for his heart to stop.

The tiny infant girl had paused long enough in her fit to look at him with glowing green eyes – the same eyes that had haunted his dreams and caused him to wake up screaming on many sleepless nights. Dreams that had eventually forced him to seek counsel with the Orianna years before.

The baby girl cried out again, which forced the motherly instincts of the only woman in the room to try to calm her down. A simple, natural act that dealt a final blow to Flag's emotions and left him completely broken. "Please just take her away," he choked out.

Horrified by the events that had taken place, Ta'mika glared at him and ran out of the room with the child in her arms. She had obviously misinterpreted the situation, but Flag didn't care.

He had lost everything.

CHAPTER TWO

Dragonira kicked a pebble and watched as it skittered across the floor and jumped recklessly into the massive trench that divided the room in two. After what felt like years of waiting, the pebble finally hit the bottom with a loud thunk that resonated off of the dungeon walls.

She flinched at the sound. In her mind it represented those unfortunate enough to have also once called this place "home" and could not tolerate it – choosing to leap to their deaths through the dungeon's only true opening.

Dragonira often wondered if she were the reason they chose to leave, but she could never expand on the concern enough to wonder why this would be. As far as she was aware, she wasn't terribly frightening. She was a short, skinny thing, with long dark hair and bright green eyes. If there was anything negative to say about her appearance, it was that she didn't take particular interest in it and looked generally unkempt. Personality wasn't likely a factor either as she was far more stable than the criminals who were sentenced to share imprisonment with her.

Her mind mulled over the disappearances of her "friends" and regardless of what train of thought she chose to follow, she continuously returned to the notion they somehow knew about her father. While his official title was palace magician, she always felt the term was too simple to explain him correctly. He was frighteningly more than the cheap trickster that it indicated and she often suspected he was the reason people wound up down here to be forgotten by the rest of the world.

Deciding that she was tired of dwelling on the ghosts of the pebble, she made her way toward the giant hole that lit the palace's underground. The cavernous dungeon was built out of the ancient aqueduct system that had been carved into the cliff. This suggested there had once been running water for at least the palace inhabitants. Now there was only a waterwheel and pulley system that brought the life-sustaining liquid up from the floor of the desert ravine. This she could see clearly from the maw of the cavern in which she stood.

"Wouldn't that be something to have now?" she marveled aloud as she studied the trench.

She walked the edge of the empty channel until she reached the rough rocks that must have once supported the rest of it. There she sat down and let her feet dangle out into the hot desert air. Like so many prisoners who lived here before, she had thought of jumping to her impending doom on the rocks below, but could never bring herself to actually do it.

Reorienting to think on the aqueducts, she leaned against the wall and watched in wonder at the waterfall on the other side of the chasm. *Had that once flowed up into the castle? Had it done so by bridge? Why didn't they rebuild the bridge?* These questions were overshadowed by a much larger quandary: "What idiot would think to build a kingdom in the desert, on the wrong side of the ravine?"

Dragonira rolled her eyes and stood up once again so she could lean out and observe the lake far below. Instead of focusing on colors reflected in the cool waters, she noticed the length of the shadows on the cliff face and realized the day was drawing long.

"Shit!" she swore out loud as she dashed back inside. Despite the fact that her father often seemed to prefer she never have existed, he had gone out of his way to make sure she was at least somewhat educated. His lessons were self-centered and often focused on ensuring that she could assist him with his spells and rituals, but she was thankful for the knowledge nevertheless. Unfortunately, she had lost track of the time she had before the lesson scheduled for today.

Her feet thudded on the berm as she charged toward the alcove that shifted the channel upward and carried it into the ceiling. Using the full of her momentum, she rebounded up it and into the tunnel above. She then crawled through the hidden spaces in the walls until she reached the stairs that would bring her home.

Out of breath, she felt that she might have traversed the tunnels fast enough to make up for missed time, but as she pushed open the trap door to his ritual chamber, she found her father waiting for her. He held a scroll that he had mangled by wringing his hands around it and on his face he wore a scowl that could send even a fighting nargazoth crawling back into its hole.

"You're late." His fiery eyes betrayed the coldness of his voice. His anger amplified by their slitted sunset hues.

She attempted to apologize, but she got stuck on the words and fell silent. Saying anything would only serve to anger him further. She wanted to drop back down into the hole she had exited but, afraid of the backlash, she instead climbed up the rest of the stairs and closed the floor door behind her.

He placed the scroll on a shelf and turned his back to her as he grabbed something else off of it. His disposition caused her to worry and she tried to see what it was even though it was impossible through the cascade of silver hair that draped around him.

"Come here."

She hesitated.

"COME HERE!"

The shout jarred her enough to take a couple of steps forward, but she froze again as he turned to watch her. Her reluctance set him off and he lashed out, causing her to stagger backward. Dragonira didn't even realize she had been cut until she looked up to see him holding his ritual dagger and felt the sting of her own blood running into her eyes.

"Be gone from my sight," he commanded in as much disgust as his voice could carry.

Shaking, she obeyed and rushed to her room to hide from his wrath. She jumped for her bed when he slammed the door, but as she heard the lock slide into place, a strange sense of relief washed over her. He was beyond the need to injure her further and would leave her alone for an unknown length of time. After a few moments passed, she thought that perhaps now was when to put in action the escape plan she had been fantasizing about. *But first...*

Dragonira ambled over to her tiny washroom – which had once been a closet – and used a wet rag to tend to the cut on her forehead. She flinched at the initial sting of the water against the shallow wound, but after a moment the pain subsided. Once clean, she inspected it in the broken mirror on the wall. It was far less severe than the blood flow had led her to believe, and she was thankful that it would likely be healed by morning.

As she finished washing up, she allowed her mind to focus on the tiny window that sat near the ceiling above her bed. When she was little, she had thought it was proof the castle her father said they lived in was sinking. Eventually she realized the shifting amounts of dirt covering it had been the work of farmhands.

The memory of this discovery always bothered her. While she remembered seeing them pushing shovels into the ground, she couldn't figure out how she had been able to view them through the window when it was so high up. It was another in a long line of memories that she had forgotten, but it was what fueled her breakout plan.

She dug around underneath her bed until she heard a loud crash outside of her room that caused her to jump to a standing position and hold her breath. After a short while she released it again, having figured out that her father had actually left their apartment and slammed the door behind him.

Not wanting to waste more time, she flipped her mattresses up and fished out the scroll she had been searching for. It contained a simple teleportation spell she had swiped from her father's journal when he had not been looking. It was apparently such a minor thing to him as he never noticed the missing pages. *It'd be nice if he doesn't notice my disappearance either*, she thought as she unrolled them.

It didn't take her long to commit the spell to memory, but she found she was hesitant of activating it without fully knowing where to go. The stable yard seemed the obvious answer, but she wasn't even sure it actually existed as she imagined.

Looking up at the tiny window, she realized she could verify her vision if she could look out it at least once. After taking a moment to calculate how far up the window was, she breathed a voice to the magic controls she learned and was suddenly falling back toward her bed.

In the split second it took for her to realize the spell worked, she was able to glimpse the window flying up past her before she collided with the mattress. With a better idea of how to orient herself for the fall, she tried again and was able to see level ground and a wooden structure through the glass during her descent.

The stable! It was there!

Dragonira jumped off of her bed and danced in a small circle as she tried to figure out what to bring with her. When she heard a door close, she looked at the entrance to her own room and realized she didn't have time to prepare for the outside world anymore. As she heard the lock slide on her door, she repeated the spell and was gone.

CHAPTER THREE

The old warden's office that Flag called home was much like the waterworks cavern in that it was once an open hole in the cliff face. Whether they were chiseled into the rock, or built brick by brick, he would never know, but the rooms he called home wrapped around a piping structure that must have once delivered water into the tower above. A false floor had been built into the large waterway and it now served as his ritual chamber. It was here that the sorcerer should be spell casting within, but the frustration with his daughter sent him outside to the veranda instead - the only "room" that didn't receive an outer wall.

Flag had slammed the door as he stepped out and, naturally, the glass within it had shattered. He swore under his breath as he turned to pick up the pieces.

He was never known for his patience. On the contrary, he was famous for his temper. "The Silver-Haired Scourge" he was called; a man who felled an entire army with a deadly glare from his fiery eyes. This absurd act was supposedly what allowed the once-young Siamera general to become the king of Libris Del Sol.

While it was true that Julian and his subordinates now lived in the kingdom of the infamous desert library, the story was pure exaggeration. Flag's eyes were the color of the sunsets, but he couldn't shoot down anything with them. The truth behind the event was that he had almost killed himself performing a simple lightning spell to take out a few advanced raiders.

He never bothered trying to correct the rumors though. The big benefit of the story was that it had elevated him out of the slave status he had spent most of his life as. It also allowed him the solitude he needed since the passing of his wife – for the most part. He still had to share his life with his only offspring; an insolent brat who had killed her mother in childbirth and was forced upon him later in life.

Flag had made it a point that she knew just how important today's ritual would have been and yet, she blew it off as she had a number of times before. He had locked her in her room as punishment for this, but largely he just didn't want to look at her anymore.

Dragonira was very much like her mother in the way of appearance. They both were small, lithe, and had hair the color of midnight. The biggest difference between them was in their eyes. Ta'nia had calming blue eyes that reminded him of a lake he once found solace in. His daughter's eyes were a haunting green that literally illuminated her disdain for him. They were also the eyes of prophecy.

Shortly before his wedding to Ta'nia, he had suffered from a strange series of dreams in which he would find himself in the middle of a burning city, face to face with an abomination made of black ink. The monster threatened to destroy everything he had loved, and selflessly he would attempt to defeat it using the same set of war-winning spells he had learned from his bride-to-be, who would throw herself in his path so as to protect the demon.

After weeks of being impaled in his nightmares, he sought counsel with the Orianna to find out if they meant anything. To his dismay, she had told him they were signs a loved one was going to betray him in death, and that it would ultimately lead him to his own demise.

On the surface, the realization of this prophecy had been less dramatic than its symbolism played out, but it had destroyed him as promised. Ta'nia's death had left a gaping hole in his heart and caused him to become a bitter shell of himself. Dragonira only served as a reminder of this.

He threw the pieces of glass over the railing and watched them fall as far as his vision would allow. The sun glittering off of the shards awoke a second, older insecurity within him. A feeling of brokenness – a sense that he had once been a part of something larger and majestic. It was a feeling that pursued him his whole life despite his many efforts to write it off as the wistful thinking of a child servant. No. There was more to it, which is why he was so upset when his daughter failed to show up when he needed her.

Frustrated, he dropped into a wicker chair and allowed his eyes to wander around the terrace. Eventually, his gaze landed on a little yellow thistle flower that sat in a jar in a little alcove by the door.

His thoughts shifted back to the day they had discovered the briar patch. The king – with his own young son – had invited Flag and an eight-year-old Dragonira to join them on a day-long survey of the outer wall. The trip was an uneventful inspection for damage that was over much faster than they expected and to kill time, they set up a picnic in the late afternoon shade of the structure. This routine event wouldn't have been of any note had it not been interrupted by Julian's son, Pavlova, screaming for help.

While the adults had been discussing the state of the wall, the two kids had evaded their caretaker to play at the top of a small hill. Dragonira then tripped on a rock and tumbled into a briar patch at its base. A more caring Flag had rushed to make sure his daughter was okay and found that her arm had become entangled in a mass of branches.

That was the first time he noticed the flower; a single dilatory bloomer that Dragonira had bled on. Late as it was, Flag had not expected to see the flower again when he returned many weeks later to eradicate the dangerous plants. Even after he burned the thorny bushes to a crisp, its petals retained all their brilliance. Stunned by this, he kept the flower and made it a point to understand why it would not simply die as the rest of the plant had. Eventually, he developed a theory that it had not been a feature of the flower, but rather a condition belonging to his daughter.

As the years progressed, and they grew increasingly more hostile toward each other, he had many chances to test and prove this theory – none of which Dragonira remembered. A part of him felt that he should regret killing her over and over for his rituals, but she really was doing the kingdom a service as he no longer needed to sacrifice the citizens for his research.

Which is why it was so important that she had been on time!

Flag jumped to his feet with renewed fervor and stomped across the terrace, not caring so much if he broke the door this time. He slammed the locks open on the door to her room and prepared to vent his frustration, but he was greeted with an unexpected sight.

She was gone.

CHAPTER FOUR

Dragonira huddled up against the sand-colored brick in the castle's shadow as the realization of what she had done hit her full force. Panic tried to settle and exhilaration fought to keep it at bay. The swirl of emotions made her dizzy.

She had escaped.

It was such a wondrous and aloof concept all those times she pondered on it in the dungeons, but now that it was a reality, she found it nauseating. *What now?* She had never planned to leave in such a rush and was confronted with the fact that she was lost in a world she didn't know, without the supplies she needed to face it.

A thought of returning home flickered through her mind and she jumped as she realized she was standing next to the window that had brought her to this point. An imagining of her father taking notice of her through it caused her to dart toward the open area in front of the stable, where she crashed into someone who had taken that particular moment to exit the structure.

"Ow! Hey! What the…!" shouted the stranger.

Dragonira had fallen to the ground in the collision and could not place the voice with a face until she rolled over and looked up to see a dashing young man rubbing his shoulder. The thin fur that dusted his skin was pale except for on his arms and around his eyes, where it gradually darkened to a near black that wrapped itself over his long ears and blended with his obsidian hair. His brilliant blue eyes were striking in contrast and she fought desperately with herself not to run away from their gaze when he reached his hand out toward her.

"Calm yourself. I won't hurt you," he said in a tone that did little to hide his own surprise.

Only somewhat assured she accepted his offer and placed a timid hand into his. The light grasp almost caused him to drop her when he tried to pull her to standing, but he brought his other arm around to catch her before she fell.

"What were you running from?" he asked as he released her.

Dragonira could feel her own ears leveling out slightly in embarrassment and she folded her arms in an attempt to comfort herself. "I'd rather not say."

The man in front of her chuckled and shrugged. "Okay then. Do you have a name? I'm Pavlova."

There was something familiar about that name, but she couldn't place what. It felt important and she paused long enough in thought to confuse him. "I know it's silly sounding, but that's the life of a noble. Big houses and silly names," he continued.

That was more than enough of a clue. *Damn it. I found the prince.* She had always just assumed the members of the royal family never left their palatial home above her own, but in hindsight that made little sense. She also should have realized their home included the outdoor area as well.

"It's not any sillier than my name," she responded, trying to sound at least halfway intelligent.

"Which is?" He smiled as he tried to draw the information out of her.

Embarrassed at how she was ruining the conversation, she barely squeaked out an answer. "Dragonira."

"What was that?"

"Sorry. It's Dragonira," she said a bit louder.

The already dark shadow on his face seemed to darken further as he registered it, but then he shrugged. "You win."

Although she had declared it, she still felt vaguely insulted by his curt response and took a step backward to show it. "Excuse me?"

Pavlova held his hand up defensively. "My apologies. You just said that… your name–" He cut himself off. "Would you like me to call you by another?"

"Well…" She had to think about her response. She wanted to end the conversation so that she could continue on with her escape. Unfortunately, she couldn't just abandon the prince without earning a level of suspicion that could land her in trouble. "A nanny once referred to me as Iri. That would suffice."

Liking that answer, he chuckled once again. "Iri it is. Would you like to join me for dinner tonight?"

Dragonira avoided his eyes as she tried to find a distraction that would allow her to turn him down. She didn't want to return to the prison she had just escaped. "I…"

The prince offered his hand out again and smiled insistently. "Consider it repayment for nearly knocking me over."

The logic of this statement escaped her, but she found herself trapped by it. "Fine," she accepted reluctantly.

They had to walk a short distance to reach the nearest entrance to the royal keep. Along the way they ran into a number of people who knew the prince well enough to suspect he was up to something. An older woman hauling a milkmaid's yoke even stated as much when she spied them. "Heckling the queen again, are ye?"

Pavlova smiled and waved to the woman, but he lowered his head and sped up his pace in order to pass her by before Dragonira had a chance to ask about what she said. They continued at this pace until they reached the doors and the prince pawned her off on a uniformed woman who was supposed to help her prepare for the evening.

"I'll see you in a little bit," the prince said as he politely kissed her hand and dashed inside.

Dragonira resembled a statue as she tried to process everything that had just happened. Her bewilderment must have shown on her face because a small voice to her right chimed in.

"He does this fairly often," the attendant said, taking a step forward to establish her presence.

"Does what often?" Dragonira asked before thinking.

"Invite random women to dinner. He even invited me once." The attendant reached for her hand in order to guide her through the palace. "The queen used to harass him to begin courting women and I think he does this to annoy her."

The attendant paused in her stride to look her over. "You appear to be from a different class from the rest of us peasant girls. What part of the city are you from?"

When Dragonira didn't answer, the attendant waved it off with a cheerful "never mind" and led her into a magnificent room adorned with wall-to-wall mirrors and a number of matching armoires. The attendant made her way to one of these and began pulling out dresses. "My name's Kinya, by the way."

"Iri." Dragonira repeated her earlier nickname absently as the grandeur of the room overtook her. She had thought the underground apartment she shared with her father had been sizable, but the dawning realization that this room existed only for one to try on clothes gave her an understanding of the magnificence of the rest of the palace. "Was this always a dressing room?"

Kinya shrugged. "It has been for as long as I've been working here." She then brought an arm load of gowns over and held them up, one by one, against Dragonira.

"Your eyes are extremely green, you know that?" She scoffed as she tossed a copper-colored gown to the floor. "It's almost like they glow. You're not going to match any of these things. Hold on."

The small attendant dropped the rest of the dresses to the ground and went to another closet to inspect its contents. The whole time

Dragonira watched her uncomfortably. *What have I gotten myself into?* She really should have run when she realized she had stumbled into the prince. *But where would I have gone?*

Kinya frowned and pulled out perhaps one of the most elegant garments Dragonira had ever seen. "I hate to put you in black because of your hair, but it's the only thing I can think of that won't clash with the rest of you."

It had a surcoat made of a light yet rich material that swallowed all light that hit it. This was trimmed with a golden embroidery that lined the hems and took her breath away. The gown worn underneath it matched the pattern of the trim, but was white. Dragonira was almost afraid to wear it, but once Kinya was able to convince her to try it on, she didn't want to bother with another dress.

From there, she was thrown into a whirlwind of beautification. Her long, silky hair was brushed back into an ornate clip and then woven into a thick black braid. She had never worn makeup before, but she decided that she didn't like how it weighed. The shoes that went with the dress were their own special form of torture and yet, even though she had gone through the process step for step, she was not prepared for the sight that greeted her in the mirrors when it was over.

Two bright green orbs blinked her confusion back at her. She had seen her reflection an innumerable amount of times in her life, but never had she seen herself like this. She felt that she looked like a painting, someone else's idea of who she was and what she looked like. It felt wrong, but she also kind of liked it.

She unconsciously compared herself to the handmaiden in the mirror, remembering what Kinya had said about going through this herself, and wondered if she had felt this awkward then. The woman seemed like she would be more suited to the affairs of high society, but the job she held and her peasant comment earlier suggested otherwise.

Kinya once again picked up on her thoughts and smiled warmly. "Don't worry about me. Go have fun tonight. Who knows, maybe something will come from it."

Dragonira nodded but couldn't shake the anxiety that had settled in her stomach. "Do you know how long this will take?"

The handmaiden shrugged and shook her head. "There's no telling. I was unfortunate and was only there for a couple of hours."

A couple of hours! Dragonira's mind reeled. She was accustomed to meals being a quick ordeal that ended as soon as the plate was cleared. What could possibly cause a dinner to last a couple of hours?

She received her answer shortly after she was ushered to the dining hall. There must have been nearly a hundred people present, and most of them were nobles from other kingdoms who had come to utilize the vast resources of the library. Others were high-ranking castle staff and if any of them used this as an opportunity to speak to the prince, she could see this night dragging out. Dragonira was not prepared for this.

Gossip amongst the upper class of Libris Del Sol started to run rampant as soon as Pavlova – cleaned up from his venture to the stables and dressed in robes that highlighted his royal status – approached her and led her to her seat. Some of what the nobles said corroborated what Kinya and the elder woman outside had alluded to; that she was just one in a line of women who temporarily caught the prince's eye. Another annoyance that displaced the traditional seating arrangement to upset the queen. She also learned that the king was unusually late for the dinner, which meant they couldn't yet begin to eat. Despite how the first few bits of gossip made her feel about herself, the later bit of news was the hardest because of something else she had figured out for herself.

The seating arrangements were, in fact, very specific. At the head of the table sat the king and queen, with the queen to the king's right. The first seat to the queen's right was where Pavlova sat and because Dragonira was his guest, she sat in the seat next to him. The queen's lady in waiting sat next to her and a few cousins after that. This was okay. It was the other side of the table that concerned her.

To the king's left sat his mother (Pavlova's grandmother). Next to her, and directly across from where Dragonira sat, was an empty seat. Beside that sat a gentleman who had been introduced as Jinto, the head of the king's guard. To his left sat the head of the waterworks, followed by an ongoing set of palace officials and their wives or children. It was the empty seat that concerned her.

"That's where my father's adviser sits," Pavlova explained when he caught her staring at it. "He usually skips eating with us, but nobody ever takes his seat when he's absent."

"Why is that?" she asked, dreading the words she knew would come next.

"Superstitious, I guess. He's also the royal sorcerer." The prince laughed. "Perhaps they think he'll curse them or something."

They're right, Dragonira thought as she grabbed her glass and gulped down a bit of its contents. At least they didn't have to wait on the king to drink.

This small action sent the gossip on a tangent. Although they thought they were being quiet, the nobles suspected she had a connection to the missing adviser. "Maybe he cursed her," she overheard one woman say to another before tying the theory to her appearance. The comments only grew more ridiculous from there and Dragonira fought to keep from sliding under the table in embarrassment.

"By the suns, if it isn't little Dragonira!" came a thunderous proclamation that immediately silenced the hall.

Every single eye in the room was on her now as Pavlova's father sat in his seat and leaned forward to greet her. "How long have you been back?"

"Been back?" She stammered an echo, having absolutely no idea what his majesty was referring to.

The king smiled, then gave his son a nod of approval before addressing her again. "Flag said he sent you off to train under the

Orianna. Am I to assume your training is now over?"

What are you talking about? Dragonira merely nodded and glanced at Pavlova for help, but found none as he too was directing his confusion toward his father. After a moment, he glanced at her and finally felt the need to speak. "Father, you know this woman?"

The king's smile broadened. "Of course I do! She's Flag's daughter. You two used to play together as kids."

If the room was quiet before, it was deathly so now. The king, however, didn't notice as he continued the conversation with his son. "Where did you meet her?"

"Outside the stables, but I–"

"Oh! So you just got back!" The king turned to address a doorman. "Ferris! Go fetch my magician! I'm sure he would like to know his daughter has returned!"

The room was still quiet at the time of the king's request, but it wasn't long before she was once again the central topic of shallow conversations. She tried not to fidget every time her father was brought up, and wound up just poking at the food on her plate, no longer hungry for any of the delicacies placed before her. Eventually, her nervousness caught the attention of her escort.

"Are you okay?" Pavlova asked.

Dragonira's attention snapped back to the prince and she forced a weak shrug. "I guess." She fought to add onto the statement and wound up using the king's previous excuse as a scapegoat. "It has just been so long."

The prince looked her over and then nodded in an almost equally unsure manner. "Ah. Okay. Well, hopefully the servant will be able to find him soon."

She wanted to tell him that her father's presence was the last thing she wanted, but it was already too late. What she really wanted was another chance to escape, which the king seemed determined to prevent.

"So, darling. Are you as gifted in prestidigitation as your father is?"

"Presti-what?" the prince interrupted, unknowingly asking her question for her.

"You know, magic. Sorcery. Fortune-telling. That stuff."

How was she supposed to answer that? She was often the focus of his spells and, even more frequently, the reason that the spells they did together worked. However, she had never really been privileged enough to see what he did on his own and there was no way she would know what services he performed for the royals. She answered the best way she could. She shrugged.

The king leaned forward. "You can do magic, yes?"

"Yesss..." She looked him in his sky-blue eyes cautiously. He was wearing an odd expression and it unsettled her. Did he want her to cast a spell now? She would never find out what the king was trying to insinuate for the room fell into a dead silence.

Her father had arrived.

With her heart in her throat, Dragonira watched as he nodded his courtesies to the guards, the guests, and then the king. Once he was seated he shot her the most sincere smile she had ever seen, and said, "I am glad to see you are home."

The play he put on had her so dumbfounded it took entirely too long for her to realize she ought to say something back. The glare in his eyes ended up serving as the reminder and she tried to match his false sentiment. "I am glad to be back."

"What a grand reunion!" The king had gotten out of his seat and placed a hand on his magician's shoulder while raising a glass in her direction. "Let us dedicate this dinner in honor of this event!"

There was a loud cheer as the other guests raised their glasses in unison and drank. Following this, the second course was brought out and it occurred to Dragonira that she had missed the start of the dinner completely.

I am terrible at this, she thought as she looked the gathering over for the millionth time. Had she a chance to do this night again, she would have run away from the prince after knocking him over. She glanced over at Pavlova and found him staring.

As if he had taken note of her distress, he sat up and loudly asked if she had been to the library. When she shook her head no, he turned his attention toward his father. "Would it be okay if I show it to her?"

There was some hesitation on the sorcerer's part, but they were granted permission to leave. Once the doors of the grand hall closed behind them, she faced the prince and let out the biggest sigh of relief. "You do not know the service you have done me. I am in your debt."

He raised an eyebrow and nodded. "Then come. You can explain it to me there."

* * *

The library was massive. A segmented triple helix that reached up into infinity and pierced the sky with its translucent glass and metal. Ivory and gold, the library practically glowed from the soft light that filtered in through the top.

Each level was a rounded shelf circling the inside of the spire's outer wall. On these shelves were innumerable sets of bookcases that radiated outward from the spire's open center. Every floor was dotted with three equidistant and round platforms that jutted out into the void. These balconies were connected from level to level by three golden rails that spiraled upward and out of sight through the center of the tower, but they did not provide a means of travel. In fact, it looked impossible to reach the other floors.

Dragonira stepped out onto the nearest balcony and leaned on the glass railing that lined it. When she looked down, she could see the massive round desk the librarians used as their base of operations on the ground floor, three levels down. When she looked up, she was hit with such a sense of vertigo that she had to balance herself on one of the plush chairs that had been placed for readers.

"Yeah, I was going to suggest not doing that," Pavlova said as he sauntered over to her. "Even without all the spirals and circles, its height is dizzying."

She lowered her gaze to watch him speak and nodded. She was able to regain her composure by the time he had finished. Standing straight, she realized a detail was missing from her memory of the view. "How do we get to the other levels?"

The prince smiled as he moved around her and placed his hand on an engraving in the railing. "We get help."

The etching lit up when he touched it and within moments the air next to him shimmered and faded to reveal a tall woman dressed in a plain white kaftan. "Greetings, prince. What floor?"

The sorcerer's daughter recognized a teleportation spell when she saw one, but to have it executed so flawlessly as to not be affected by the displacement afterward was astonishing. "How did–"

"The librarians of Libris Del Sol are special," Pavlova interrupted. "I'm not part of the order, so I don't know the details, but they can just… do that, and without incantation or recoil! They can also bring others with them when they do so."

Dragonira was struck speechless as she recalled her attempts at something similar earlier in the day. Her spell casting was so clumsy in comparison to the exit she just witnessed. While her spell fizzled and popped, the librarian's was an exercise in grace. She had to see more.

"Floor nine and five, where the books on flying are." The prince took her hand and nodded reassuringly as he held his other hand out for the librarian to take. In the blink of an eye, they were standing at the end of a long row of shelves. Much to Dragonira's disappointment, their escort was nowhere to be seen.

"Wait," she interjected before he could take control over the conversation again. "Where did she go?"

The prince shrugged apologetically. "I'm afraid that I don't know for sure. We are not the only people in the library who need her services."

"Soooo…" she blinked at him, "you are saying she cannot only carry us here, but she does not have to drop the spell and recast it to go elsewhere?"

Pavlova looked at her uneasily and she felt bad for assuming he knew significantly more about spell casting than he obviously did. "I apologize. That was just… fascinating to me."

"Would you like to see something I find fascinating?" He took her hand and guided her down the row, away from the center of the spire. At the end of the bookcases there was a large balistraria-style window that he directed her toward. The view through it overlooked the entire kingdom from a little bit above the palace wall. To the right she could see the southwestern tower that her father's apartment was buried beneath. Beyond that was the curtain wall, with a marketplace at its base. Just over the barrier, she could see the village. A large vacant area separated the townsfolk from the massive outer wall that protected the kingdom from the desert winds. Dragonira assumed this was filled with smaller structures that she couldn't see from their current angle. It was beautiful and she found she wanted to view it from a greater height.

"Quite a sight, is it not?" Pavlova leaned on the wall at the window's edge. "You can see the parts of the kingdom that matter from here. Any higher up and you're disconnected, superior. Any lower and you're buried by it."

Having spent all her life underneath it, she didn't really understand the first part of his sentiment, but she didn't want to question it. "That is an interesting perspective."

Pavlova's smile faded a little and he left the window. "You still owe me an explanation."

"I know, and I'm sorry, but I don't feel like this is the best place to discuss it."

"Because it's public?"

She nodded.

"I can understand that. What I want to talk to you about is fairly sensitive as well."

"Pardon?"

"You were never at the Orianna's, were you?"

She gaped at him. "Was I so obvious?"

"Perhaps not to the others, but they didn't find you hiding out behind the stables." He shook his head. "I spend pretty much every morning tending to the taratins and there were no new ones checked in. There's no way that you arrived recently without one."

"I could have teleported."

"Not unless you're a librarian. Nobody else can do that," he retorted.

She dropped her gaze and looked out the window again in an attempt to avoid his eyes. "Doesn't matter. You already know the story told at dinner was not the truth."

"What were you doing by the stables?"

She glanced around and lowered her voice, half out of embarrassment and half from not wanting to be overheard by anyone who could report to her father.

"I was trying to escape."

"You were planning to steal a mount?"

"No." She shook her head. "I didn't really have much of a plan."

He looked at her warily and for long enough that she became

uncomfortable.

"What?"

"You were acting rather suspicious back there."

"Excuse me? I was trying to leave the very same people who you sat me at a table with. How was I supposed to act?"

He shrugged and let out his breath. "I suppose my father's paranoia is rubbing off on me. Normally he's the one watching for nervous twitches and the like when someone's in his presence, but he seemed rather happy to see you."

"Yeah, that threw me off, too. Why would he be watching for twitches?"

"Oh. Well, because he actually has quite a number of enemies and he worries they might use me to get to him. Nobody I've brought to the table has meant us any harm though."

She blinked at him. "Why would anyone wish him harm?"

"You do know he didn't inherit the kingdom, right?"

She nodded. Although she hadn't talked to her father much over her lifetime, she had learned he had been in military service to King Julian when he overthrew the tyrant king and took over his reign.

"Well, there are still some people who secretly support the previous king and even more who are afraid of your father."

She shot him a look. "You say that, and you still think my behavior at dinner was unfounded?"

He laughed. "You're right. Sorry."

"You're forgiven." She paused. "I still mean to leave."

He shook his head. "After my father's outburst back there, you won't be able to get very far."

She raised an eyebrow. "And why not?"

"I'm sure you noticed they like to talk. By morning you'll be recognized the second you step foot in the city."

"Is that bad?"

"You'd have to suffer more awkward situations like tonight, or worse… your father's enemies would find you."

"If he's so hated, why do you keep him around?"

The prince shrugged. "To be honest, I don't see anything in him that the rumors suggest. He's been a perfect gentleman with my family and a wonderful mentor for my father."

Dragonira gawked at him, completely taken aback. She had spent her life either hiding from her father or obeying his every command to avoid his wrath. She discovered she was jealous of the prince for being able to say such kind things about someone who had been so horrific to her.

The prince noticed her reaction and his own internal conflict showed on his face. "Is he really that bad?"

"I can't go back there," she responded quietly.

He placed his hands sympathetically on her shoulders and pushed her back so he could look at her with sincerity. "I'll see what I can do, but you might have to spend at least one more night with him. You could survive that, right?"

Her heart sank and she slumped against the wall. "I don't–"

"I'll send a messenger with you to explain to him that we have plans in the morning."

Dragonira looked up at him. "We do?"

He shrugged. "We do now. Meet me here and we'll come up with something."

"That… just might work." She nodded. Her father absolutely had to obey the royal family, which meant Pavlova's half-baked plan might actually ensure that he'd let her leave the apartment again. "Okay. Let's do that."

With the serious talk over, the prince felt obligated to show her around the library. While much of it looked the same, she was please to discover that many alcoves and spaces hidden amongst the shelves were converted to house a wide range of activities. On the thirty-fifth floor, there was a ring of stools and tables where kids were busy painting each other while a single instructor tried to keep up with their antics. On the forty-second floor they found an enclosed study occupied by a bunch of elderly scholars shouting at each other. Although they couldn't hear them through the glass, they could see they were vehement.

"No doubt they're in a heated debate about life, the universe, and everything," Pavlova quipped, and rolled his eyes.

Dragonira chuckled and they moved on to the top floor, which was the only one housed within the spire's glass dome. Unlike all of the levels below, this one had no hollow point. The clear floor upon which they stood spread all the way across the library, and the view through it was just as vertigo inducing as looking up from the bottom had been. She made a point not to look down, which wasn't hard for the view outward was breathtaking.

From this high up, the desert had the appearance of a great golden ocean frozen in time. As the three suns began to set, the waves shifted from yellow and orange hues to deep purples and blues. The sky matched them for a brief while, but as the morning sun kissed the horizon, the clouds caught fire. This was amplified as the second sun – the brightest sun – followed. It wasn't until the third star of the asterism set that the sky opened up to the moons and stars. Dragonira could have stayed in the library forever, but once the suns were gone, they were called away to rejoin the nobility in the dining hall.

CHAPTER FIVE

"Stupid pompous jerks," Tom muttered under his breath as he gazed through his binoculars. "I mean, look at them! Eating their full-course meals without even so much as a thanks to the hard workers who put it there!"

"What are you going on about now?" came an unexpected voice from below.

Tom rolled so that he was on his back, supported by the large branch he had perched on, and peered down to see who had spoken. Upside-down and below him was a redundantly spectacled man who was standing chest-deep in the grass bushes that lined the desert's only river.

"Oh, hey Eric. What do you think?! Those palace morons have my little sister trapped, waiting on them hand and foot!"

"You don't have a sister," the much older Sivoan replied flatly.

"Fine. My girlfriend then!" Tom retorted.

"Does Kinya know about that?" Eric stated as he readjusted the string that held his long hair back.

Tom threw his binoculars and sneered down at him in annoyance. "It doesn't matter. I still can't stand royalty." He paused. "Can you bring those back?"

Eric looked at the field glasses at his feet and shook his head. "You should really be more careful with this thing. I doubt the Earthers would give you another one."

"Shut up."

"Fine, then I'll keep it." Eric snickered as he picked up the discarded object and placed it in his rucksack. He then grabbed a branch and hoisted himself up next to the fired-up calico nut-case, who nearly knocked him out of the tree when he dove into his bag after the binoculars.

"Seriously, you should treat your stuff–"

"Who is that?!" Tom interrupted his lecture and pointed across the ravine.

"I wouldn't know. I can't see into the palace like you can," Eric retorted, a little upset that he couldn't get his point across.

"Here, look! The chick walking to the library with the prince."

Eric took the powerful lenses from Tom and glanced through them. He saw the couple crossing the sky bridge that connected the spire of learning with the royal keep, but he couldn't figure out why the girl was a "chick" or what that entailed.

Perhaps Tom's biggest problem was that he was often hard to understand. Years ago, he had stumbled upon the Earthers when he ran away from an entertainment caravan and into the large oasis that lined the southern edge of the ravine. Although it was supposedly against the hidden intruders' code, they adopted him into their small colony. Eventually, they learned each other's languages, which unfortunately meant the young calico's speech had turned into a hybrid mess of Ogaitian and Earthling.

It had its function as well. Tom's bi-lingual abilities worked in favor for the future liberators of Libris Del Sol since they now held their important meetings in a language that could not be found anywhere else on their planet. This meant that if anyone in support of Julian the Drunk were to listen in, they would not be able to learn anything important.

He would have asked Tom to clarify his means of address, but the girl in question turned around to face the window as though she knew she was being watched. Eric caught a glimpse of her frighteningly green eyes before wrenching the binoculars away from his face.

"What?"

"She looked at me," Eric replied.

"Who is she?"

The older man paused before handing the tubular lenses back to his friend. "I think she may be the sorcerer's daughter."

If Eric had a continuance of that thought, he never knew because Tom jumped up to stand on the branch, causing it to sway with his irritation. "What the fuck!" he shouted in the general direction of the palace.

"Calm down."

"You trying to tell me that THAT asshole is able to score a lay whenever he wants and I CAN'T!"

"No, I... what?" Eric floundered.

"Judging from the way she looks, her mom MUST be a piece of ass!"

Eric waited for Tom to finish his rant and quiet down before speaking. He couldn't understand the boy anymore as he slipped into a dialect he doubted even the Earthers knew. After several minutes had gone by, Eric decided to take a gamble on what his friend was complaining about. "It's common knowledge around the castle that his wife is dead."

Tom stared at him blankly. "And?"

Eric sighed. "He probably hasn't 'gotten laid' once since then."

Tom stopped to stare at him. A small smile soon spread across his face and the resulting grin sent shivers down Eric's spine. "What are you thinking?"

"Think she'd like me?"

Eric's hand met his forehead so fast that he nearly knocked

himself over. "Considering who her father is, I would strongly advise against that."

Tom lowered the binoculars and glared at him before dropping into a deadpan stare. "I was joking, you dumb fuck. No girl, no matter who she is or how well she performed in bed, would be worth that."

Eric blinked at Tom as his mind blanked and he turned his attention toward the river. No matter how hard he tried, he couldn't read the kid and it was annoying. "Yeah... okay. Come on. There's a meeting tonight."

"How come you know so much about people there?" Tom asked, causing Eric to pause.

The older Sivoan gestured across the ravine to the centuries old castle standing on one of its many cliff faces. "I work there, you idiot. Did you forget?"

"Doing what? The girls say they never see you there."

Eric sighed and started down the tree. "I take food and water to the prisoners in the dungeons. They work in the upper levels. It's natural that they never see me."

Tom raised an eyebrow at that and finally started following his friend down the tree and onto the path to the rebel camp. "Can you get anyone out?"

Eric just shook his head.

"Have you ever seen him?"

There was a jump in thought Eric had missed. "Seen who?"

Tom had taken on a giddy tone similar to that of a kid wanting to hear more bedtime stories. "You know! The Silver-Haired Scourge? The Flag of Death! The–"

"Yes. I've seen him," Eric said gruffly, rolling his eyes.

"And?" Tom asked excitedly.

Eric remained quiet in an attempt to shrug off the calico's enthusiasm.

"AND?"

Eric stopped so suddenly in his frustration that Tom almost crashed into him. "He frightens me, so I keep my distance. Now stop this inane babbling and let's go."

Tom gave up the fight and obediently followed Eric to the clearing at the river's edge. There they were greeted by a raised platform that led to two ropes stretched across the river.

"Ugh. Can't we just build a real bridge?" Tom voiced his complaint.

Eric shifted his bag so that it sat on his lower back before grabbing the top rope. He then placed one foot on the bottom one to gain a feel for it. "You know we cannot. If scouts were to come up from the ravine, we would need to be able to quickly prevent them from crossing."

"If they can teleport, it wouldn't matter anyway."

Although Eric hated to admit it, the calico had a point. While those with such powers were usually reserved for work in the library, it wasn't unheard of for the librarians to take up soldiering roles. This occurrence was very rare; happening only when the library spire itself was perceived to be in danger, but there were always exceptions. "If nothing else, this is hard to spot."

Tom, who was now concentrating on carefully walking down the single-rope bridge, merely nodded.

The last time the world saw militant librarians was when the wandering nomads of the oasis convinced the kingdom of Lieron to protect them from the tyrant king almost two decades before. The now-nameless ruler of the library kingdom had sought to burn the oasis as his mind turned mad, and the desperate Siamera tribes retaliated by sending a call for help in all directions.

When the northern country came to their aid, they started in with siege weapons and wall breakers, which the librarians saw as a danger to their spire. Within the span of a couple hours, all of the catapults, battering rams, and ballistae were nothing more than a fractured mess at the bottom of the ravine. Eric shuddered as he recalled the memory of that extremely one-sided battle.

Thankfully, the librarians had removed themselves from the war after that. The Siameras had continued their campaign against the tyrant's kingdom and eventually succeeded in placing the current drunkard on the throne. Although the rebels had grown to hate Julian, they could hardly fault the nomads for their choice in ruler. He had started off decent enough. It had been he who the tribes had sent north to seek the help of the Milmordas. He won over Lieron's ruling family and they agreed to help as long as he oversaw the military campaign himself. They then sent him back to the library kingdom with a troop consisting of their own nomadic tribe – the Cafras.

Another caveat in this arrangement was that Julian took over rule of the library kingdom and marry the Lieronese princess when he did. This gave the Milmordas power, in a remote capacity, over one of the most sought-after kingdoms in the world. Even with his own opinions on the drunken lord, Eric didn't like the fact that Julian was a puppet to another land.

Frowning, he joined Tom in the hand-over-hand shuffle across the river. Eric and Tom jumped from the precarious "bridge" and wound their way up the hidden paths toward a group of tents similar to those the nomads lived in. Once within the camp, they made their way toward the centralized food tent, and stumbled upon Bik – a natural human, born on Sivoa – waving his arms around in frustration.

"It is impossible to shoot them from here!" The lanky archer slammed his hand on the table that sat between the group's leaders and himself. "Can't you just ask them to give us something with more range?"

Ka'say ran a hand through his fiery red hair and flicked his tail in annoyance. "No. It would be against the Earthers' code and you know it."

"But this affects them too!"

Ka'say's twin brother, Ka'ren, jumped in before his brother unloaded on the stubborn man. "Actually, no. It does not. They can leave whenever they want."

Bik lowered his voice to a grumble before continuing. "If we had something more than arrows, we'd be able to pick off the royals from across the ravine. I cannot understand why you are fighting me on this."

"Do you not remember what happened the last time projectiles were launched at the palace?" Eric stepped in and placed a calming hand on the archer's shoulder. "We wouldn't want that again, would we?"

Bik was too young to remember the event, but he had been taught some of the kingdom's history. After several moments' pause, he figured out what Eric was alluding to and resigned himself to the fact he had lost the argument before excusing himself from the tent.

"Thank you," one of the twins addressed Eric as soon as the archer was out of earshot. "I understand his enthusiasm, but I do wish that he would stop with his wild plans for a while."

"He should remember his position here. We already have a tactician," the other twin spoke up as he emphasized Eric's role within the rebellion. "Bik should be training the others to shoot arrows."

Tom stepped up then and called attention to the reason for his arrival. "Eric said there was a meeting?"

One of the twins nodded and then Ka'say lead them through the food tent, to a smaller fabric structure on the other side of the clearing. Unlike their previous shelter from the suns, this one was closed in on all sides and guarded. They pushed aside the tent flaps and sat on the carpet that served as its floor.

The older Sivoan reached into his satchel and pulled out a few rolled up sheets of paper as the others situated themselves around him. Tom sat to his left, while the twins sat across from him and to his right. As he smoothed the maps out, he couldn't help but feel a level of respect for the rebel leaders.

Ka'say and Ka'ren Wiltafoir had lived with a third brother in Libris Del Sol since the time of the tyrant king, whom their family had actually sided with in the previous war. When their kingdom fell, they were thrown into the dungeons and subsequently experimented on by the sorcerer. They survived, but their identical brother Ka'lee had not. Eric never asked them for the details.

"Are these not lining up?" Ka'ren asked as he turned some of the pages to try to make more sense of them.

"Unfortunately, they don't, but that might not be a bad thing." Eric chose his tones carefully, not wanting to disappoint anyone with the veiled news. But before he could speak Ka'say caught onto what they were talking about and frowned. "I thought the ladies said that the maps were done."

Eric nodded. "They are. The levels are not lining up because passages have been closed off or changed into other spaces over the years. There may even be secret passages that we can make use of."

The room had grown quiet as they eyeballed the papers, silently hoping to find the palace's secrets within the hand-drawn lines. Eventually, they all came to the realization further exploration was required and that was discouraging.

Only a select few were allowed in every part of the palace, and the majority of them had been brought in from Lieron. It had taken years for the few ladies they had to first get accepted into the stewardship and then carefully pace out these maps in secret.

"So, how do we find out if these exist?" Tom broke the silence.

Eric glanced at him and then turned an inquisitive eye toward the twins. "We may have to ask the girls to do a bit more."

Ka'say nodded and Ka'ren shook his head. "They aren't going to like that."

"True, but what other choice do we have? They already know how to sneak about to gather information. Nobody is more qualified," the eldest Wiltafoir told his brother.

"The girls are going to need coordination," Ka'ren fired back. "This will make them much more vulnerable, yes, but we can't rely on their information otherwise."

"What about Ta'mika?" Tom suggested.

"Won't work. She resigned from the palace," Eric reminded the young calico, whom he suspected brought up her name only as an excuse to later harass her for food.

"Damn. Do we have anyone else who can get past the iron gates?"

They all looked at Eric who stared back blankly until he realized he was silently being volunteered. "Whoah-ho. No. I can't do it. I only have access to the lower levels and it would look suspicious if they were to come visit me. It's bad enough that they have to relay packages to me through the market."

Their stares continued, but shifted in meaning as Eric's method of communication became clear. Like Tom, they had assumed he had direct contact with their spies. Instead, messages were sent via a complicated hand-over game that started with the drudges and moved through the knowing members of the kitchen staff, on to the errand boys, and then through the marketplace, to Eric. While they could ask him to try to expand his reach beyond this, his being caught would be a devastating blow to their organization.

"Let's send Bik!" Tom joked.

It was his turn to receive stares and he melted underneath them. "I was just kidding."

Rolling his eyes, Ka'say spoke. "While I would love to give him something to do, we can't afford to give him the chance to launch a doomed assassination attempt. I'd rather have you go instead, but–"

"Wait. Why couldn't he go?" Ka'ren turned to his brother. "I know his appearance is unusual, but we could disguise him as well as we would anyone else."

Eric raised an eyebrow at the suggestion. "How would that work? He doesn't even live on that side of the ravine, let alone work in the palace."

Ka'ren smiled. "I have an idea. Just leave it to me."

CHAPTER SIX

Even though she was armed with a message, a messenger, and a plan, she immediately regretted ever having left Pavlova's side. While her father may have put on a convincing act for the royals, Dragonira knew he would be angry over her disobedience. She took a deep breath in an attempt to alleviate the tension in her chest, but she was still afraid of what he might do.

They turned the corner at the base of the stairs and the presence of a young boy interrupted Dragonira's thoughts. He was sitting against the wall, staring dejectedly at his feet. Faded fuchsia hair fell in front of his face, so Dragonira could not see his eyes, but it did part nicely around his almost-oversized ears. They were of the brightest white that she had ever seen. In fact, all of his fur was like that and should have clashed with the dingy and dark walls of the dungeon, but somehow didn't. It was as though he were a relief sculpted on the wall. He belonged there.

She expected her escort to stop and say something to the boy, but he kept walking as though he didn't even notice someone else in the hallway with them. He just continued on and she had no choice but to follow, leaving the mystery behind.

Dragonira wasn't exactly sure what to expect once she arrived at the apartment, but it was certainly not what she got. Her father was running all over his study like a lunatic. Picking things up, putting them down somewhere else, as well as a number of other things she couldn't fully comprehend.

She was about to ignore this and head to her room to ponder on the strange sight in the hallway when he spotted her. After casting a dirty glance her way, he noticed her escort who then, before departing, relayed the message about her morning meeting with the prince. She attempted to retreat to her room, but her father leveled a finger at her. "No! You stay there!"

She froze, watching as he tore up their apartment in his search for something. Eventually, she realized he was looking for multiple somethings and that they had one thing in common; they were components for a spell – a big one.

When he finally finished gathering his supplies, he returned his attention to her, noting the borrowed gown she wore. "Get undressed. Meet me at the circle."

With that, he shoved aside the bookshelf that obscured the entrance to the ritual chamber and disappeared, taking whatever hope Dragonira had for the evening with him. She glanced at the door and considered running away again, but decided against it in fear that the effort would undo whatever plans Pavlova had for getting her out of there permanently. She resigned herself to assisting with the ritual. After all, he was ordered to make sure she was able to meet with the prince. How badly could he hurt her? Worried about the details of the spell, she secretly cast a numbing charm on herself and left her borrowed dress on the desk in the foyer.

The chamber was cylindrical in design, with only one visible entrance way. The floor was composed of the same large brick slabs that the rest of castle shared, but was painted. Done in dried blood was a diagram comprised of a large circle touching three smaller circles, which sat equidistant from each other. This was all enclosed by one more, even larger, circle.

When her father noticed her enter the room, he grabbed her arm and practically flung her into the center of the blood drawing. Then he reached into the pockets of his robe and produced three large oligoclase gemstones of different colors.

She could feel the energy of the spell course beneath her feet as she watched her father pace the diagram, pausing at each circle to place a stone within it. As he rounded the last circle, the energy intensified and lifted her into the air, startling her. She looked at him, panic written all over her face, but as he returned her gaze she suddenly felt faint. Within seconds, her vision blurred and darkness overcame her.

Flag watched his daughter intently to make sure the sleep spell he cast had taken hold. When he was certain it had, he pulled a triangular golden amulet from his pocket. Within it, sat four oversized diamonds arranged in a manner similar to the circles on the floor. The largest stone sat in the middle, while the smaller ones, all identical in size, sat on the points. It was one of his greatest achievements. A simple piece of jewelry that kept record of every spell he cast and, in some cases, allowed him to perform without ritual. Most importantly, it allowed him to tap into extreme energies without backlash.

Often referred to as "recoil," magic always came at a price. The payment for power was often random, and in Flag's experience, painful and steep. The spells that he cast when he served in Julian's army would leave him incapacitated for days. Considering the intensity of some of those spells, he was lucky the recoil hadn't killed him. Back then he didn't have time, or even the wherewithal, to prepare payment in advance. Now he was more cunning.

His rituals over the past decade had grown more complex and were highly experimental. Preparing payment for them was practically impossible, so he had to seek out a means to offset his debt – indefinitely. This was no easy task. Research showed that some paid more for power than others because they were less naturally attuned to the sources. Flag wasn't tuned into anything outside of his own wonder, so he had to pay heavily. His daughter, on the other hand, didn't have to offer anything at all.

He noticed pretty early into her training that she was able to do small spells with no effort or consequence. This continued even when they moved onto more complex works and rather than let it annoy him, he decided to try to take advantage of it.

At first, he did so directly by having her do all the conjuring, but as she grew more and more insolent, this chore fell back on him. Eventually, he formed the idea to overlap her presence onto the tools he used and, with her unwilling assistance, the amulet was forged.

He walked over to where Dragonira was floating and clasped the pendant's delicate chain around her neck. The sorcerer then walked over to the first of the smaller diagram circles he would have to pace in order to begin the impelling process. There, he took a deep breath and spoke the name of the smallest sun.

"Adeen."

The light blue oligoclase near his feet illuminated, flickering on like a soft candle flame. Of Sivoa's three celestial bodies, the light was from its weakest, but because his path would next lead him to its strongest, he needed her help.

"Mask my presence."

The blue light flickered in acknowledgment and he picked up the gemstone before he continued his trek along the diagram.

The blood circle began to glow and he traced its circumference until reconnecting with the larger center ring. The light followed him as he walked along to the next peripheral loop. There he hesitated.

For reasons he would never know, he found it impossibly difficult to work with Sivoa's primary sun. By logic, she was the easiest to see and thus hear. She should be the least troublesome to speak to. Millions of others could. They even amassed, forming a cult whose leader was essentially an open channel to the dominant star. If they could communicate with her, why couldn't he?

His past attempts had always met with violent consequences and was why he needed Adeen's aid. Flag reached out, putting the light blue gem between him and the clear stone on the floor.

"Orianna."

White light exploded out of the small gem, washing out everything in its brilliance until it scaled back to the luminance of a campfire. Flag held up the blue gem in his hands and spoke a command through it.

"Awaken Auvier."

The white light pulsed and dimmed even further, its patron

losing interest in the happenings of a desert basement at night, but still acknowledging the request. Flag wrapped his hand in a cloth and picked up the Orianna stone before moving on.

The morning sun was the second largest in the sky. Despite its daily early arrival, it was the least enthusiastic. If it transmitted any signal to anyone, it was exceptionally weak and easily overlooked. It did respond to Orianna's presence however, so Flag – in need of all three to power the diagram – practically ran to bring the second stone's fading light to him.

"Auvier."

The orange stone came on, but barely. Flag touched the clear gem to it and it brightened considerably.

"Stay with me," Flag said as he picked up the rock and followed the path of blood back to the first circle, completing the circuit. There he placed the Auvier rock down and moved to the second circle, where he returned Orianna's gem. He put Adeen in the third circle. This unintentionally switched the starting positions of the morning and evening suns, but that didn't matter.

The sheer amount of power now coursing the painted lines on the ground made Flag dizzy and he became wary of tripping. The air sparked and he realized the feeling in his gut from earlier had been correct. There was an unidentified presence amongst them, as he had hoped. He needed that presence but, unfortunately, was not strong enough himself to manipulate the suns' energies needed to capture it – even with protection from the recoil.

He frowned and looked at his daughter, somewhat frustrated she was the only one who could perform this ritual. He knew it and had previously gone out of his way to ensure that she would via a subjugation spell she never discovered. As he had once himself been a marionette to such a spell, he was not proud of this, but the need outweighed the cost. He couldn't afford for her to strike up against him now.

He took his position in the center circle – where the

concentration of energy would have killed him if not for Dragonira's presence – and spoke. "Now as I stand before the asterism, I make heard my request!"

Flag studied the expressionless face of his unconscious daughter. Her calm face was a complete contrast to his own emotions and he reveled in the fact that she would not know the excitement he felt at being able to move his research further – or how much she contributed to it.

"Bind the ethereal presence roaming our halls within this vessel before me!"

The sorcerer then muttered the words that allowed him to control his daughter's actions and watched as she grasped the amulet and held it to her lips. Although he couldn't see it, he knew she was drinking in the ritual's energy as well as being trapped within it.

An uncomfortable amount of time passed and Dragonira threw her head back, gasping for air. Flag knew she had it – or at least enough of it to where he could intervene and trap it. He pulled his dagger from the sheath in his sleeve and grabbed her wrist. When the trapped consciousness within her caused her to twitch, he took that as his signal to act and slit her throat.

There was a thunderclap of sound as the energy supporting her exploded outward, dropping her to the ground in a crumpled heap. The necklace remained in the air as a failsafe, devouring the powers he had summoned. He had just enough time to catch it before it hit the ground.

Flag held his breath as he searched the amulet for the being that was supposed to be within it. After a little while he realized there was nothing there. "Impossible!"

His thoughts were interrupted by laughter, which he realized was coming from his daughter, who was dying at his feet. Despite her severed flesh and flooded windpipe, she was laughing at him. The being that escaped had hijacked his hex on her and was using her to mock him before it took its leave.

Flag felt his enthusiasm exodus out of him and he sighed before going around to gather his supplies. He had believed his ritual had been perfect and yet, it failed. Now he would have to go over every aspect and possibility of what happened to see where he went wrong.

CHAPTER SEVEN

There was little that Julian hated more than listening to people's grievances. Had he known that this would have been part of being king, he might have forgone the offer altogether and let the tyrant king burn the desert library to the ground.

That was an exaggeration.

Julian sighed as he listened to the last of the village folk complain at him for the day. He was a windy fellow, upset about having to wait so long to say something about the bazaar's rapid growth and it encroaching on his property. After about ten minutes, the king waved the man toward Marboe, his chancellor, whom he hoped would tell the man where he could stick his bazaar.

When they had left the grand hall, Julian stood up from his sandstone throne and stretched. He didn't know what time it was, but if the morning grievances were over, then lunch was next and he was hungry. He tried to sneak off before Boris noticed, but failed in his attempt as he ran into the chamberlain in the passageway.

"Damn it, Boris, can't I just eat in this? It's cloth, just like everything else I wear. It washes."

"I'm sure it does, your highness, but shall I remind you of how difficult it would be to get a replacement in the event that it doesn't?"

While Julian would run the kingdom in the nude if he could, his in-laws from Lieron insisted that he "run the kingdom properly," which unfortunately meant he had to dress the part no matter what he did. The uniforms he wore for listening to the villagers complain had been specially selected for just that purpose and the frivolousness of it drove him insane.

"Fine." A frustrated and daring tone jumped into his voice. "You can have this. I'm going to eat." The king stripped down to just his undergarments and left Boris to pick the fine silks off of the floor. He might have felt bad for the steward and complied had his appetite not been so great.

As per the daily routine, his court (excluding the chancellor) had been seated in the council chambers, awaiting his arrival. They all exchanged glances when he entered but said nothing about his lack of clothes. *Cowards*, he thought. *Every one of them. It might just be time to replace them.*

"Marboe will be late. Let us start without him," he said as he sat, signaling the command that their food be brought. Unlike the village grievances, he could genuinely ignore the complaints of his council for they generally only repeated themselves from day to day.

"A whisper has come in from the north, my lord," the records keeper announced, ruining his plan to sleep with his eyes open. "Your wife has arrived."

A tension that Julian didn't know he had washed off him with those words. "Wonderful news! Any word on how her father is doing?"

Elcin continued solemnly. "Yes. But it isn't good. His health is continuing to fail despite the return of his children."

Julian's heart sank. The queen of Lieron had sent them a whisper several weeks ago, when her husband had initially fallen ill. She had believed his symptoms were caused by his depression over his grown children. Normally their visits would cure this, but according to his records keeper's further reading, this was something more.

"How long will Chiarina be away?" the king asked, already suspecting the answer he would receive.

Elcin shook her head. "I do not know."

They sat in silence as their lunch was brought out. One of the servants noticed Julian's attire and chuckled, breaking the somber atmosphere. *She can replace Elcin,* he thought as he pulled some meat off of its skewer. About that time Marboe had entered and restored a little bit of the faith he had lost in his council. "The desert heat prove to be too much for my lord?"

Julian waved the comment off, smiling. "What of the bazaar incident?"

"Good question." The chancellor shrugged and took his place at the table. "After some words with Jinto, he ran away with his tail between his legs."

They all had a laugh at that. One simply did not mess with the monster of a man who headed the palace guard. Julian could only imagine how quickly the fight left the peasant when Marboe introduced them.

From there, the meeting dipped back into normalcy. Nuha reported that the library was shifting its focus toward the annual Gala of the Suns. Caiside informed him that the bank was doing exceptionally well for this time of year and allowed the others to pat themselves on the back while Nathara pointed out that this was likely due to the allowed increase of hanging gardens in the city. Gared piped in with something about his contributing water toward the effort.

It blurred together as the food in Julian's belly began to make him sleepy and he positioned himself in a way to fake interest while his mind wandered. It was then Tenoch said something that genuinely caught his attention.

"Dassous reported that an abnormal amount of food was purchased from the market district for a tavern in the farmlands."

Excitement swept through the king, though he kept his face calm. "Am I to assume they did not follow gathering procedure for this?"

"They did, but hastily and in less time than is allocated for such things," Tenoch reported.

Julian was no longer able to contain his smile. Although he had enjoyed many things about ruling, he was much better at war, and little reports like this excited him more than he cared to admit.

The rebellion in Libris Del Sol was a subtle one and had he not been the target of its attacks, he might have overlooked it altogether. The first attempt on his life had been by a man raving about how he ruined the kingdom that Lord Shoa had built. Julian had him dismissed as a lunatic for he knew the tyrant king had stolen the kingdom all the same. He hadn't built anything and in fact, had tried to level it when he couldn't dictate the order of the library spire itself.

The detention of the lunatic attacker had been a sort of cue and their wall inspection crew was mobbed by masked swordsmen. He couldn't recall the details of that skirmish, but he did remember how intoxicating it was to disarm and dismember his assailants. Unfortunately that was the last time they tried to kill him directly.

Over the years, people attempted to bring him down via arson, poisons, hexes, rocks, knives, etc. The closest that anyone had come had been an archer that, ironically, saved his life by knocking him off of his mount with an arrow in the arm. Had Julian stayed in the saddle, he would have been impaled by the volley of arrows that followed.

After many conflicts, over many years, they had taken to some unusual means of digging the vermin out of the city. One such way was to monitor the businesses in the bazaar. While some shared goods on a black market, it was the vital resources that told on people the most.

Being a kingdom in the middle of the desert meant necessities like food and water were easy to track and they noticed large amounts of it would go to a single establishment shortly before the attacks. That, or personal celebrations. Julian hoped the current news would lead to the former. "Do we have a plant at the tavern already?"

Tenoch nodded. "He will send a messenger with his report later."

"Speaking of messages, I was summoned?" A tired and irritated voice made itself known.

They all turned to see the palace sorcerer standing in the doorway. Julian hadn't called for Flag, but that mystery was soon solved as Elcin stood to greet him. "You were. The king has need to send a whisper to Lieron."

Flag nodded and reached for the paper and quill that occupied his spot at the table more often than he himself did. "What is this message?"

"Oh, right." Julian stared at his friend, puzzled by how formal he was being until he remembered they were in the presence of the council. "Please send the queen – both queens – my best regards and a charm for the health of the king."

The sorcerer leveled his eyes at him. "I can't send a charm on a charm, but I'll relay the thought. Anything else?"

The king glanced around the council and shook his head. "No. I think that will be it."

"Then I take my leave." Flag bowed and made true on his words.

When the sorcerer had left, Tenoch sneered. "I don't see why you let him have so much leeway around here. He should be sitting on council with the rest of us."

Gared shot him a knowing glance and Julian held a hand up to silence the head of the city guard. "Don't worry about him. He comes when we call him and that's plenty."

The constable was not pleased but stayed silent as the king addressed the rest of the council. "Is there anything else that needs to be addressed?" When nobody answered, he stood up. "Then you are all dismissed. I'm going to go get dressed."

CHAPTER EIGHT

Two kids were playing in a dusty field, exploring all manner of games and hidden adventures. After a particularly tiring game of tag they plopped down on the withered grass and watched the sky.

"What'd you say your friend's name was?" the boy asked the girl.
"Dodihuatu," she said matter-of-factly. "Dodihuatu Naftali."

"That's a stupid name."

The girl scooted closer to the boy and punched him in the arm. "Don't say that! You'll make him mad!"

She glanced over at a third child with fuchsia hair who may or may not have been there before. He smiled back at them before returning back to the miniature fort he was building out of sand and sticks.

"But it is a stupid name." The dark-haired boy rubbed his arm as he tried to defend his point of view.

"Your name's stupid," the girl retorted back at him.

"Oh, yeah! Well, at least my name doesn't mean demon's wrath!" he shouted, attacking a known point of contention for her.

The little girl went silent and ran off, leaving the dark-haired boy all alone in the dusty fields to watch the clouds fly overhead.

* * *

Dragonira awoke from the strange dream to find herself still lying on the floor in the center of the diagram. A large dried puddle of blood shared its space with her. The fresh wash of red over old, dried hues was startling and she attempted to back away from it, but found she lacked the energy to even try.

Giving up on escaping the pool, she tried to recall where it came from and drew a blank. There had not been an animal brought in to sacrifice. She then remembered that she had to undress – was still undressed – and rolled over to see if she had been cut.

She found nothing.

None of this made sense. There was the ritual; check. She had to take off her dress; but it wasn't her dress. If it wasn't her dress, then whose was it?

Dragonira visualized the dress in her mind and as she did so, was flooded with memories of the previous day. While there was no physical blow to it, the mental activity caused a blossom of pain to take root over her right eye and she rolled over in an attempt to escape it.

"Our plan…" she whispered to the ground, wondering if it was too late for her to meet Pavlova. Unable to move, she replayed their conversation in her mind and was troubled when she found that she wasn't remembering it right. The prince was saying things that didn't fit into the context of the conversation. Things like "We were to meet yesterday" and "Is she okay?"

It wasn't until her father's voice answered that she realized the voice belonged in the here and now. "I'm sorry, Prince. She hasn't been feeling well these past two days and is still resting."

She uncurled her body and rolled so that she was lying on her stomach with her head resting on an outstretched arm. She tried to call out, but only managed a small squeak.

"I wasn't aware… is she all right?" Pavlova's concerned voice asked. Surely he would push his way in and find her here, in the strange room behind the bookcase.

"She will be fine. It's probably something she ate," her father answered back so sincerely that her heart sank. He sounded genuinely worried about her. *Don't believe him!* she thought as hard as she could.

"But everyone else from the banquet is just fine." The prince sounded suspicious and Dragonira tried to smile. *That's right! Call his bluff! Do it!*

Her moment of unfounded victory came to a crashing halt as her father laid out a perfectly reasonable explanation to back up his claim. "The Orianna has a very strict diet, so she probably wasn't used to such a feast."

Dragonira reached out her other hand toward the doorway of the chamber where the voices crept in from. *Wait! Please don't fall for it!*

Pavlova didn't hear her thoughts. "I guess that makes sense. I wish I had considered that before. Please tell her I hope she gets well soon."

"I will. Goodnight, Prince."

She heard the door to the foyer shut and realized Pavlova was now walking away. She chased after him with her heart, called to him in her head, but she could still feel the distance between them growing.

Dragonira dug her nails into the cracks between the stones in the floor and tried to follow him, not caring that she would tear up her bare skin in the process. He couldn't get away. He was so close!

Fear overtook her when she heard the sound of heavy boots coming down the steps toward her. As her father stepped into her line of sight, it was all that she could do to lie still and close her eyes.

"Overheard that, did you?"

Even though he knew she was awake, she kept her eyes shut and didn't answer him. His anger radiated off of him and she didn't want to see it. Seeing made it real. Instead, she braced herself for the assault she knew was coming, and waited.

And waited.

She stole a glance upward and saw her father looking off into the distance in thought. Then he let out a heavy sigh and cast his eyes back down at her, muttering something she couldn't make out.

Her eyes, like the rest of her, became inexplicably heavy and gave up. She heard a shuffling and was rolled over so that she was lying on her back. As everything went black, she felt her father's strong arms scoop her up and carry her away.

CHAPTER NINE

Eric awoke to the distant sound of laughter, followed only by what could be Tom's voice. At first, he blamed the pain in his head on the racket, but after he opened his eyes, he realized that he was lying on the floor and not in the cot he was supposed to have been sleeping in. It took a while, but he was eventually able to piece together what caused him to be in such a position.

He had arrived back in the camp late the night before and was almost immediately accosted by the twins, who needed him to compare the maps to something that another rebel had found in the library. It was an interesting find that showed just how much the palace had changed over the course of eighteen different rulers, but it had kept him up most of the night.

The strategist remembered seeing the faint light of the first sun illuminate the floor of his tent, but after that he couldn't remember anything. He had been sitting at his desk, which he was now underneath, meaning that he had fallen off of it in his sleep. Even though nobody had been around to witness it, he was embarrassed by the blunder.

He felt around the ground for his glasses and was relieved when he was able to confirm that they hadn't been broken. His hair tie, on the other hand, had come undone and his dirty-white hair had knotted itself into a false beard. It had been a rough sleep.

Unable to find a brush, he used his fingers to comb away the mess and tied it back with a string. He then used the desk that dumped him to stand, and spotted the maps strewn across it. "No," he told the papers affirmatively before he went to exit the tent and nearly ran into someone who had been standing outside. He subconsciously waved at the familiar figure before recognition and a sense of dread kicked in. He was face to face with the prince of Libris Del Sol.

"Good morning!" the noble said with a level of enthusiasm that did not match the demeanor of one surrounded by his enemies. "You totally missed all the fun!"

Eric knew he was tired, but he now suspected that he was still dreaming. "Tom?"

The prince smiled a big goofy grin and held his hand out to show off. "Yup! Isn't it great?"

"It's somethin..." the strategist mumbled. "Why are you dressed that way?"

Tom pointed over his shoulder, toward the food tent where Eric had been planning to go but was now reconsidering. "This was Ka'ren's crazy idea from the other night. We had some of the women put it together. They think this might help us get information as well as bring shame to the royal family."

"It'll definitely do one of those things. Now move, I need something to wake up with."

"They're out of brew."

Those four words had more of an effect on his morning than everything else he experienced so far. Today hadn't even started for him and he was ready for it to be over. "Then I'm going back to bed. See you later."

Prince Tom grabbed his arm before he could leave and guided him toward the open marquee where the others were eating. "No. You have to be in on this."

Reluctantly, Eric followed the disguised calico up until the point where he could ditch him to speak with one of the cooks. While he was waiting for his meal, Ka'say arrived to place his dishes in the wash bins. "What do you think? Quite the resemblance, eh?"

"I think that you would look more like the prince than he does," Eric answered bluntly, not wanting to admit that in his sleep-addled haze, he had totally believed the disguise.

The more social of the twins shrugged. "Maybe, but you know that my brother and I can't be seen in the city. Too many people willing to turn us in for the sorcerer's ransom."

Eric nodded even though he felt the twins had been overly paranoid on that front. He knew more people hated the sorcerer than wanted his money.

"Besides, we aren't trying for the prince. The disguise is actually supposed to be of Arminius."

"Who?"

"The cousin who got in trouble for slumming under the prince's name. Remember? He looked enough like him to fool half of the brothels."

Eric remembered. According to rumor, the nobles had been so embarrassed that they had a librarian line of sight teleport him back across the continent, which was logistically infeasible and likely untrue. "So, we're not planning on entering the palace with this. Why do it?"

"Well, the name is just in case we are caught. Otherwise, we are going to try to play the royal connections in the market and library. That book we gave you last night was a fluke. The real city records would be what we need."

"I see," said Eric. "That could work. If the librarians are busy and Tom plays his part well, they'd believe he was the real prince and take him right to the fourth floor."

Ka'say nodded, then stopped and shot him a look. "Wait. How do you know it's the fourth floor? Isn't that kind of low?"

"I don't know how long it has been since you visited the library, but that's the floor they won't let anyone visit." Eric's food had arrived and his sudden need to eat it was making him testy. Ka'say picked up on this and allowed him to sit at a table while he went over to speak with his brother. It wasn't long before they were both sitting in front of him.

"Was this the grand idea you came up with at the last meeting?" Eric asked Ka'ren.

He nodded and then shrugged. "Honestly, it was Ta'mika's idea, but I dismissed it because it was so high profile, but now with the need to get to the records as well, it seems like a necessary risk."

Eric paused in chewing his food long enough to look at him but said nothing. The twins knew he didn't want the tiny Sassin family to get wrapped up in their politics as the first war had done them enough damage. "Is she planning on getting involved?"

This time Ka'ren shook his head. "She provided us with some of the prince's clothes as well as a charm of illusion, but she–"

"Wait," Eric interrupted Ka'ren. "She's in the camp now?"

The twins glanced at each other and Eric jumped to his feet to go search the camp for the woman. It didn't take him long as he simply followed the sound of Tom's obnoxious voice thanking her for her work.

When she saw his approach, she held her hands up. "I know what you're going to say. Don't worry about me. I just stopped by on my way to visit the family."

Very few people were able to leave the city gates without escort, but Ta'mika had special ties to the royal family by proxy of the nomads. She and her daughter were free to come and go as they pleased, though Kinya was usually forced to stay and take care of the house.

Eric shot her a look and pressed his lips into a thin line. "Just be careful."

She rolled her eyes at him. "I'll be fine."

"And Kinya?"

Ta'mika leveled her gaze at him. "She still doesn't know anything about all of this outside of rumor. If I get caught for any reason, it shouldn't reflect on her."

"That's not what I meant," he addressed sternly. "I mean, if you get caught, she'll be without a mother and I don't think she can handle that. You really should just be enjoying your retirement."

"How do you expect me to do that when the Scourge is manipulating that corrupt idiot king of ours? Making sure they are removed from life is ensuring that my daughter has a decent future!" the plump Sassin vented.

Eric sighed. He had known her for long enough to understand that when she dedicated herself to a cause, it would be difficult to deter her off her war path. He also knew this grudge of hers was an old one.

Ta'mika had been in charge of the kitchens when he came to work in the dungeons. He was a broken man and she managed to find a way to comfort him through work. Her daily routines for him were to get groceries from the bazaar, fetch water from the waterworks, wash the dishes so they were ready for lunch and dinner, and then finally deliver the food to the prisoners and overnight workers.

Even though she kept him busy, there were always pauses in the routine where they would simply sit and chat. He learned she had been indirectly related to the sorcerer through her cousin, who had married him when the nomads and the northmen took the kingdom. She and her cousin had been raised as sisters and because of their kinship, Ta'mika served as her handmaiden.

"I never liked him," she would often say in regards to the sorcerer. It was a fact she didn't keep from her cousin either. Proximity and her cousin's fondness for her husband never changed her mind, but it wasn't until he murdered his wife and abandoned their newborn daughter that she had any justification for her hatred of him.

She had wanted revenge ever since. Eric even suspected she was the one who had organized the start of the small insurgent group he was now a key member of, but he would never know for sure. The only thing he was certain of was that she should just let the younger rebels carry on for her and that she get her family out of the city.

"Is the tribe planning their migration?" he asked, connecting the thoughts in his head.

"They are, but in following with the seasons; they will not leave until the Gala of the Suns."

"You and Kinya will go with them this time, correct?"

Ta'mika reflected his frown at him. "I'd rather not, but even the twins are pushing us in that direction."

Eric nodded, thankful for once to Ka'say and Ka'ren for their secret meetings with her. "Good…"

The Gala of the Sun was the perfect time for them to invade. It was one of the three times of year the villagers were allowed past the inner wall and the only time that revelry would mask their invasion. The palace itself would still be sealed off and guarded, but the discovery of secret entrances could help as long as they stayed out of the library's jurisdiction. His biggest worry right now was that the nomads would not travel far enough to outrun the city guard when the time comes.

"You've informed them of the coup, correct? Why will they not leave earlier?"

Ta'mika answered him with an expression he could not read, but was in no way comfortable with. "Tradition," she answered flatly before nodding a goodbye and taking off in a choice direction.

He started after her but stopped when Ka'say stepped in his way. "Just let her go. She's already late."

Eric complied, but as he watched her turn down a path, a weight settled in his stomach. There was something suspicious about her answer and he hoped that it didn't mean she was deliberately withholding information from him so she could be more involved with this war.

CHAPTER TEN

A familiar rumbling caused her to stir in her sleep, ruining her dreams of kids at play and of annoying princes in libraries. As she opened her eyes, she realized the sound was not coming from outside, but within. She was hungry.

Unaware of what time of day – or even what day – it was, she sat up and looked around the room. "I need food," she said to the walls and made the effort to climb out of bed. She noticed then that she was nude and that confused her. Where was her sleeping gown? What happened to her undergarments?

Damn it all. She remembered the start of a spell, then the prince coming to check on her. After that, she drew a blank and panicked. Racing to get dressed, she cursed at herself for not meeting up with the prince, who so generously offered to help her... escape...

Dragonira paused as she slid her foot into a shoe. She had been so afraid of her father that night because she had been brought back into the castle, but now that she thought about it, all she had to do was teleport out to the stables again. This epiphany was interrupted by the sounds of her stomach reminding her that she was still hungry. "Okay, fine," she told herself as she tested her room's door. When she found it unlocked, she was a little startled.

The foyer was empty. Further investigation showed that she was alone in the whole apartment and might well be for a few days given the amount of her father's things that were missing. The silence was uncomfortable but she really couldn't place why that was the case. With as much as she wanted to leave him, she should have been glad that her father was gone. It took her a long while to understand that the situation felt very much like a trap. While her father leaving on unannounced excursions was common enough, it felt odd that he would do it so shortly after she had broken every one of his rules.

Her feeling of dread turned to those of excitement as she revisited the rooms of her apartment. He really wasn't there! There was nobody to stop her from leaving and she now knew that she had the means of doing it. In a flurry, she had packed a bag with a few garments she believed would be ideal to travel in and then she ran across the foyer into her father's room, where she grabbed his military knife and scabbard along with a small bag of coins. He would flay her alive if he knew she had these, but she didn't intend on seeing him again.

In a heartbeat she was standing outside of the stables, more prepared to face the world than she had been before. She had briefly considered stealing a taratin to help her on her journey, but she dismissed the idea when she remembered that she had no idea how to ride one. She did, however, check to make sure there was nobody in or around the stables before she made a mad dash across the courtyard toward the massive wall she knew separated her and the village.

She had gotten as far as the gate when she ran into her first major obstacle of the day: a lock. She tried yanking it open before concluding that she could reuse her escape spell. She had gotten most of the way through the chant before she noticed the people in the tunnel on the other side of the gate and stopped. How would they react to someone who could openly do what the librarians did, but was not actually one? Her brief excursion around the palace had revealed to her that her magic abilities were a rare commodity on their own, but it was unheard of for non-librarians to do what they do.

Darting to the side of the barred opening and peeking around the corner every now and then, Dragonira waited until there was a lull in the crowd and repeated her words. She had barely finished her breath when she found herself standing in the tunnel, between a fountain and a doorway labeled "baths." She would have dwelled on the practicality of a community sharing its water resource in such a way had the crowd not returned.

She stood out like a sore thumb. Even though she had attempted to dress down, she was still wearing the clothes of a more noble class and she knew it would cause her problems. Instead of standing in the open to be gawked at, she ran into the bath hall and found herself somewhat unprepared for the sight that greeted her.

The washroom adjacent to her father's bedroom had been large in her eyes. It was also extremely private and apparently something most households lacked. Although there was a wall to divide the men from the women, there was an entire community in here, washing, wading, and playing in the water. Dragonira hadn't imagined anything like it.

A woman who had entered the bath behind her said something mean under her breath and pushed around her so she could get undressed. Embarrassed, Dragonira followed suit and placed her bag on a stool that stood against the wall. Next to it there was a bucket and a grate in the floor. Once undressed, she continued to mimic the other woman's actions and used the bucket to haul water from the bath back to the grate. She did the best she could to wash herself without sand or a cloth and, after rinsing, entered the pool.

Now what? She sank into the water up to her chin as she stared off into her thoughts. *I know that there's a market out there somewhere. I could buy some new clothes there. Perhaps I could even trade what I have in so that I don't look so...*

As the word "royal" popped into her head, so did the image of the prince. Guilt hit her then and she sank further into the water. She really should find some way to let him know she was okay.

Someone to her left giggled and she realized that she had been blowing bubbles in the water. She looked to see a little girl clinging to her mother, grinning from ear to ear. The mother smiled helplessly and shrugged on the girl's behalf. "I'm sorry," she said. "I'm afraid she doesn't have a grasp on manners quite yet."

Dragonira shook her head and smiled back. "It's okay."

"From the palace?" the mother asked all of a sudden.

Dragonira shook her head furiously and stopped before she

overdid it. "No. Why do you ask?"

The mother nodded her head toward the stool that Dragonira had placed her bag and dress upon. "Your dress and the way you carry yourself... I just assumed."

"You can have it," Dragonira answered before she really thought about it.

The little girl, while young, knew what was being offered and she tugged at her mother's ears. "Dwess!"

The mother looked lost. "You would just give it to me?"

Dragonira nodded.

"But what would you wear?" the woman asked.

There was the issue with the offer right there. Dragonira could put on a different dress, but she would be back to her initial problem of looking more regal than she wanted to be. "We could trade," she suggested.

The woman mulled the idea over in her head, all the while her daughter yanked at her ears and hair. "It is a lovely dress, but I'm afraid I just couldn't accept it. It is too fine for someone like me."

Dragonira shook her head. "I think it would look nice on you. I'm serious. If you want it, you can have it."

The woman narrowed her eyes. "Is it stolen?"

"What? No. Why would it be?"

"Then why are you trying to get rid of it?"

"It..." She sighed. "I am from the palace. I just don't want it anymore."

The woman stared at her incredulously. "You left the palace to get rid of a dress?"

"No!" Dragonira rubbed her hands together. "I don't want any of... the... palace anymore. I want to leave."

"If you're really from the palace, which family are you from?"

Dragonira stared at the woman in disbelief for a moment and was about to say something when she realized that she couldn't answer. Not only did her father not have a last name, but she knew almost nothing about her lineage. There was also the fact that mentioning the palace sorcerer might not go over so well.

"I thought so," the woman said when she didn't answer. "I'll let you know that I'm going to report you to the guard when I leave."

The woman's warning did not fall on deaf ears and before long a fully dressed Dragonira found herself, and her bag back in her room. All that effort, wasted because of a single dress. She wanted to cry and hit something and scream, but instead she just sat on her bed feeling drained of all her energy.

I'm still hungry...

She gave in and uttered the words that would bring her to the library. She wasn't really sure why she had picked this as her destination, but it was better than her father's apartment. As she wandered the bookshelves, she remembered seeing people with food at the top of the spire and decided that she'd give it a try.

When she couldn't find someone to deliver her, she used her trusty spell again to enter the atrium. This turned out to be a mistake, for when she appeared, she was mobbed by a crowd of angry people who wanted to be somewhere else. Here, the manner in which she was dressed went unnoticed as everyone mistook her for a librarian.

While Dragonira was comfortable with breaking herself down molecule by molecule and flinging herself across space, she did not want to get other people involved. She had very little experience with it, but from her readings she understood very well what the consequences could be.

The crowd grew larger and, in overhearing the various

conversations around her, she found out the librarians haven't been up for quite a while. After a little bit of shouting for the crowd to calm down, she explained that she was only a trainee and couldn't teleport others yet. It was a lie, but it worked. She promised the crowd that she would investigate what was wrong and teleported to the first floor.

She found all three of the librarians on duty there, huddled on the edge of the large circular reception desk. They were talking to someone else who she couldn't make out at first because he was also leaning in. When he stood up straight, however, she had to pause.

There stood the prince. No. Someone who looked like the prince, but she knew wasn't. The resemblance was so close that she tried to remember if Pavlova ever mentioned having a brother.

One of the girls busted out giggling and reminded her the people many floors up were about to riot. Dragonira smacked the counter to get their attention and the three of them whipped around, both annoyed and shocked they had been caught. When she told them about the mess upstairs, they straightened out and thanked her for letting them know about it.

She then turned to 'Pavlova' and raised an eyebrow. "Who are you?"

The man shot her an arrogant grin and replied, "I am the prince."

"No you're not."

"I know, but you have to admit that I look the part."

She stood there blinking for a few seconds before giving into the fact. "Well… yeah. You do." Then the question that she really wanted to ask popped, fully formed, into her mind. "Why are you claiming to be the prince?"

The man pointed upward and winked as he gave her his answer. "Wanted to impress the ladies."

"Do you know them?"

He nodded and explained that he visited them fairly often, and thought it would be fun to show them his costume for the party, which caused her mind to blank. "What party?"

As soon as the words left her mouth, she regretted speaking them for the man shot her the most disturbing grin she had ever seen. Thankfully, he didn't get to elaborate as another voice interrupted the conversation.

"I heard there was an impostor down here."

Dragonira spun around to face Pavlova and smiled. She wanted to explain what had happened since she last saw him then and there, but the expression on his face suggested that it wouldn't be a good idea.

"Cousin! It's been a while! How goes it?"

Both Dragonira and Pavlova stared at the impostor.

"Who are you?" It was Pavlova's turn to ask.

The doppelganger flicked back a lock of hair and responded. "Uh… your cousin, Arminius. Come on! We used to play together as kids all of the time!"

The expression on Pavlova's face indicated his disbelief. Dragonira would have agreed with his silent stare had she not had that dream, that memory, of them as kids. She stepped up to Arminius and asked, "Did you used to have pink hair?"

The prince's cousin frowned. "I did once, but I've decided it wasn't for me."

Dragonira glanced at Pavlova, who still looked confused about all of this. "Do you remember playing with a small pink-haired boy when we were little?"

Pavlova shook his head. "I'm afraid I can't remember anything that far back. I just know that I don't like people pretending to be me." He narrowed his eyes at Arminius. "Go change out of my old clothes. If I catch you pretending to be me again, deportation will be the last of your problems."

Arminius pouted and then turned to walk off. "Okay, cousin… be that way!"

"Before you go." The prince caught his elbow and stared him down. "If you don't want to anger my father, you better show at dinner. He'll want to hear word of Lieron."

Pavlova's cousin paused awkwardly before dashing for the door. Once he was gone, Dragonira turned to find Pavlova smiling down at her through his perplexity. She shot a comforting grin back. "That was weird."

He glanced at the doorway and nodded. "Yeah. It was." The prince started to say more, but decided against it. "I just hope that he actually quits this time."

Dragonira raised an eyebrow at the statement, hoping that Pavlova would elaborate, but he never did. She found the situation amusing, but considered how Pavlova felt. Having someone running around pretending to be you was a bit of an unnerving thought.

Her stomach growled, breaking the silence that had settled on the near-empty lobby. Pavlova broke out into a musical laughter and gently grabbed her hand. "Come. Let's get you something to eat."

CHAPTER ELEVEN

As soon as the street had cleared, Tom made a mad dash for the door of a two-story adobe in the middle of town. When he got there he banged on the heavy wood that prevented him from getting inside. "Kinya! Please say you're in there!"

After an excruciating amount of time, he heard a tiny voice say, "Hold on! Hold on! I'm coming!" Minutes later, there was the sound of a latch sliding back and the door swung inward. He shoved his way inside before the home's youngest resident could issue a proper greeting.

"What the fuck, Tom! I just–" Kinya interrupted herself to bust out laughing. "Haha! Oh, shit! You look just like him!"

He glared at her but was otherwise too out of breath to respond. Catching the hint, she led him into the kitchen and sat him at the table. "I'm guessing that the plan failed. What happened?"

The pendant that colored his hair and fur to match the prince didn't carry much weight at all, but when he pulled it off it felt as if he unwrapped himself from a blanket. It was good to feel the hot air again. "I was an idiot."

Kinya smirked at him and shook her head. "Got caught up in Arminius' reputation and chased the wrong girl?"

"Plural. Girls... at the library."

"Oh. Oh, no. You didn't?!" She gaped at him. "You went after the librarians?"

Tom shrugged. "Not intentionally."

Kinya shook her head. "By the suns. You really are a moron. Ha!"

He sat up to defend himself. "Well, I figured that if I could trick them, I'd be able to fool anyone. It actually worked!"

"Until?" she continued for him.

"Until the actual prince showed up," he finished quietly. "I might have hit on his girlfriend by accident."

"Seriously? You met the prince already and... wait. Girlfriend?"

"You know, the dark-haired girl with the creepy green eyes. She showed up to yell at me about tying up the teleportation queues and then he came along and he–" He sat back in his chair. "Suns. What a creep."

"He's really not so bad. He was probably just annoyed at the fact his look-alike was causing problems again." Kinya winked at him. "I don't know much about her though."

Tom smiled as he interrupted what was certain to be a year's worth of gossip. "You confuse me, you know that?"

"I do?" She smiled at him and raised an eyebrow.

He didn't want to admit he loved when she made that face. "Well, yeah. You work and stand up for the royals, but your mother is working to lead a rebellion against them. Aren't you afraid of backlash?"

Kinya shrugged. "My mom likes to think I'm clueless to her war and I'm fine with that. You guys know not to hurt me, and the royals don't see me as anything more than a faceless servant – if they notice me at all. Their money pays for this home. I can't really complain."

Tom glanced around the tiny apartment and sighed. She had a point. If one turned a blind eye to certain plights in the city, it would be easy to forget about the tyranny of those running the kingdom and live a normal day-to-day life like she did.

"Do you work today?"

"Not in the palace. Amma left me with a bunch of clothes that needed mending and delivering." She frowned. "She was supposed to help with that yesterday, but she hasn't come back yet."

"Oh?" Tom sat up. As far as he was aware, Ta'mika had left the camp days ago. "Need help?"

Kinya grinned. "In fact, I do. Come on."

Tom had expected maybe a dress or two when he volunteered to help, but when Kinya ran outside to "get the cart," he knew he was in trouble.

They spent the next couple of hours sorting clothes based on how damaged each article was. Most had small holes that didn't take Kinya long to close up, but some were damaged beyond repair. The chore had taken them up to the point where the suns were beginning to set. "Okay. I'll have to do the rest tomorrow. Come. We need to get these to Marl's before he closes."

As Kinya prepped the cart, Tom donned a disguise. While the prince disguise wasn't ideal, it was better than allowing his natural markings to show through. Instead of the royal robes, however, he borrowed some of the leftover clothes and covered his head and mouth, leaving only his eyes visible.

Kinya approved. "You look so uncomfortable. Will you be okay?"

Tom shrugged. "It's hot, but I'll survive."

The first of the three suns had already kissed the horizon when they finally made it to the market and most of its patrons had left. According to Kinya, this was the best time to do business because it wasn't so busy or hot, but it also didn't allow for much time. For this reason they had to bypass any extraneous shopping and made their way straight to Marl's.

If there was any kind of dark market here, Marl was definitely at its forefront. His shop had a few items out for display, but there was no level of consistency to them. It was also attached to a building nobody was allowed in and out of.

"What kind of business does he run?" Tom asked when they finally left.

Kinya sighed. "I was told not to ask, but I suspect they're slavers."

Tom stopped in his tracks and looked over his shoulder at the now-closed store front. As much as he hated wearing the layers, he was suddenly very thankful for his disguise. The people behind shops like that were the kind he spent a good portion of his life avoiding. "Seriously? Why would you deal with them?"

She shrugged. "The slaves need clothes too, you know."

Tom had to admit she had a point.

Hungry, they stopped at a small food stand that was in the middle of closing. The merchant had just about thrown out all of the day's perishables, but he had an assortment of things on a stick that made Tom appreciate how long ago lunch had been. Unable to sit in the marketplace, they took their food to go and wound up eating it on the roof Kinya shared with her neighbors.

"This isn't much of a view," Tom said as he stared at the four-story wall next door.

"That's because you're looking in the wrong direction, moron."

As he turned he saw the wall of another large home, the empty rooftop of a similarly sized adobe, and the walls of the buildings across the street. "I'm sorry, but the views are still lacking."

Kinya rolled her eyes and dragged him by the arm to the furthest corner from the rooftop entrance. Under an awning here was where Kinya kept her modest vegetable garden and it overlooked the street itself. With the new angle, Tom was able to see similar gardens lining the street until they dead-ended at the marketplace and the palace wall. "Okay. That's better."

Kinya punched him in the arm and took a seat next to a flowering plant. She shook her head at him as she munched on her kabob. Following her lead, he bit into what had to be the burnt remains of some sort of bug.

"Shit. That's terrible," he said as he spat it out into the street.

"You can't be happy with anything, can you?" She chuckled.

Tom stuck his tongue out at her and sat close enough to threaten her with the burnt bugs on a stick. "I'm just spoiled. The Earthers and the camp cooks make some really good food."

She nodded in agreement as she finished off the kabob in her hand. "I have to say that these are unusually bad, but I might be spoiled as well."

She was of course referencing the food in the palace and the expression she wore confirmed it. Unable to help himself, he found himself following her gaze to look at the lavender sky above the wall.

Kinya wore the faintest of smiles. "I wonder what they're having."

CHAPTER TWELVE

After Arminius had fled, they found themselves feeling awkward about remaining in the library. Something about the ground level of the imposing spire instilled a sense of duty that they really didn't want to act upon and they fled through one of the many archways that held it up. Pavlova wasn't sure how they ended up at the market, but when he saw Dragonira holding back her excitement at the diversity of colors and wares, he knew this was where they should be.

The part of the market that spilled into the inner wall was vastly different from its counterpart on the other side. The heavy security forced upon the vendors ensured that only the finest of products greeted noble eyes and the prince took comfort in knowing that his date wouldn't encounter anything unpleasant.

"If you see anything you like, it is yours," he offered, and was surprised when she appeared embarrassed by the gesture. After assuring her that his treating her was okay, she began looking at the shops. However, it wasn't until she stopped at a fruit stand that she showed any genuine interest. "What is that?" she asked, pointing to a large melon sitting toward the center.

Having to explain fruit caught him off guard as it was something he generally took for granted, but further consideration of the desert climate made him aware of this simple privilege. "It's an orloro melon. Would you like me to buy it?"

Dragonira nodded and Pavlova had the merchant cut the melon into pieces for them, which turned out to be a mistake. As they continued through the market, the juices of the plump fruit soaked the bag they had been given and dripped onto a decorative rug they then had to buy. Not wanting to repeat their unintended purchase, they climbed up a set of stairs that brought them through the inner wall, to sentinels lookout that oversaw the village.

Pavlova dropped the rolled-up carpet on the floor and sat on it. Dragonira followed his lead unenthusiastically. "Sorry. I didn't mean for you to have to buy such an expensive rug. I just–"

"Don't worry about it. We'll just put it in your room so you can think about what you did."

She rolled her eyes before taking the piece of melon that he offered. As the flavor hit her tongue, her entire demeanor changed. "By the suns! That's delicious!"

The prince chuckled as he watched her transformation and took a bite himself. Although thirst-quenching, it was unbearably sweet and he had to set it down. *Leave it to a woman to like something like that.* The fact that she enjoyed it as much as she did amused him on a level he didn't fully understand. It was as if he had forgotten that she was allowed to enjoy the same pleasures other girls did. She just seemed more important than that.

She caught him watching her and paused. "What?"

"Nothing." He shook his head and looked out over the city, but watched her from the corner of his eye. As she bit back into the melon, he found himself wondering if he ever relished something so much. He then wondered if perhaps the melon tasted different to her and if so, what that was like. As he spied on her, he realized that what he really wanted to taste was her lips.

This hadn't gone unnoticed. "I can stop if my eating is bothering you," she said as she placed the fruit down.

Aw... Pavlova smiled and sighed. "My turn to apologize. You may have the rest. I find I'm having difficulty with it."

"It is a bit much." Dragonira smiled at him and shared in overlooking the city. "That first bite was amazing, but it quickly wears on you. I don't think I can finish it either."

"That's kind of a shame. That little fruit traveled such a long way to get here."

The look she shot him demanded clarification and he couldn't help but laugh a little. "I mean, that it's imported. We can't grow those here in the desert because we don't have enough water."

"Ah." She nodded and then frowned as something crossed her mind. "Do we import everything?"

"We grow our own crops as well. " The prince shook his head and then pointed out a green roof several city rows over. "See that house over there? They're part of the rooftop gardeners' guild. They probably grow some of the smaller plants that we eat. While over there," he gestured toward the outermost of the city walls, "is where our larger crops are."

Dragonira followed his gaze and ingested the knowledge as readily as she had the melon. The child-like wonder in her vibrant eyes suddenly reminded him of a trip to the outer wall when he was small. She had been there, accompanied by her father, who was there at the behest of his own. They were there to see what was going on with an irrigation system – or something like that.

From a kid's perspective, the doings of the adults was unimportant. What was important was the large field they ran around in. If he remembered correctly, she was a fast runner and hard to escape, so he was glad when it was his turn and he tagged…

"Wait! I DO remember a boy with pink hair!"

Having not been privy to the thoughts running around his head, she smiled at him with a confused mix of emotions and took a deep breath before letting it out in relief. "Okay. I thought I might have been delusional and made that up. It's not exactly a normal hair color."

The prince was stunned. *How could I have forgotten about someone so odd?*

He tried his best to recall all of the details about that day but was only able to recall her face even though there had been three kids there that day; the pink-haired kid, Dragonira, and himself. As he tried to place names with the unknown figure, he remembered why the subject of hair color came up in the first place. "I don't think Arminius ever colored his hair."

She shook her head. "I agree. His name doesn't fit my memory of him."

A silence fell between them as he thought about his few encounters with his cousin. There was not a point that he could ever recall him ever having a hair color different from his own. In fact, Arminius took pride in how much they resembled each other. Pavlova frowned at the thought. "That means he lied to us."

"Could it possibly have been another of your cousins?"

He shrugged and stood up, having enough of the midday sun, even in the shade. "Possibly. My mother's family is fairly well known for being eccentric. It might have also been a villager."

"Perhaps we can ask your father?"

The prince shrugged. "We could ask him at dinner tonight, but I am unable to promise that he will be sober. He doesn't take Mother's absences well."

"Is she away often?"

He shook his head. "No. Unfortunately, my grandfather is unwell and she went to see him."

They had left the outpost and continued their conversation on the Lieron family as they descended the steps. Now that they no longer had to worry about melon juice getting on everything, they continued shopping around the inner market; stopping to investigate taratin saddles, incenses and spices, and to watch a potter play music by lightly tapping a wooden dowel on his wares.

It was already growing dark by the time he realized they should have been changing into dinner attire. The thought caused him a momentary panic, but he calmed as he watched Dragonira make her way toward the dry fountain at the end of the row of vendor tents. The simple white dress she wore reflected the last of the suns' light and made her radiant against the night's rising purples and blues.

His breath caught in his throat as she pointed to the ancient structure and turned toward him. "Ever notice that the palace was designed around a huge amount of water that we do not have?"

"I never thought about it," he admitted. Architecture was the last thing on his mind but, like with the melon, he was somehow attracted to her fascination of it. He was attracted to the face she made as she pondered it and other things beyond his grasp.

If asked, he would have to admit there was something about her that lured him in; made him want to help her. She was pretty, but there was also an air of mystery to her. Add the challenge that her father was the most terrifying man in the kingdom and she was practically irresistible.

Without fully realizing his actions, he reached out and brushed her arm and caught her lips with his when she turned to see what he wanted. She pulled back instantly, but after some consideration, she returned the kiss.

CHAPTER THIRTEEN

Flag hated dealing with the librarians. The way that one had to surrender absolutely to their whims in order to switch floors was ridiculous – and dangerous if one happened to be on the library's bad side. While he never did anything to earn their ire, they always kept an irritatingly watchful eye on him.

Learning how to teleport himself was an act of defiance against them as much as it was convenience to himself. It should not have come as a surprise when his daughter did the same – nor should he have been caught off guard when he saw she had used the trick to meet up with the prince in the marketplace.

He sighed as he closed and shelved the book he borrowed from the floor of records. A part of him knew that he should be impressed by his daughter's ability to captivate the royals as she had, but her becoming close to them meant that he could lose his most precious tool. Perhaps it didn't really even matter. As much as he wanted to continue his research, his other plans were finally starting to pick up momentum.

The sorcerer had just started down a row of shelves when a thunderous voice shouted at him from across the library. "Have you seen your daughter?"

Flag turned and watched King Julian march out of the palace passageway, around the interior balcony, and toward him. "I'm afraid that I have not," he lied, assuming that feigning ignorance would rid himself of the monarch quicker.

"Damn." Julian stamped his foot. "My son missed dinner and I was told that he was with her."

Flag raised an eyebrow at this. "Is this really such a concern?"

Julian shrugged. "Maybe not, but I had also received word that

Arminius was back."

Flag rolled his eyes and turned so that he fell in pace with the king as he circled the fourth floor of the library. "I don't see why this is an issue."

"You're not at all concerned?" Julian's sky-blue eyes glanced in his direction.

Flag kept his gaze forward. "Arminius' reputation is unflattering, but your son is a decent kid. He wouldn't let your nephew do anything out of line."

Julian stopped and considered his words for a moment. "Perhaps you're right." The king then glanced back toward the entrance to the palace walkway and grimaced. "Would you mind taking me back to my suite?"

Flag deadpanned for a full moment before sighing in the face of the king's laziness. "Fine."

In the blink of an eye, they were standing on a terrace overlooking an indoor garden, before a large ornate door. The wrought-iron and glass structure served as the entryway to a series of equally imposing rooms that Julian normally shared with his wife. The prince had a similar residence one floor below.

Jinto, the king's doorward had practically jumped out of his skin when the two of them materialized in front of him. Now that he had regained some of his composure, he pushed the heavy door open for his king. He only offered Flag a look of malcontent, which the sorcerer returned.

Completely over dealing with the two of them, Flag teleported back to his apartment. There he flopped between the stacks of books that he had forgotten to clear off the bed. He didn't bother removing the satchel that he had been hauling and left it draped across his torso. The ordeal with the king had drained whatever lingering energy he had left over from his trip.

He would ditch Libris Del Sol to make a new life elsewhere if he could. Somewhere where a possessive psycho-king wouldn't abuse his abilities to support his laziness, cure his hangovers, or provide meaningless entertainment – such as random battles with other sorcerers who just happened to wander into the kingdom.

He frowned as he remembered one such battle. The visiting magician had threatened him with a timed-return curse similar to the spell the librarians used in order to make sure their books didn't permanently wander. Flag had shot him down with a lightning bolt, but as fast as he was, the opposing sorcerer was still able to get his spell off. To this day, Flag couldn't leave the kingdom for more than a month at a time.

Initially, he had believed it to be a lame trick, but when it did not vanish upon the death of his rival he figured out there was more to it. The battle had been set up by the king with the intent of keeping him in the kingdom permanently and had tied the spells debt to himself somehow. This meant that Julian still had a vested interest in keeping him close. Routine checks, scheduled outings, and impromptu visits only served to verify this. Flag's secret excursions had to be planned with all of this in mind and the fact that his daughter had run to the royals made them even more difficult.

Another problem was that she could potentially divulge the details of all the things he subjected her to. Sorcery wasn't a taboo subject in the desert kingdom, but the meanings and methods behind his rituals would raise more than a few of the wrong eyebrows. At least he could take comfort in knowing that everything she said in this regard would be taken with a healthy dose of dubiety. Anyone learned in the arts would know she would not have survived the things she did.

The tug of the satchel strap started grating on his nerves and he sat up to place it on the floor. He then started to undress for bed and paused as he glanced at his journal lying open on the bed. It was a black leather-bound thing with metal studs and a clasp that only he could unlock. He must have left it out for a large circular design was staring back at him. It was the same diagram that he had painted with his daughter's blood in the ritual chamber. He knew now that the diagram was wrong, but it still had put him in contact with a being that he only suspected existed before. A star-given sentience? A being of pure energy? A singular example of a greater consciousness? He knew not what it was, but he wanted to interrogate it.

Flag brought his gaze up to the stack of books from the library. It had diminished in size as some of the books had returned to their homes on the shelves, but the weathered hand-written one he had tucked a number of notes into remained. He plucked it out of the pile and opened it to a page that showed two feline beings and a tower. Above and behind it was the same symbol he used in his rituals, save for a triangle that connected the three outer circles. On the opposite page was the briefest mention of a story that served as the foundation for almost all of the wedding ceremonies on Sivoa; the Siameran ceremonies in particular, as the nomads even took that symbol as their clan crest over a properly conjured one.

Idiots, Flag thought as he unconsciously scratched at the tattoo on his left palm. The day before their wedding, he and Ta'nia met the matchmaker from the cult of Orianna in the apartment they were to share at the top of the southwestern tower. They had picked this location because the ceremony was supposed to bless the home in addition to bringing it together.

In what would be their dining room, the oracle placed a massive oligoclase between them as they kneeled facing each other. Flag had tried to listen to the woman's incantation, but was distracted by his beloved's giddiness and the tingling in his hand as he placed it on the gem. The tingling then turned to burning and the both of them had to fight to keep their hands down until the end of the ceremony, which had cleanly seared the most beautiful pattern he had ever seen into his flesh.

In contrast, Julian and Chiarina had their unification ceremony publicly and at the start of their wedding ceremony. They used a circular iron to burn their joined and wrapped hands into a bloody mess. The end result was a raised and irregular scar that was offensive to look at. How this – and the Siamera's refusal to include

Lieron into their clan by magic – failed to insult to the northern nobles was beyond his understanding.

He stared unseeingly at his palm for a while before a tremendous yawn overtook him. As much as he hated devoting the time to it, he knew he needed to sleep. There was much that he would need to be awake and ready for.

CHAPTER FOURTEEN

There were only two of them. They stood on an imagined precipice and watched the light of those who slept flicker in and out as they dreamed. She was once like they were, part of the luminous mass, but boredom dictated a change and she became the first of her kind; radiant and singular.

This change was exciting, but she soon grew tired of experiencing it alone and sought someone to share it with. She called out to the others, but none woke to her pleas and she gave up, wishing an eternity for a companion. In time, her prayers manifested in the form of a being she named Ragnar. He was almost a complete contrast to her; he was dark where she was light, cold while she was warm. She wore her fire for all to see (if they would), while he kept his inside, only to come out in sporadic fits of brilliance. Her elation over him had been everlasting – until now.

"What do you mean you're leaving?" She fixed a monochromatic gaze on her son.

"I'm sorry, Mother, but I must find my place."

Orianna blinked slowly and deliberately. "Your place is here with me."

The shimmering son blinked in his own time. "My father's place would be with you."

Orianna was silent. She had created him out of her own life stuff – a bad idea for now she was incomplete, as was he and she never intended to fix that. Had she a partner before, he would have had more to grow from, but her impatience doomed them. He had resented her for that and now he sought completion elsewhere. She couldn't fathom an existence without him. "Please don't leave me."

Ragnar had already started to turn away, but paused at hearing the sadness in her voice. "I must."

With that he vanished, taking her passion with him. This enraged her and she cursed loudly into the darkness, finally kindling an awareness within those who slept. "You will never find what you are looking for! You will never belong anywhere but with me! Nothing can love you such as I! You are nothing without me!"

CHAPTER FIFTEEN

Elainia had been trying to sleep when her subconscious showed her an image of two celestials. *Not again. You promised me one day a year.* The vision faded and she believed the goddess had heeded her request until she suddenly found herself surrounded by fire.

With a hunger beyond what was natural, it devoured buildings and chased people. It turned toward Elainia and she barely had time to flinch before she was engulfed. Through the flames she saw a darkened figure with bright, envious eyes scream in a rage that physically burned.

The oracle awoke to find herself tangled in her sheets, on the floor. *That was uncalled for. You could have woken me up the normal…*

As she sat up, she noticed the suns had not even teased at the horizon. Her windows were pitch dark with the moons being the only things she could see. To make things even more surreal, all nine of them where visible from her bed.

Adeen?

She felt a tiny warmth spark in the back of her mind, but it was gone just as fast. Even still, it managed to relay a sense of urgency that would have gone unnoticed on any other night – drowned out by Orianna, her patron goddess. Not tonight, however. This night belonged to the anniversary of Elainia's birth and it was the one day she owned. *Try again, little sun. Her attention is not on me today.*

For the briefest of moments, the moons shined brighter and the nightmare of fire played out in front of her eyes again. This time Elainia was able to place where she had seen it before and she understood why she had not been contacted until now. *The sorcerer's vision. What about it?*

Instead of an answer, she only received the vision again before it faded completely. The Orianna glanced out the window and noticed a thin sliver of blue light beginning to define the horizon. Auvier, the unconscious sun, had returned for the day. The others would soon follow.

But I don't have to talk to any of them. Elainia smiled as she stretched and dove back onto her bed. When she first heard the voice of Orianna, she had been asked what she would like in exchange for her servitude. An annual chance to simply be herself was all she had asked for. Her peers thought that it was a risky request (for who would ever want to dismiss their goddess?), but it was granted.

Try as she might, she found going back to sleep impossible. She had awoken too close to her own schedule and found herself dwelling on the sorcerer's vision from long ago. Best to think on it now, for she would have to put it out of her mind come the day's end unless she wanted her patron deity's wrath rained down upon her.

She got up and paced across the circular room until she reached her vanity. As she brushed her ridiculously long brown hair, she pondered on the encounter in which the sorcerer confessed his fears to her. His vision and the new one had differences. He wasn't in Adeen's at all. Only a village, some strangers, and a monster... No, not a monster. A child of perhaps sixteen.

This clarification of the dark figure spelled out what the smallest sun had been trying to relay and she staggered backward over the bench she was sitting on as the knowledge overwhelmed her. She cried out and Ja'kal, her assistant who must have been standing watch, was there in an instant. "Is everything all right, my lady?"

She took his procured hand and pulled herself up. "Please prepare the caravan. We must leave for Libris Del Sol by nightfall."

Ja'kal stared at her in confusion. "The library kingdom? But why? It's such a long way."

"That is why we must leave today!" the Orianna interrupted. "We do not have time to spare!" She paused and glanced sadly around the room. "We may not be returning."

That woke the young apprentice up. This location at the edge of the desert had played sanctuary to the Oriannas for generations. To suddenly have their lead oracle say that she potentially would not be returning home was serious business indeed. "Right away, my lady."

With that, he turned and bound out of the room, setting in motion the gears for their departure. The Orianna stood up and walked to her balcony to take in the view, certain it would the last time they ever saw it.

* * *

Dragonira was jolted out of a deep sleep by screams she only realized weren't real as she sat up. While the visions had been surreal and defied logic, the large Sivoan-like beings that were arguing in them felt so real, it was disorienting.

Or perhaps it was her surroundings throwing her off. She was in the library again, but this time she was pressed against Pavlova's side as he slept comfortably on the couch hidden amongst the bookshelves.

In a moment of panic, she couldn't remember why she was there, with him, in such a compromising position. She then remembered the day she spent with him in the marketplace, and the kiss by the fountain, which wound up drawing more attention from its patrons than was comfortable. They ran to the library in order to avoid the crowds, but even in the impossible spire they were limited in their privacy.

They wound up on the floor that connected to the palace, where they sat and talked in a furnished nook between shelves. They didn't bother paying attention to the time and, considering her current situation, they both must've fallen asleep there.

Embarrassment took over and she shuffled to the other side of the couch, unsure of what would be the proper response to this situation. Was she supposed to wake him up? Did she need to leave?

The notion of abandoning Pavlova here threw her thoughts into a dizzying spiral that brought her back to the dream that had awoken her in the first place. There was a familiarity to it that she found troubling and she dwelled on it until a small set of feet stepped into her view. Glancing up, she met eyes with someone dressed as a librarian but could not possibly have been more than ten years old. "Uh... hello there?"

The little librarian simply nodded a greeting and then turned toward the prince. "Master Pavlova. You have overslept. It is time for your lessons."

The prince groaned and moved only as far as the arm cushions. Dragonira laughed and glanced back at the girl to see if she shared in her mirth and found that the girl's eyes had never left her. Even when she spoke again to wake the prince, she kept her unwavering gaze on her. It was unsettling.

The prince finally sat up and waved a hand at the girl impolitely. "I know. I heard you. I'm up." He yawned and glanced at Dragonira, whom he was surprised to see. "Good morning."

"Good morning." She echoed while keeping an eye on the librarian. She smiled as well, but it was hard to keep it genuine with the strange audience of one.

"Did we spend the whole night here?"

Dragonira nodded, but wasn't able to elaborate further. She had fallen asleep as well. In fact, if she remembered correctly, she had fallen asleep first for he had been talking when exhaustion hit her like a wave. It was as if her dream forced her into unconsciousness, rather than it happening naturally. She felt there was something she was supposed to pull from it, but she had no idea what.

Her silence was loud enough to cause both the prince and the librarian to stare at her. When she noticed, the thoughts running through her mind evaporated in the heat that spread across her face. "Sorry. What was that?"

Pavlova smiled apologetically. "I have to attend to my studies, but I know that you don't really have anywhere to go now. She will escort you to my suite. You can stay with me there until we get things sorted out."

What?! It was true that she didn't want to return to her father's, but she didn't particularly want to move into the palace proper either. "I... uh–"

"This way, my lady," the young librarian instructed and grabbed her hand. Startled by the girl's sudden action and the situation in general, Dragonira allowed herself to be led around the inner balcony and through the aerial passageway to the palace, where they parted ways with the prince.

Wait a minute! Dragonira gasped as his offer caught up with her. Did Pavlova just say that she could live with him?! Wouldn't that be against some sort of social law? He was the king's son! The heir to Libris Del Sol! She was... what was she? Technically she could be a noble, but she knew nobody in the kingdom. She was an outsider on the inside – an inside outsider!

"Is this permissible?" she asked awkwardly.

"They are my rooms. I can do with them as I please," he said before departing, leaving her with the little librarian and without a say.

They traveled through a passageway that she recognized as being adjacent to the dining hall until a turn brought them to a large atrium at the heart of the palace. It was similar to the library in that it was comprised of many balconied floors, stacked one on top of each other, except these were square and connected by stairways in each corner. They used one of these to reach the cactus garden on the ground floor.

Is nothing in this place small? Dragonira marveled at the architecture. She would have loved to stay and look at the plants, but the librarian had marched on ahead of her to knock on the glass and metal doors on the other side of the garden. She had to run to catch up. By the time she reached the entrance of the suite, the doors had been opened and a handmaiden greeted her. The tiny librarian was nowhere to be found.

"This way, my lady." The handmaiden grabbed her wrist and tried to drag her inside without giving her a chance to catch her breath.

"Whoah, wait up," Dragonira said, snatching her hand back. "I didn't agree to stay in the prince's room. I just..." She trailed off as the handmaiden looked her over with a bemused expression. "What?"

The woman's hair had been bundled up in a number of cloths that threatened to topple over as she moved aside so that Dragonira could see the hall that lay beyond the door. "The prince has many rooms. You will not be sleeping in his bed," she teased.

I am not awake enough for this, Dragonira thought as she crossed the threshold into the suite. She was too flustered to continue combating the situation and followed the handmaiden to a set of doors off to their right. The second they entered the guest room, the servant closed the door and grinned slyly as she nailed her with another awkward instruction. "Undress."

Dragonira deadpanned at the woman. "Why?"

The handmaiden pointed to another door in the room. "For your bath. You haven't bathed already, have you?"

"Ah," she replied unenthusiastically, "I can bathe myself."

Obviously disappointed at losing the chance to get some gossip fodder out of her, the handmaiden bowed and backed out of the door. "As you wish, my lady."

Finally alone, Dragonira stripped and entered the bath chamber. It was similar to the one in her father's apartment and not something she would have given a second thought to, had she not seen what the common people of Libris Del Sol dealt with. Unlimited water (even if it was recycled) and private places to enjoy it was a stark contrast to the noise of the bathhouses. *This really isn't fair*, she thought as she stepped into the almost-cold pool.

She recalled yesterday's fiasco and sunk in until the water was up to her chin. What a wimp she was. Even if she had been arrested, she still would have succeeded in escaping her father's domain. Instead of embracing her freedom, she had run back to the familiar.

Dragonira thought of the darkened being from her dream and discovered that she envied him. He had done it. He had gotten the courage to leave. She needed to do the same.

* * *

Flag skipped breakfast in favor of asking the king to allow him to search through his private study. It was a place that never ceased to amuse the sorcerer, for Julian treated the grand office as nothing more than a giant storage space. Anything important, like political work or items that required thought were always taken care of in either the library or the council room, so the study remained largely unused.

For this task, Flag probably would have gone to the library himself had it not been for the dream he had. The two beings in it reminded him of something that he knew to be in Julian's possession and might be what he needed to tie the Siameran traditions to his research. Finding the statues from the king's wedding was turning out to be quite the challenge, however, and after what felt like hours of picking meticulously through the dust, Flag dropped into one of two heavily upholstered conference chairs in the middle of the room.

Where the fuck are they?

When he had asked, Julian assured him that his study is where he kept them. The king even stopped drinking to help him search when they weren't on the shelf he had thought them to be. When this effort turned up nothing, Julian supposedly left to ask his mother if she had seen them. Flag suspected the king had actually left to refill his mug.

The sorcerer allowed his eyes to wander around the room again. A final, half-hearted attempt to find his current objective before his thoughts took over.

The last time he had seen the delicate statues was at Julian's wedding. They were another thing that Flag had paid little attention to at the time as he had his own marriage to deal with.

A number of alliances had been forged through such arrangements and the new monarchy of Libris Del Sol had decided it would be best to overwhelm their new kingdom with celebration by honoring all of the unions at once. Flag had gone from slave to captain in a day so that he could marry Ta'nia. Julian united the desert with the ice mountains by way of the Northerner's daughter. The whole affair was long-winded and Flag had ignored most of it to flirt with his new wife.

He tried to remember the story that precluded the king's union and failed to recall more than the snippet from the book he found. Nothing suggested the statues would be of any significance either, but the lingering feeling from the dream he had wouldn't let them go. They simply had to be the next piece in the puzzle that was his research.

"Hey, Flag!" Julian's voice echoed in from the hall. "They're not here. They went back to Lieron."

Damn it all! That was his luck. Every time he gained a clue that would help him possibly solve the mystery of his tortured existence, he hit a wall. The only way that he would gain access to the statues and their story, in the time that he had left to research them, was by attending another Siamera wedding, which was impossible. There was only one unmarried member of the royal family left in the kingdom and the prince seemed determined to be a lifelong bachelor. Even if he did find a lady to court, it was unlikely that Flag would be invited.

Unless... Flag jumped to his feet and dashed out into the hall as the groundwork for a plan fell into place. All he needed to do was arrange things with Julian – if he could find him. The sorcerer stopped in the middle of the large empty room and found himself alone. This was awkward since the king had just addressed him from here.

"My lord?" He spun slowly around and found no sign that anyone had been there. No doors were open and the king's half-eaten breakfast was still sitting on the table. He was about to leave when he found himself restrained by arms wrapped almost lovingly around him.

"Julian, what are you doing?"

There was a pause and Flag could feel the arms relaxing their hold. Then suddenly they shifted forward and there was a weight on his back. "I'm looking for a companion."

"Are you really so drunk?"

He felt Julian shrug. "Can't be helped. Chiarina left for her mother's kingdom and I've been without."

"You have concubines."

Julian slid off him and sighed. "Actually, I don't. She sold them off some time ago."

Flag felt a twinge of remorse at this news, but he didn't let it show. "Pay a visit to a brothel. There are ways of getting in unseen."

The drunken king shook his head and sighed. "Not with news of Arminius hanging around."

"Then tap the staff. There are plenty who—" Flag's advice was interrupted as Julian's drunken clumsiness shoved him against a wall.

"That's complicated," the king whined. He then reached up and caressed Flag's cheek. The smell of drink that had been lacking a few minutes ago was now back in full force. "You look enough a woman. I can make it more an effect."

Flag placed a palm on Julian's face and shoved, knocking the king to the floor. "I look no more a woman than you."

"Impel quiescence…"

The sorcerer looked down incredulously. "What?"

The drunken king smirked and tried to stand as he stumbled over more of the repudiated spell. "Impel Obsequi—"

Sovereign or not, Flag was done with this nonsense and he used his foot to return Julian to the floor. It took an extraordinary amount of willpower not to kick him a second and third time. "That no longer works, remember?" He stepped past the temporarily crippled king and made his way toward the door. "We will talk again when you're sober."

By the time that Flag made it to the cactus garden he was in such a foul mood that he had forgotten why he had left the study. As the heavy door slammed shut behind him, it all came back and he dropped his head back in disbelief. "Damn it…"

Julian was prone to being an agreeable drunk and even with the strange come-ons, it would have been more than easy to convince the king that their children should wed. Instead, Flag had allowed his temper to get the better of him and now he would have to find another time to push this arrangement.

He ran his schedule through his mind and frowned. Another secret trip had been on the agenda, but the timing for it was now a problem if he wanted to motivate the royals to back this idea. The people he was supposed to meet with, however, would not wait for him to push something so trivial.

What he needed was a big enough distraction to occupy both parties for a time. As he looked at the cacti in front of him a solution presented itself.

They were due for some rain.

* * *

Julian pressed his forehead against the door and eyeballed the empty flagon in his hand. *Damn it! Why did I do that?*

He didn't mean to upset the sorcerer. In fact, he had meant to explain to his friend just how frustrating things had been for him since Chiarina left, but his drunken state took over and focused on his physical complaints. Complaints that would have been abated had his wife not left, or dismissed the harem.

Fuck. What sense did any of that make? Didn't he go a significant portion of his life managing just this situation? He stood up straight and paced back toward the study, where he grabbed an empty wine bottle before leaving it again. He then threw the bottle across the foyer and sank into a chair facing the balcony.

He immediately regretted this. Now he'd have to clean it up – or make someone handle it while trying not to say what caused the mess. Did it matter? Would anyone actually question it? He was the king. He could just command and have people obey.

That was the complication of his position. The previous ruler of the stifling desert kingdom ruled with that mentality. He was the king, what he said was law. Julian couldn't afford to remind his subjects of the tyrant he had saved them from.

He sat back and remembered the night that they had finally won the city. They had scoured the palace to finish off whatever loyalists they could find and stumbled upon the harem, buried beneath the royal suite.

That was an awkward situation. First off, there was something of a language barrier. Being from the north, he was versed in high and low Nyanyranall, which allowed him to speak with the nomads he commanded. The women spoke a dialect of Surla and, at the time, he had to find someone in his ranks to translate for them.

The women were glad they didn't have to withstand the tyrant's beatings anymore, but they argued that they liked their little community and did not want to leave. Even when they were invited to come celebrate, they had chosen to stay in their little coven. It utterly baffled him.

Despite the awkwardness he granted them their wish. He had the locks on their doors broken off and requested that the library offer them protection from unwanted intruders. No longer his concern, he had almost forgotten about the strange group until the one year anniversary of their takeover.

He had taken his wife back to their chambers, where they celebrated in private for several hours. Instead of returning to the festivities outside or sleeping, they decided to explore the rest of the inner palace. A set of steps down from what is now the cactus garden brought them to the suite that the harem girls occupied. Chiarina had stared him down hard over their existence, but she also happened to speak Usan – another dialect of Surla – and was able to get the full story from the girls. She also received a proposition, which she accepted, much to his surprise.

Embarrassing as it was at first, both he and his wife visited the women for experiences they couldn't replicate on their own. They would visit separately as well, but they didn't really talk those forays. Chiarina lost interest in their company after the birth of their son and it had been she who offered the location to Flag sometime after his wife passed.

Julian shifted position and adjusted himself as he recalled the sorcerer's wife. *By the suns, she was gorgeous.* The desert and the night wrapped up into one beautifully vibrant being who just happened to be completely beyond his reach in every possible way. A sand-born child who was picked up and adopted by the Cafra tribe they were warring on behalf of, she was the chief's daughter and tribe liaison. If he laid one finger on her, their war pact would be over.

She was a damned good battle magician too. Perhaps that was the problem. With her providing support to the front lines, she was continually nearby. Her beauty always shoved in his face. He could hardly stand it.

At his breaking point, he had sent his subordinates to find him a whore from a nearby town. Whatever the debacle was, they came back with an unconscious, tall, skinny, silver-haired man in a dress. Julian had wanted to publicly pummel them to death, but he bit back his wrath when they presented him with a red leather book.

The spells within it were supposed to force the man whore into compliance while altering his appearance to fit the desires of its owner. After signing his name into the tome, Julian had tried the spell and found its effects staggering. He freaked out, threw the book, and assigned Gared and Jinto to digging the piss pits. When his new servant awoke he threw some armor and a sword at him and told him to join the ranks.

That turned out to be a mistake.

In the next battle the strange man showed an aptitude for wielding lightning and struck down a couple of riders before being overcome by the recoil. Julian, excited to have another potential battle magician in the ranks, placed him with Ta'nia for training. Little did he know they would fall for each other.

One night he passed her tent and overheard the sounds of their pleasure and became enraged. The unfairness of the situation was overwhelming. HE had wanted to court her, give her everything she could want, protect her, lay with her... it was unfair that, of all people, HIS concubine made it into her bed.

Julian had been upset enough to wait most of the night in the soldier tent that Flag had been assigned. When the new magician had returned from his romp, the commander read off the spells in the book and enacted his revenge on an illusion. After he was finished, he threatened the man whore to keep quiet and continue paying such dues, lest he take out his forbidden desires on their mutual object of affection.

And damn it, he honored that agreement too...

Julian took his lust for Ta'nia out on Flag more than he cared to admit and it had turned him into an emotional wreck by the end of the war. When they finally won the city, he was so happy to be over it all that he drove to drinking right away. When Ta'nia and Flag approached him to demand the man's freedom he was more than glad to give him away.

What happened?

The weddings happened. The year following the liberation of Libris Del Sol was busy. He had established a court to manage the city, reconciled with the library, organized the rebuilding of the walls and irrigation systems, and finally had to deal with an arranged union that ensured Lieron had claim on the most desired library in the world.

It wasn't that Chiarina was a bad match for him. He grew to appreciate her on his own, but Ta'nia absolutely stole his breath and broke his heart when he saw her ascend the steps for her and Flag's small ceremony.

He knew then that he had to keep tabs on them somehow. At first, he did it by befriending the couple. Why not? She was technically royalty and an ally under his care. Then she and Flag started venturing out of the kingdom together, making it impossible to monitor them.

This plight was cured when a magician he hired to fight Flag (for the amusement of the nobles) came up with the idea to curse the sorcerer with a timed-return spell. Though the visiting magician had died, his plan actually worked! He no longer needed to worry about his friends leaving the kingdom permanently!

Or so he thought.

He had never expected that she would die in childbirth. Julian was devastated, but not anywhere near as wrecked as Flag had been. That was when he sobered up to the situation and finally left the ruined family alone. He also became even more dependent on his drinks.

The king stood up and walked over to the pile of broken shards, wracked with guilt over the morning's event. He went to pick up the glass, but changed his mind and instead sought out the kitchen. There he'd find lunch, a drink, and someone to clean up his mess for him.

CHAPTER SIXTEEN

The worst part about traveling to the camp was the ravine. The desert's scar wrapped around the southern edge of Libris Del Sol, blocking it from the oasis that served as the region's life blood – an architectural blunder that someone had once corrected by way of a convoluted waterwheel system.

If one was crazy, they could use this series of pulleys and buckets to scale the north wall of the ravine. The idea terrified Tom, so he opted to use the extremely narrow set of stairs that had been chiseled out of the rock in eons past. There could be a long-winded debate over which was safer but Tom at least understood how to use one.

Scaling the ravine took an entire day, so when Tom ran into Eric at the top, he was utterly baffled. He had left the Sassin household just as the sky started to lighten and the dungeon worker was nowhere to be found. "How do you do that! We were both kingdom-side yesterday and I know I left before you did."

Eric shrugged. "I left last night."

"Seriously?" Tom gawked at him. "That's insane. It was way too dark."

"All nine moons were out last night. It was bright enough."

The calico puffed his cheeks. He would admit that under normal circumstances, traveling to and from the camp at night would be ideal since there was always the possibility they would be seen climbing the walls during the day, but the path was rough and far more dangerous in the dark.

"If you left so early, how come you're hanging out here?"

His elder friend pointed over his shoulder and sighed. "The nomads are realigning with the sun trails and the library is helping."

Tom felt himself make a face and Eric chuckled at it. He had been told plenty of times that there was a schedule to this, but he could never figure it out. "Was this why you left last night?"

"Yeah. I tried to beat it…" Eric nodded as he gazed out over the ravine. "They started early."

The two of them watched the suns finish their trek across the sky. The wind kicked up just as the smallest sank behind the horizon and stirred them into action. Once they were sure the oasis was void of librarians, they continued on toward their destination.

There was an eerie silence to the camp that caused a slight panic to settle in Tom's chest. It threatened to grow until they rounded a corner and found one of the twins talking with a stranger dressed in earthen clothing.

"One of yours?" Eric asked from somewhere behind him.

Tom shook his head, but then corrected himself and shrugged. He might have been adopted by the visiting humans, but the colony they brought with them was so large there was no way that he met everyone. The only thing he knew about this individual was that he was some sort of high-ranked officer based on the uniform he wore.

Ka'ren nodded a goodbye and finished his conversation with the stranger and turned toward Eric and Tom as if he had known they had been there. "Good. You guys made it here. We should get to the tent. I think Bik might have talked my brother to death by now."

"What was that about?" Eric asked, gesturing back to where Ka'ren had been standing.

"When the librarians showed up we had to ask the Earthers for help to hide the tents. They used their magic–"

"Science," Tom interrupted.

Ka'ren nodded. "Right. Science. They use it to hide us from view. It worked."

"Ah." Eric turned toward the tent, no longer interested in the conversation. Tom on the other hand paused at the news. The strangers to their planet exercised a large level of precaution when it came to their interactions with the natives. Hiding the rebels from the library wasn't likely something they would do unless a greater threat loomed.

Tom caught up to Ka'ren to ask him about it when the sound of thunder rolled in the distance and caught every one's attention. They watched the sky for a long moment before the young leader suggested they "go inside."

They jogged across the campgrounds in order to catch up with Eric and entered the council tent as a group. Bik was rambling on about something and Ka'say shot his twin a silent plea for help.

"I've trained them as best as I could. They can hit targets on the horizon, but if we can't carry the bows up the lifts, then there's no point!"

"Calm down, Bik. I understand your frustration with having to train everyone, but what—"

The irate human marched over to Eric and snatched a map from his satchel. He then held it up and pointed at a spot on it for Ka'say to look at. "There's our problem."

"The water lifts? I don't get—"

"How do we hold onto those lifts?" Bik retorted.

Ka'say held his hand up in the air and sighed. "Just say what you want, Bik. I don't have the patience to play your game."

The master archer stood straight and held his hand, palm-down, out to his side. "Our bows are about this tall. We can carry them slung over our shoulders well enough, but they still stick out. I can pretty much guarantee they will get caught in the nets."

"We can have them brought to the top of the cliff through the marketplace. It's not that big of a de–"

"How are you going to get them into the castle after that? We're riding the lifts all the way in."

An awkward silence settled in and the twins glanced at each other before they shot Eric a look. "Would you be able to smuggle them in?" Ka'ren inquired.

The tactician shook his head. "Ever since the first botched attempt on Julian's life, the palace guard have made it a point that no weapons go in or out of the place."

"What about teleporting them in?" Ka'say ventured.

"Pardon me?" Eric tilted his head in confusion. "I don't think the library would–"

Bik shook his head. "Come now. We know that you can conjure."

This news threw Tom for a loop, but if he stopped and thought about it, it made a level of sense. The man was able to get around rather quickly. He turned his gaze toward his friend and found that he looked as bewildered as he felt.

"That's news to me." Eric adjusted his glasses and shook his head. "I might wish I had the ability to manipulate the forces, but I assure you that I cannot."

Ka'say cocked his head. "It would explain a few things."

The elderly tactician shrugged. "Even if I could, I'm not a librarian, so I would not be able to teleport. My work also places me in the vicinity of the Scourge, so if I were able to use such talents, I would surely be caught by him."

Tom knew this was a sore spot for the twins and was not surprised they dropped the matter. He was just a little surprised Eric would bring it up so casually.

"Moving on." Ka'say directed his attention toward Tom. "Were you able to get what we needed from the library?"

Tom froze. "Uh... no."

"Did the disguise not work?" Ka'ren asked quietly. His disappointment with his idea was evident, but premature.

"Oh, it worked. I just ran into the prince before I had a chance to get anywhere."

"What was that?" Eric interrupted.

"I said that the disguise worked."

"No, I mean that noise."

They all paused and could hear it now that they had stopped talking. A low thrumming coursed through the tent and resonated off of the wooden supports.

Bik was the first to understand it and panicked. "It's the ropes!"

The wind had caught the canopy of the tent, causing it to strain against the ropes and making them vibrate. The people inside barely had enough time to register what was going on when the first rope gave and sent a stake through the tent, clipping Eric in the face as it flew past. They all dove for the ground just in time for the rest of the tent to become uprooted and go sailing into the brush beyond.

"Over here!" a voice shouted from somewhere to their left. A human woman was carrying a lantern and waving people toward a thicket of trees. "It's safer over here!"

The camp leaders scrambled against the dust-filled wind to get to the light and joined the woman in a lean-to situated between some boulders and the trees. It was crowded as much of the camp had already taken shelter there, but the atmosphere was friendly despite the raging storm outside. Tom was just glad he didn't have to worry about any more projectiles and went to share a smile with his older friend, who he quickly realized wasn't there.

"Wait! Where's Eric?"

* * *

They had watched the storm roll in from the balcony outside of the prince's suite. At first the clouds held little of their attention as dust storms were often enough, but when the first roll of thunder greeted their ears they gave it notice. Overall it had taken about two hours for it to roil around and build before it reached them and they had spent most of that time watching it from the railings.

Now Dragonira was watching the rain slide down the window in amazement. "I can't even remember the last time I saw rain!"

Pavlova followed the course of one droplet with his finger as he nodded in agreement. He then smiled and leaned back against the cushions on the couch they had pushed in front of the window. "If it weren't for the lightning, I'd say we could stand outside and enjoy it."

Dragonira allowed her jaw to drop a little at the thought of standing out on the balcony, getting soaked. She hadn't even considered the idea, but now it was all she wanted to do. She turned her eyes upward, looking past their reflection to see the clouds beyond. She was angry at them for being so noisy and, for a moment, she felt as if they understood.

Then light exploded across the sky as electricity shot down into the ravine, causing the couple to jump back from the window. The wind picked up and the storm became increasingly violent, setting fire to the line of trees that sat on the horizon across the ravine. Dragonira stared at the yellow glow as Pavlova grabbed her hand and gently led her further into the suite. *Did I do that?*

A part of her felt guilty for the thought, but an unexplainable excitement had settled in her chest and sent her heart racing. She remained focused on the storm through the retreating window until Pavlova stepped in front of her and slid the door shut. Then she snapped her attention to her surroundings and discovered they were standing in the prince's bedroom.

She arched an eyebrow at him. "What are we doing in here?"

The perverted thoughts racing through her mind where shot down by the look of concern on the prince's face as he stared into the foyer through a gap in the door. "The storm's getting really bad. I probably should have shut the outer doors, but we'll be safe in here."

Suddenly she felt bad for her previous state – even if Pavlova was unaware of it – and she placed a hand on his shoulder. He didn't fully acknowledge her until the thunder calmed enough for him to tear his attention away from it. The warmth behind his smile mixed with the thrill she felt from the storm and she moved to embrace him. She could not recall when they locked lips, but she did notice as he picked her up and carried her toward the bed. The exciting atmosphere stirred something within her and she consented to ride out the remainder of the storm with him there as they undressed.

CHAPTER SEVENTEEN

"Ragnar... Why did you leave?"

The great being's paws had cracked and started to bleed on the rough terrain her son left in his wake. She had been following this path for an incomprehensible amount of time and the loneliness was setting in.

She was about to die.

"Damn you, Ragnar," she vocalized as the last of her strength ran out and she collapsed onto a sharp rock. It had impaled her, but the pain she felt was nothing compared to the emptiness inside.

"You shall suffer, Ragnar, for this," she cried silently as the first few sentient creatures formed from her blood and gasped at the wasteland they were to call home.

She cried, and rivers and oceans formed. The sentients rejoiced, not fully understanding what was going on, and ran to the beautiful blue of the water. Almost immediately they ran out of it shivering. It was cold, something to appreciate but also something to be wary of.

Just as Orianna's vision started to fade, another being appeared and knelt beside her.

"Ragnar!" She tried to jump up to meet him but was unable.

The being shook his head and reached out to wipe away a tear. He was not her son, but he was beautiful and glowed warmly. Despite her great despair, she was at peace.

"Who are you?"

"I am Auvier and I have heard your cries."

He moved away somewhat and extended his energy outward in

invitation. "I too have known loneliness, and want it no more. Will you come with me?"

With his aid, she abandoned her broken body and her soul leapt up to join him. The two playful lovers chased one another through the newly formed sky. Their revelry eventually formed another life, a daughter, who they called Adeen.

Orianna, however, did not forget her suffering and its memory festered inside her. She wanted to lord her new family over her former son and to show him what they could have been. She wanted him to regret abandoning her.

CHAPTER EIGHTEEN

Elainia groaned as the pain in her head forced her into consciousness. At first she thought it was the result of her goddess finally taking note of her unexpected excursion, but she came to realize the discomfort she felt was not in her head at all. It was in her legs.

She reached out in an attempt to turn and see what the problem with them was, but found no purchase as her fingers plunged into sand. She was pinned into place and she couldn't see past the dune she was lying partially in. Whatever happened, she was no longer in the sled.

"Ja'kal!"

The storm last night had come on them so suddenly that they had no time to prepare for it. She remembered lightning striking the ground nearby and spooking the taratins. The sled had lurched, but beyond that she couldn't recall anything. She suspected that she was now under it, pinned against the sand and with no help in sight.

She called out for her understudy again, but was only met with the quiet howl of the wind through the dunes. Perhaps he was knocked out as well. The Orianna didn't like that she hoped this was what his silence meant, but if anything fatal happened to him she was going to die here – in the middle of nowhere. It was a horrifying image, but also one that did not match up with the visions that led them to travel in the first place.

"Ja'kal! Damn it! Where are you?!" She screamed until her throat was raw. She let her head hit the sand and she sulked. He had to be alive. He simply had to be.

There was a muffled noise somewhere behind her but she

couldn't see what it was because of how she was trapped. She silenced herself and froze, praying whatever caused the sound had no intention on harming her. A familiar shadow appeared to her left and she released her breath.

"Oh, thank the suns! You're alive!" She turned her head toward the shadow's point of origin. "For once I don't know what happened since we last saw each other."

His ugly sandals disappeared from view as he knelt down and smiled in front of her. "There was a demon in that storm. It tossed the sled and threw me down a dune. I twisted my ankle in landing, so it took me some time to make it back here."

Elainia blinked at that. "I'm so sorry, Ja'kal." This hazardous trip was all her fault. To make matters worse, she had failed to predict its course, which she should have been able to do. She was the world's top oracle, after all.

Ja'kal merely shrugged. "I'm okay, let's just get you free."

He got up and walked over to the sled. At first she couldn't tell if he was doing anything, but then she heard a low creaking noise and a sharp pain shot through her legs and up her spine. She called out and slammed a fist into the sand.

In a heartbeat Ja'kal was beside her. He had pushed the sled over so that it was no longer on top of her, but she still couldn't move. When he saw that she was struggling, he offered a hand to help her up but she refused it. "I can't. They're broken."

The faint smile he had attempted to comfort her with had vanished. She knew he had suspected her legs had been crushed and hoped to deny the fact by remaining silent. Now that it was out, the weight of their odds of survival pressed in, making her head swim.

"Wait here," he instructed, and once again disappeared from view. A grunt and the sounds of wood snapping greeted her ears. This piqued her curiosity and using the abilities that the goddess Orianna granted her, she saw that he planned to re-purpose the demolished sled into a shelter.

She didn't know how much time had passed from when he started his project, but when he was done he braced her legs as best as he could, with the few supplies he had and gently carried her inside. Although he was silent, she could see he was fighting panic over their situation.

Poor thing. She reached up and placed a hand on his cheek. "Calm down, my friend. I'll take care of us."

* * *

A powerful yawn overtook Julian as he waited for his breakfast in the small alcove next to the kitchen. It had been a long night. The storm, which they thought would be more wind than anything else, wound up being a torrential downpour with an unexpected amount of lightning.

The thunder had woken him up long before he was summoned by his steward to join in an emergency meeting with his council. The storm sparked fires and mudslides all over the city and whispers arrived almost immediately. They had to tap the royal guard and the library in order to form a small task force to help with the larger issues – such as the flooded field threatening to take down a portion of the outer wall. Everyone else had to wait.

The storm had tapered off shortly before sunrise and it was only about an hour ago that the council retired in hopes to catch some sleep before they would all take shifts in hearing out the villagers' complaints. Julian would sit in on the afternoon session, so he had some time to himself to rest as he saw fit. He decided that he needed food and stopped by the palace kitchen before he sought out a bed to sleep in.

That was where Flag found him. Although the sorcerer looked his usual sleep-deprived self, he was handling the morning with more energy than the king could muster. Julian found himself envious of this as he nodded a greeting in fatigue.

A look of confusion settled on Flag's face and after a long moment of silence he spoke. "What are you doing down here?"

The palace kitchens were stacked on top of each other, but originated one level below ground and were positioned at the top of the stairs to the basement levels. It was common to see the sorcerer here for that reason, but was rare for Julian to visit. "Just wanted to grab something to eat before I go take a nap. That storm last night was something else."

Flag nodded before he grabbed his daily basket of food from the serving window. He appeared to be irritated at something and Julian could only guess that it was his presence. He couldn't blame him for it. "Hey... I want to apologize for my actions yesterday."

"What?" The sorcerer paused his inspection of the basket to shoot him a quizzical look, throwing Julian off his line of thought.

"Uh... yesterday when I was drunk... I... Sorry."

Flag stood up straight and paused in thought for a moment before nodding. "You really should cut back on the drinks."

"Yeah," Julian agreed, but still found himself dumbfounded at Flag's indifference over something he knew would throw him into a rage normally. What was he upset about if it wasn't that? As he thought the scene over, he realized the sorcerer had tried to start a conversation beforehand. "You wanted to talk to me about something, right?"

"We can discuss it later."

The king shook his head. "I have time now. I can't guarantee that to be the case later."

"Fine." The sorcerer huffed as he set down the basket and gave him his full attention. "Are you aware that my daughter has moved in with your son?"

Naturally Julian had no clue. "When did this happen?"

"Yesterday."

Julian rolled his eyes and chuckled under his breath. "Figures.

No. I was not made aware of that yet, though I am sure that it would have ended up on today's meeting agenda."

The sorcerer was not amused. "I was intending to bring it up then."

"Oh." Julian fought off the urge to make a quip about the sorcerer's attendance (or lack thereof), but those terrifying sunset eyes suggested that it would be best to avoid it. "I'm not sure that we're going to have a normal meeting today. The storm last night disrupted quite a bit and we'll be observing grievances all day. Boris is handling that right now, actually."

As Julian studied his friend, he noticed that look again. Perhaps the storm had caused some sort of problem for the sorcerer. "Did it affect you?"

Flag scratched at a small cut below his eye that Julian hadn't noticed. "Yes, but it's nothing worth noting. Since you are determined to talk now I would like to propose a union between our children."

"Are... are you serious?" When Flag continued to stare him down, he could see that he was. "What would you get out of it?"

"Not a lot, to be honest, but Dragonira would be close to home." He paused. "You'd benefit from it far more."

This sent Julian's mind reeling. What could he possibly gain from having his son marry within his own kingdom? The point of such things were to make a kingdom stronger by merging its resources with – "Oh, that's brilliant! If my son married your daughter, we wouldn't have to fight off claims to the kingdom or the library!"

Flag held his hands out as he performed a shallow bow. "This was why you had been secretly shooting down Chiarina's efforts, was it not?"

Julian smiled and marveled at the sorcerer's insight. The queen had begun to grow impatient with the prince's lack of interest in a wife and had attempted to arrange marriages with some of Lieron's major trade partners. This, however, did not sit well with Julian. Libris Del Sol was so far away from the northern kingdoms that the only benefit he could foresee was gaining timber from Arlogate. This was a valuable resource, but the northern states had made it clear they wanted a say regarding the ownership of the desert library's valuables.

Even if the library had been under his complete control, he knew this would cause him to lose his only real bartering chip. He needed the other kingdoms to pay for access to their knowledge if he wanted to keep Libris Del Sol afloat. He had mentioned this to his wife a number of times, but the spoiled northerner insisted everything would work out.

Her flippant attitude about this resulted in Julian advising the prince to bring random village women to dinner whenever he wanted. This way, even if she managed to succeed in bringing a potential bride-to-be to the table, she would be overshadowed by the prince's choice of the day and shamed until she was sent home.

Of course, marrying within the kingdom posed its own problems. The most immediate would be the over-ambitious nature of its inhabitants. Any of the low-lifes his son dated could lay a claim to the throne simply by producing a legitimate heir. Marrying him to someone within the court, on the other hand, was an immediate way to avoid such drama.

"Before I agree to this, I want you to know that I am aware it would put you in line for the throne..."

"You don't trust my intentions?" The sorcerer read him like a book. "If it would help appease, my lord, you can strike my name from the beneficiaries. I don't want to rule a kingdom and I already have everything I need."

"Okay then. I agree to this union." Julian held his hand out to shake on the agreement. "I'll have a servant go fetch our children."

* * *

"Hold on! I'm coming, I'm coming!" Kinya shouted as she climbed over a pile of boxes that she had carried out of storage and dumped into the common room.

Rain had come in through a hole in the garden wall and collected on the stairs, from there it spilled into the large closet they stashed things they either never saw again or never intended to unpack. Despite these little truths, Kinya didn't want the forgotten collection to be destroyed by water. She had been haphazard in her efforts to save it and now wished she had taken the extra effort to keep the hallway clear.

Her mother was shouting obscenities by the time she had unblocked and opened the door. "Calm down! Yeesh! I had to... what happened to your hair?!"

Kinya stared in disbelief at the disgruntled ex-nomad who stood in the doorway.

"I had to exchange it to make sure I crossed the ravine safely," Ta'mika said as she pushed her way past her daughter and into the mess she had made.

"The librarians wouldn't bring you back?"

"When the storm rolled in, they told us to stay in the tents and left." Ta'mika sighed and shook her head. "You're going to clean all of this up."

Kinya gawked at her mother, ignoring the new chore assignment. "Why didn't you listen to them? Scaling the cliffs at night! What were you thinking?"

"I wanted to get back to you!" Ta'mika snapped back. "There was nothing natural about that storm and I needed to make sure you were safe!"

Kinya melted under her mother's gaze and shut the door. "You know, it's safer here than pretty much anywhere else I could have been."

"Have you looked outside?"

"Nooo..." Kinya reversed her actions and opened the door to look through it. The neighborhood was trashed. Debris was everywhere and the only reason that the larger house next door hadn't crushed hers was due to a mystery rock formation that wasn't there yesterday.

It took her a moment to realize her mouth was hanging open and she spun around to face her mother. "Did you! You did! How! What?"

Ta'mika held up a hand to silence her daughter and smiled. "I read a warning in the sand, but was unable to make my appeal to the librarians before they left. Thank the suns I was able to get here in time."

Kinya was flabbergasted. Her mother often claimed she could predict the future and tell fortunes, but she never gave it any merit because generally, the woman was terrible at it. Now the young housemaid was confronted with proof to back the claim and it was like she met her mother for the first time. "But, you're not a magician..."

Ta'mika smirked and gently grabbed her daughter's hand and tugged her inside. "Of course I'm not, but anyone can do magic if they appease the right forces."

"But... the exchange... the recoil." Kinya was going to bring up what she had been told about having to pay the forces to use their power, but something clicked. "You traded your hair!"

Ta'mika nodded. "I did. The winds kept the path dry for me so I could come home."

"What about the rock?"

"That wasn't me. It was one of the palace guards," her mother explained while looking a little defeated.

Kinya was able to piece together that her mother had wound up asking for help. Considering her mother's disdain for the royals, asking one of their minions for help must've required swallowing a lot of pride. "Thank you," she replied, unsure of what else to say.

Ta'mika smiled and hugged her daughter as she should have done when the girl first opened the door. "I'm just glad you're not hurt."

When they separated, the elder Sassin surveyed the piles of stuff with a different eye than she had before. "What happened in here?"

"Nothing major. There's a roof leak and water got into the storage space." Kinya chuckled. "Pity there isn't a natural force behind cleaning."

Ta'mika smiled. "You would have to sacrifice the mess."

"By cleaning it? Real funny, Mom," Kinya snarked as she began stacking boxes. Her mother moved in to help and they worked in silence for a while until a loud chime sounded just outside the door.

"You have got to be kidding me!" Ta'mika exploded. "All this damage to our homes and they expect you at the palace!"

"Calm down. For all we know, it could be telling me I have tomorrow off as well," she said incredulously as she once again opened the door.

In the frame floated a soft purple orb of light that smoked as it strived to burn itself out. Kinya waved her hand through it and the gruff voice of the sorcerer spoke. "This message is a call to duty for the following: ALL palace guards, outer ring agriculturalists, outer ring carpenters, rooftop farmers guild members, Aliram of Laifer, kitchen staff levels A through D, public bathing facility managers, and inner rim housekeepers. Please report to your assigned posts immediately."

Kinya glared at the spot in the air where the whisper smoldered and evaporated. She could feel her mother's misplaced temper burning a hole in the back of her head and had to take a deep breath before turning to face her. "Yeah, yeah, I jinxed it. Don't worry, Amma. I'll be home as soon as I can."

The little housemaid gave her mother a hug and pushed past her to retrieve the cleanest uniform she could find in the laundry room. She didn't care that her appearance wasn't pristine. Based on the list of people being summoned and the events of the previous night, it wasn't like she was going to have to prepare for some high-society event.

"I'll be back later!" she called back as she skipped out the door and jogged down the street. She stopped to make sure her friend Alnara received the message as well and power-walked the rest of the way to the palace. If she were honest with herself, she would have to admit that she was relieved to get away from her mother's overbearing presence – even if it did place her under the watch of Huruga, the "kitchen overlord."

About an hour had passed before Kinya finally made it to the little alcove outside of the ground-level kitchen. She had allowed her mind to wander on the trip and was trying to figure out who Aliram of Laifer was when a panicked voice caught her attention.

"There you are!" Vika grabbed her elbow and stooped to catch her breath. Her uniform was even more disheveled than Kinya's, making the young Sassin feel better about herself. "You were the last to attend on the sorcerer's daughter? Correct?"

That's an odd question. "I helped her get ready for dinner a little while back, but–"

"Good enough." Vika used her grip on her arm to drag her toward the laundry facilities and handed her a large wooden box of the type they only used for special occasions.

"Are you serious? They're going to have a ball tonight?!" With the damage that the lightning and mudslides caused, it would be irresponsible to host a feast.

Vika shook her head. "Not quite, but I'm sure there will be one later. They're announcing the prince's engagement tonight, but nobody wants to take the dress down to his fiancé."

Kinya blinked at the woman, trying to process all of the

information she had just been fed. "Who's he getting married to?"

The other housemaid's brain visibly quit at her question. When it jumpstarted again, Vika was borderline furious. "The sorcerer's daughter, you idiot! Go take that to her!"

Vika shoved Kinya out into the hallway and abandoned her to take care of some other task, leaving her alone with her confusion. That was sudden. While the green-eyed woman's presence at the dinner table was unusual, nobody in housekeeping thought it was going to go anywhere. To hear that she was now going to marry the prince was...

SHIT! She's the sorcerer's daughter!

Kinya cringed as she realized she would have to go down to his apartment to fetch her. *Ugh. No wonder nobody else wanted to do this.* The man was infamous for being the reason servants were never seen again – despite the fact there was no proof to the claim.

What was true was that he had a terrible temper. Kinya knew a little more of the reasoning for it than most, but that didn't mean she wanted to see it firsthand. When she had descended the right amount of stairs and traversed the right amount of corridors, she stood face to face with his door. An eternity later, she gathered the courage to knock on it.

Nobody answered.

Now what? Do I knock again? What if I leave that package here in the hallway for them? She shook her head and decided that was a worse idea than making sure it and the message was delivered. This time she knocked on the door harder.

It flew open and she cowered back in anticipation of the lashing that would befall her. When it didn't happen she opened one eye and saw the sorcerer shoot her a look of surprise before settling into his normal grump. "What?"

Kinya held up the box and darted her eyes down the hallway. "You're uh... your... this is for your daughter."

"She moved in with the prince." His voice was unusually dry and raspy as he redirected her. Kinya realized that he was still sending out whispers when she interrupted him and she attributed his odd reaction to her appearance on that.

"Oh. Uh... Thank you." She bowed slightly and turned as he slammed the door shut.

Suns... just how much activity can happen in one night? This is insane! She made her way back to her station and explained the daughter's new living situation to Vika, who stared at her in disbelief for some reason. When the other handmaiden reclaimed the package and set off to deliver it to the palace royal attendants Kinya went home.

She couldn't help but laugh at her odd adventure at work. *Imagine if mother heard about this!*

* * *

It had only been a handful of days since the first time a royal attendant had prepared her for dinner, but the experiences couldn't have been any more different. Dragonira watched begrudgingly as a dress woven from dreams and stitched from air was draped over her twiggy frame and her hair was yanked and pulled into a braid so tight that it threatened to pull her ears from her head. Days ago she might have wandered through this alteration of appearance with a sense of stunned wonder, but right now it was all she could do to keep from punching the handmaiden through the mirror.

It wasn't that this attendant was far rougher than the timid girl who helped on that first night, but rather what spawned this need for formal attire. Earlier in the day she and her now husband-to-be had been summoned to the king's suite, where their fathers had been waiting to tell them of their plans for the future.

It had been horribly awkward. Despite how they spent the previous evening, Pavlova appeared shocked at the news and had only gawked at his father until it was pointed out that the prince was being rude. Dragonira hadn't responded much better. Her father had found a way to keep her within his grasp despite all of her intentions and she reacted by glaring at him as the king relayed a number of details she ignored.

A prick on the scalp brought her back to the present and she flinched away from the attendant, who was holding a small metal comb in shock. "Forgive me! I did not mean..."

Dragonira waved it off and stood straight again to allow her to continue upon the task of sticking things in her hair. She tried to keep her eyes off of the mirror, but eventually they found their way there anyway and she spied the reflection of the prince in the doorway. He looked so helpless that she melted. "Oh come in."

He took a sheepish step forward and made his way toward the trunk under the window. There he pretended to be interested in it for a minute before he came to his senses and faced her. "I'm sorry about earlier... I just... It's–"

"Quite a shock? Don't worry about it. I behaved poorly as well." She tried to turn toward him, but was not yet free of the handmaiden's grip.

The prince nodded, then shook his head and then shrugged as he gave up. "I just wanted to say that I'm not displeased."

A small laughed escaped her painted lips and she bit down to keep it from growing. She knew exactly what Pavlova was trying to say and found it amusing that the master of all things social was having trouble saying it. They were both trapped by this arrangement, but on some level they were both okay with it. "At least we'll get to leave for a little while."

While she hadn't been paying attention to the king, he had and on their way back to the suite Pavlova filled her in on their itinerary. The wedding would be taking place in forty days. This was supposed to launch a festival that they would miss altogether because they would be heading north to Lieron to stay with the queen's family. There they would stay until it was time to come back for the Gala of the Suns festival.

"That's a lot of partying..." the prince said under his breath, causing her to give up the restraint on her laughter. Although not yet married, they were already thinking on the same wavelength.

"It really is." She waved off the handmaiden and sat on the trunk next to him. "Makes doing all of this for tonight's family dinner kind of senseless."

"Yeah, but that's the family tradition for you. Everyone will be wearing their second best to the table and only the four of us have any clue as to why." The prince shrugged. "They're probably trying to weasel the information out of the staff as we speak."

The attendant nodded through a smile of her own before making a small gesture to indicate that they've sworn to keep the secret. She then pardoned herself as she cleaned up the assortment of accessories that the sorcerer's daughter hadn't let her put on her. The sight was somehow sobering and the dread at facing the nobles again settled in Dragonira's stomach. "I wish we didn't have to be present for tonight's announcement."

"Especially since we're going to have the big engagement event in ten days." He sighed. "Unfortunately, it's the nobles who will be paying for that, so we need to impress them now."

Dragonira blinked at him. "They are? But, I thought your family controlled the riches."

"Eh..." Pavlova hovered his hand in the air a moment and dropped it. "The council manages the economy under my father's guidance, but we can't lay claim to the kingdom's money. That isn't to say that we are without funds. The Milmordas, my mother's family, is the wealthiest in all the realms."

"Then why do we need the nobles?"

The prince shrugged. "I think it's more symbolic than anything. Gives us the ability to see who our allies are with this and where our priorities with them lie."

Dragonira felt her chest tighten as she remembered the overheard conversations at her first dinner. "Couldn't this be a bad thing? I don't think they like me much."

Pavlova smiled and pulled her close. "I wouldn't worry about their gossip. They always make up wild speculations when they don't know who someone is. You just caught them off guard last time."

She pulled away from him and frowned. "It wasn't much better after they found out who my father is."

"It is true they don't like him much, but that works in your favor."

She raised an eyebrow at him. "How so?"

His sapphire eyes smiled down at her. "You don't have to pretend to like him for their sakes. You can just be yourself."

Dragonira's mind blanked as his words hit home. He was right. She could visibly disown her father in front of the whole kingdom and be better off for it, but the mere concept just felt so... wrong. "I don't know if I can do that," she admitted as an entire lifetime of fearing the man settled under her skin, causing her arms to prickle.

Pavlova hugged her again. "Don't worry. I already promised that I would protect you from him."

Dragonira nodded and glanced at the doorway where another attendant was waiting for them. "It looks like it's time."

"Yeah," the prince agreed. "We better be on our way."

CHAPTER NINETEEN

The dream of fire had, once again, jolted the Orianna out of her sleep. This startled Ja'kal, who had been taking care of her since their sled had flipped over a couple of days ago. After a brief moment, he realized what had happened and simply offered some of the water they had left over. She thanked him and hastily downed the offering before going back to sleep. He frowned at the empty canteen and sighed. There was still one more skin of water that he could ration out for perhaps another day, but they weren't going to last much longer without help.

He had wanted to chastise her for going through their reserves so recklessly, but he pitied her. Even in her sleep she could not rest. The pain of having her legs crushed, combined with the vision of everything burning, had made her restless. This was then amplified tenfold by the goddess, whom was greatly displeased at their having left the spire they were supposed to oversee.

Poor girl. Ja'kal attempted to soothe her by running his fingers through her hair, but she simply swatted him away. He withdrew his hand and decided to use this opportunity to go outside and think. There wasn't much he could do there either, but the hot wind made him feel slightly less confined.

He sighed, noting that the suns had already begun their descent. Ja'kal was thankful he wouldn't have to deal with the day's heat much longer, but he wasn't looking forward to the evening chill either. He scoured the area around their shelter for anything to burn and had given up after finding nothing suitable. A distant voice suddenly caught his attention.

"Hey, you there!" it cried.

There's no way I'm that lucky. He knew there wouldn't be anyone calling out to him when he turned around. There wasn't the last time he checked, or the time before. Why would now be different?

"You there! Is everything all right?"

Ja'kal was shocked to see a single individual wearing beige robes and riding an extremely large taratin slowly toward him, and he answered the man in a daze. "Our carriage was overturned during the storm and our mounts fled. We would very thankful for any kind of help."

The rider nodded his dust- and cloth-covered head and dismounted the two-legged desert runner once he got close. The stranger then offered a canteen of herb-infused water, which Ja'kal accepted gratefully before running it inside to the Orianna. The robed man didn't appear to mind this rudeness and simply followed him into the makeshift shelter.

The Orianna had looked a little worse-off than Ja'kal had remembered her and had to fight back panic so that he could wake her. When she opened her eyes, the veil of desert sickness pulled back and she smiled up at both of them as she reached for the canteen. "Thank you, Ja'kal… and you, Rinsk, for the water."

Ja'kal was used to the Orianna knowing people's names without introduction, but he wondered what the stranger felt about it. Surely that had to be something awkward for him. When he looked over to see the rider's reaction he was greeted with a calm he had not quite expected.

Rinsk caught onto his confusion and attempted to clarify. "Your mistress had called for us on the shifting dream sands."

"The what?"

Rinsk smiled and shrugged, then continued to speak in a heavy accent that Ja'kal imagined to be northern. "I don't know how to explain. Sand has magic and she used it to speak to us."

The apprentice felt that he should relate to that, but it didn't really make any sense to him. Despite having grown up in the desert, there were a lot of properties to it he couldn't understand, which he chalked up to a protected life on the Orianna spire. How can sand carry messages?

A faint chuckling emanated from the woman sitting across from them. She was asleep once again, but had found something funny. Ja'kal could only guess that she was laughing at his own inexperience. As usual he could never be sure.

He turned to Rinsk and saw that he had dropped his mask to reveal a cream-colored face, with dark stripes that traced along the edges of his nose to the corners of his blue-green eyes. His head was awkwardly shaped, which Ja'kal had originally first attributed to the dirty wrappings he wore around it. "Are others coming?"

Rinsk nodded. "They are on their way. I must go meet them."

Ja'kal nodded and sat silently as the rider made his exit. He lost track of time and must have fallen asleep because it felt like only a moment had passed from when the traveler left, to when he returned. Night had fallen, but the winds had not yet held a chill.

"Are you able to carry much weight?" Rinsk inquired as he slipped halfway into the shelter.

Ja'kal simply nodded as his mouth was still feeling the effects of sleep.

Rinsk smiled a disproportionately large smile and stepped aside. "Good. You can help us with the sun blessed."

The alternative title for the Orianna lent credence to Ja'kal's prior assessment of the traveler's accent and he marveled at the notion that they may have crossed the desert just to save the oracle. When he inquired about it, however, he discovered that they had been much closer. As they carried Elainia to the palanquin that had been brought for her, he noted it was emblazoned with the crest of the royal family of Libris Del Sol – a large circle that encased and connected the points of an equilateral triangle. Inside of this was a set of three circles that were connected on the innermost points by yet another circle. "So you are nobility?"

Rinsk laughed and shook his head. "Hardly. We're Cafras. The caravan is on permanent loan."

Cafra was a name that Ja'kal remembered from his history lessons. According to his studies, the Cafras had once been a noble family who repeatedly fought amongst itself over land claims. These arguments ended up on the doorstep of a previous Orianna who became enraged over the petty disputes. In order to weed out their lineage and end the in-fighting, she cursed the family in a manner that only allowed the women to give birth to female children. She then went a step further and made it so that only one girl from this bloodline was able to carry the family name at a time. This ultimately wiped the true Cafras off the map, but many nomads have adopted the name by either self-proclamation or marriage.

As Ja'kal had never seen any such vagabonds at the spire, he honestly had assumed that the story was simply that – a story. Being with them now felt strange and outside of reality. This feeling stuck around until they arrived at a small camp that featured tents also decorated with the Siamera crest. "Why do you have their stuff?"

"Those lazy north bums moved into the library. Let us have it because they don't plan on traveling any time soon."

That threw Ja'kal off. "But you... your accent..."

Rinsk laughed as they set the palanquin down beside one of the tents. "Born and raised in Mizzaltolte. Joined the Cafras during the war. I guess the accent stuck."

"Ah."

A couple of other nomads had carried the Orianna into her tent and Ja'kal had prepared to follow them in when he was stopped by a young woman he hadn't noticed before. She had a darkened face and vibrant eyes that matched those of her patron tribe, but her hair and ears were a reddish-brown instead black. Just like the Siameras, however, her air of regal intelligence was lost as soon as she opened her mouth. "Ya can't come here."

Ja'kal tried to ignore her and push on through, but she stepped directly in his path and pushed hard against his chest. This caused him to stagger backward and it was only by a stroke of luck that he didn't completely topple over. "What are you doing?! Why can't I go in there?"

The woman had obviously had enough and pushed him again for good measure. "Uhhh… She needs to be bathed and prepped for her surgery."

Surgery? He knew that her legs were damaged, but the full inflection of that hadn't dawned on him. "Are you… You're going to cut them off?"

The non-Siamera woman eased in her stature and nodded. "We have to. They're beyond saving."

Ja'kal stared helplessly at the tent. He had put them in a splint to keep them from moving around, but he was no medic. Even with his best intentions, he had no idea how to mend anything more than a minor cut.

He heard shuffling around in the tent and realized that he probably didn't want to be so nearby while his master was suffering through an amputation. Instead, he wandered around the small camp until he heard a loud banging coming from just outside it. As he rounded a tent he was able to see the nomads were breaking down a sled. His sled. "Hey! What are you–"

He was interrupted by a couple of kids running past him with the splinters that had already been broken off. Not thinking, he took off after them as they led him back to the center of the camp. There they threw the pieces on a stack and spun away from him as he nearly plowed into the growing pile of wood.

There was a loud shout as a dark-eyed woman appeared out of nowhere and waved her hand over the mound. She was greeted by two other shouts from elsewhere in the camp and a fire burst forth from the pile, causing Ja'kal to lose his footing and fall backward onto the sand. A voice behind him started to laugh and he turned to see that Rinsk had caught back up with him.

"It is quite a sight, isn't it?" Rinsk asked once he had finished mocking him.

Ja'kal looked up to see what Rinsk was talking about and found that the three women who had shouted, were now dancing around the fire their voices created. The air rippled around them as they moved to a rhythm only they could hear. They punctuated some of their motions by throwing sand, which never reached the ground and instead colored the air with hues that told a story he also couldn't detect.

Soon they were accompanied by a couple of musicians who played their strange instruments based on their movements, instead of trying to lead them with their notes. This produced a song that was as disjointed as it was beautiful and Ja'kal became mesmerized by the performance.

The next thing he knew, a strong hand on his shoulder was shaking him awake. As he sat up, he saw the dancers had gone and the fire was being attended to in the normal manner by one of the musicians.

"They are done with the sun blessed. She's asked to see you," Rinsk informed him gently.

That woke him up and he jumped to his feet to run to the tent that he remembered as hers. The non-Siamera was standing out front again, but this time simply pushed the tent flap aside so he could enter.

The tent was carpeted and furnished with more than Ja'kal thought was possible for a band of travelers to carry. In the middle was a ceramic wood stove that was accompanied by two different containers holding water. Beyond that was a large wooden chest that had a padded lid, which allowed it to double as a bench. Not far from it was a large cot adorned with a heavily padded straw mattress that the Orianna lay upon.

He ran to her side and was shocked to see she was completely awake and coherent considering everything. "Mistress, you called for me?"

"Yes." She nodded her head and grasped his hand tightly, betraying her appearance and indicating to him just how much pain she was in. "I have a large favor to ask."

"Anything," he said without hesitation. "What would you like me to do?"

An apologetic smile broke across her features and she pulled him close. "The goddess is preventing their medicines from doing what they're supposed to, so I'll need you to confer with her for a little while. Perhaps hours at a time."

"Is… is that possible?"

The Orianna shrugged and tilted her head. "I do not know, but she has agreed to try." She paused and sighed. "I have to apologize, though. She is a misandric entity and I am afraid it will hurt quite a bit."

Ja'kal unconsciously took a step backward. History had taught him that the largest of the suns was vengeful, but to find out she would already have a predisposition against him made him uncomfortable. However, as he looked at his friend, mentor, and master, he could not deny her request. "I'll try."

"Thank you. I have requested that Zellyth watch over you and return you to me every couple of hours so that you can return the burden to me. We will switch off like this for a few days."

"Who's Zell–" he started to ask when an intentional cough at the door informed him the name belonged to the non-Siamera woman. *Great.* He then shook his head to clear his thoughts and consent to his master's plan.

She nodded back and pulled him close so that she could touch her forehead to his. Lightning exploded into his brain, followed by fire and thorns. He saw the goddess' rage and it compounded in his chest, knocking the wind out of him as it forced him to the floor.

Visions of many different men flickered through his mind and he hated all of them without reason. This feeling consumed him and he found himself wishing all sorts of torture for them – no, for him. All these different faces belonged to the same someone; a rare someone with sunset eyes.

CHAPTER TWENTY

Tom had liked staying in the camp. The rustic feel of the tents reminded him of the better parts of his time in the traveling freak show. Now that his own was gone, he was back "home" in the sterile apartment/storage closet the Terrans had generously provided him.

The walls were close and padded, so there was no reason it should have been so loud when someone pounded on the door. "Wake up in there!"

"No!" Tom shouted back as he fumbled around for the button that would shut off the alarm clock. He then realized that was wrong and rolled out of bed to slide the door open when the noise continued. "What?"

"Boy! I wish I could sleep half as well as you do! I've been banging on your door for half an hour now!"

Tom blinked one eye at her as he tried to comprehend what she was saying. "What time is it?"

"Before dawn."

The realization that he should still be asleep slowly washed over him and he glared at her. "Why the hell would you wake me up now? I only just got to sleep!"

The petty-officer returned his gaze and stared him down, making him regret the whole confrontation. "Your superiors called for you. Get your ass out of bed and go to them."

He didn't need clarification there. The militaristic mentality of the ship's regular crew made it clear they believed the Wiltafoir twins to be the highest ranked officials in the "army" of the rebellion. Once Tom had tried to explain that they were more equally matched and casual than that, but it never really registered.

"Fine." Tom pressed the button to shut the door again and stood in thought for a long moment. The rebels were normally most active after the day settled because the sun-worshiping tribes were the busiest then and whatever action the palace sentinels could witness from the walls seemed as part of that routine. To step outside of that cover meant whatever they wanted to talk to him about, it was important.

He found a pair of pants in a questionable state of clean and put them on. The calico was about to dash out the door when he remembered that the desert air was chilly at night and stopped long enough to grab a tattered vest that had also been on the floor.

Ka'say was standing outside the Terrans' unperceivable fortress with a lantern. "About time. We need you to get to Ta'mika's immediately."

Whatever sleep had managed to cling to him leaving the ship, was gone now. "Why, what happened?"

Ka'say turned and led him up a path. Soon the two of them were racing toward the cliffs at a haphazard pace. "We just got word that there's a big gathering of the royals tonight and we need you to be there."

"Why would I need... oh." They were going to send him in disguise again. "What's the occasion?"

Ka'say slowed and glanced over his shoulder as he spoke. "Rumor has it that the prince will be getting married."

Tom frowned. "He's getting married tonight?"

The rebel leader shook his head and returned his focus to his foot placement. "No. This is the formal announcement. We should find out when the actual wedding is at it."

The calico was still having difficulty in keeping up in both gait and conversation. "Why do we care about the wedding?"

Ka'say stopped so abruptly that Tom plowed into him, causing him to drop the lantern. When the light went out, Tom realized just how dark the oasis was right then and gulped. Climbing down the ravine was going to be a nightmare.

"If this is true, it would be a better time to launch our attack," Ka'say said as he bent down to relight their way. "We would be less likely to anger the library."

Damn it. He was right, which meant Tom actually did have to go through with their craziness again. "Hey. Wait. I have to get something to cover my face. Last time I was already disguised before I hit the village."

"Already thought of that." Ka'say unloaded the satchel he wore and handed it to Tom, who managed to hide his annoyance at having his attempt to stall thwarted. He really didn't want to brave the deadly climb in the dark. "You won't need that 'til you get to the bottom anyway. Here."

Tom found the re-lit lantern shoved into his hand and he gawked at the rebel leader. "You really want me... I..." He handed the lantern back. "I can't climb down with this. I need both hands and I'll be spotted besides."

Ka'say nodded and took the light back. "Sorry... for both the rush and the danger. However, it is crucial that you get this information for us."

"Is it? Couldn't we wait until the kitchen wenches find out?"

"Honestly, I think the women in the palace are giving us the run-around. I've gotten more information from the black market scouts than I have them – including this bit of news. I also learned that if Arminius doesn't show up at the event tonight he will be exiled, so you absolutely have to be there."

The calico finally gave in to the fact he was going on this mission and nodded. "Okay." He grabbed the post with the rope to climb down and had just waved goodbye when Ka'say stopped him. "What's up?"

Ka'say looked across the ravine and bit his lip in thought. "Don't tell Eric about this."

Tom had nodded agreement before he was fully aware of what the request entailed and Ka'say was gone by the time he actually thought to ask. Instead, he mulled it over as he carefully put one foot in front of the other on the narrow path.

Eric was likely aware of the dinner and he was definitely aware of the disguise. *So what am I supposed to keep secret, exactly?* The call for "Arminius" clearly meant that he'd have to attend the dinner or else risk losing the rebellion's only chance at the royal records. After mulling it over, his best guess was that Ka'say didn't want Eric to know that he sent Tom down in the dark.

The early morning stretched into infinity. By the time Tom was able to see where he was putting his feet he was little more than halfway down the cliff face. Once the light settled, he was able to travel down with much more speed. The trick now was to make it to the palace waterworks without dying.

The "short ass" river (as he named it) ended in a waterfall that threatened to deafen his ears as he waded into the pool at its base. Invisible hands grabbed at his clothes and satchel with the intent to pull him under the surface forever. The fight to stay afloat exhausted him before he even had a chance to start the most enduring part of the trip. *This is insane!*

Just as he thought about giving up, he was greeted with a rocky structure that supported one of the waterwheels. He reached out and was able to hoist himself up upon the weathered stones, where he collapsed in exhaustion.

He lay there watching as large buckets carrying water were pulled along a huge conveyor belt up the ravine and into the palace so far away. He remained that way until the suns beat down on him mercilessly from their pinnacle point in the sky and the heat became uncomfortable. *Ka'say... you fuckin' owe me for this.*

The next step was to catch the netting that held one of the buckets in place and stuff himself inside before he got too high up. He watched the timing as they scooped water for a bit, and then shook his head, reminding himself of the absurdity of this plan. Just as reason was about to get the better of him, he remembered that his destination would bring him back to his favorite person in the world.

Maybe Kinya would like to crash the dinner with me. Tom smiled inwardly at the notion of "Arminius Milmorda" taking a serving wench to one of the biggest royal events he'd be likely to see. It was so in character that it almost hurt. It wasn't that Tom thought little of Kinya's position. He respected her immensely for supporting her mother by working amongst her enemies, but he knew the royals wouldn't think much of her – or the fact she accompanied the family outcast.

Inspired, Tom launched himself at a passing bucket and missed the drawstring. A quick scramble allowed him to catch a hand and a foot in the netting and from there he was able to climb into the container. He didn't like being wet again, but it was honestly easier than attempting to cling to the exterior the whole ride up.

He was shivering by the time the bucket upended and dumped him into a massive water basin. The splash that he made was loud and startled him to where he dove under the water to avoid being caught. When nobody reached in to retrieve him, he realized he was most likely in the clear and he climbed out of the pool.

It made sense. This part of the waterworks had been automated for centuries. Nobody had to pay it any mind unless something happened to stop the belts – a thought the rebellion itself had entertained until it realized it would hurt everyone in the kingdom and not just the nobility. This system supplied water to the fountains, the bathhouses, and the farms way out against the outer wall. It was in the kingdom's best interest to leave it intact.

The structure the pool was housed in was connected to the castle by a massive water screw powered by the same ropes that carried the buckets. The spiral within the diagonal tunnel carried the water up to the massive cistern atop the palace's perimeter wall. Everything was automated, which meant there was nobody on staff that he could steal dry clothes from.

Instead, he hung the garments from his satchel over the ledge and sat on them to keep the heavy winds from snatching them away. He watched the shadows on the wall start to grow long before he gave up and decided that damp clothes would just have to do.

Tom probably should have knocked as opposed to barging through the door of the Sassin household, but he didn't have much time left to change and he was done with being wet. "Hello!"

"By the suns! What gives you the right to bust into my house like this?" Ta'mika grabbed his ear and twisted as a means of defense, but let go when she realized he was of no threat to her.

The move had brought the calico to his knees and he was fighting back tears as he answered her. "The twins... want me to... crash dinner..."

The plump elder Sassin stared him down a moment as realization started to set in. Then she turned toward the kitchen and shouted at him over her shoulder. "Sit down. I gotta get the supplies."

Tom followed her instructions and sat in a chair at the warped, wooden table in the center of an abnormally messy room. He raise a brow at the clutter and wondered why Kinya would allowed it to happen. *Oh right!* He about jumped out of his seat when he thought of her again, but Ta'mika's orders were not to be ignored. This didn't stop him from wanting to talk to her though. "Where's Kinya?"

"She already left." Ta'mika's voice streamed out from the kitchen and had a hint of annoyance in it.

Damn. Tom slouched in the chair as low as he could without falling off of it. It seemed he was doomed to observe the festivities by himself. "Is she going to be coming back any time soon?"

Ta'mika shuffled out of the back and dropped a large bucket of supplies on the table, which threatened to collapse. "I don't know! Her new shift is all over the place. She might be on her way back right now or she might not come home 'til tomorrow morning. This last week has been crazy, which is why this room is still a wreck."

"Couldn't you do it... OW!" Tom's mouth had spoken his thought before he could stop himself and Ta'mika made him aware of it with a large spoon she had stashed in the bucket. She, however, didn't say anything further to defend herself. He rubbed at the spot on his head where the impact happened and watched her set the spell components on the table. "I apologize. That was rude."

She chuckled and shook her head. "Don't worry about it. I shouldn't have hit ya."

Once the bucket was empty, she proceeded to fill it again by upending a few bottles and a couple of herbs into it. The concoction filled the room with a stench that made Tom's eyes water, but she remained unfazed by it. "By the suns! What is that stuff?!" he choked out as he attempted to wave it away.

Ta'mika shrugged nonchalantly. "It's hair dye. Without the other women to help, I can only cast enough of an illusion spell to cover your face."

Tom nodded a second before her words sunk in. "Wait! That's going in my hair? I can't wear something that smelly!"

The elder woman shot him a glance that made him feel like a toddler again. "Don't be stupid, Tom. The smell will go away when you wash your hair. The color will stay."

The calico nodded defeat and remained silent as she went about glopping the stuff in his hair. The closer she got to his scalp, the more he imagined it to burn. He cringed as he felt the cool goop finally make contact with his skin, but he was surprised to find that the tingling sensation he expected never arrived. After a while of sitting uncomfortably with this stuff on his head, Ta'mika sent him outside to wash it off.

The gunk had exceeded all of his expectations. He practically dunked his head in the bucket he pulled from the fountain to get rid of the stench and was certain the color was going to wash out. He was shocked to see how wrong he was when Ta'mika handed him a polished steel plate to see himself in. "How did you know how to do this?"

She smiled. "Picked it up from the carpet makers and just changed a few ingredients. Sometimes I sell bottles of this stuff to the neighborhood women for a little extra income."

Tom glanced at the bucket and then thought back to the night he spent mending clothes with Kinya. "Your daughter works all the time and you're part of the rooftop farmers' guild. Do you really make so little money that you need to do all these extra things?"

Ta'mika smiled a weathered smile back at him and sighed. "Ever since Hogan passed, we've had a hard time keeping up financially. Doesn't help that things have gotten more expensive over time."

The calico frowned at this. The Sassins didn't try to live outside of their means. They shared a hovel connected by walls to their neighbors. They only bought the basics when it came to food. In fact, if it had not been for their nomadic connections, they might have wasted away years ago.

"Okay. The illusion spell's been cast. Should stay with you as long as you're awake."

He blinked up at her and then glanced at his reflection in the plate. There, a semi-familiar face stared at him and he marveled. "That's really something..."

"Yeah. Yeah. You said that last time. Now go put on one of the uniforms we pulled out for you. It's time you got going!"

* * *

Kinya's run-in with the sorcerer turned into multiple run-ins with him over the past week. Her co-workers mistook his lack of violence toward her as a sign that she needed to be his personal attendant. Now she was repeating last week's daunting chore and running an ornate package containing clothes down to the dungeon level. "Damn it, Vika," she whispered under her breath as she descended the stairs.

All in all, it hadn't been a bad week. Flag, the sorcerer, had attempted to dismiss her when she first knocked on his door as his housekeeper. He wound up finally allowing her in after she held his laundry hostage.

His apartment was small and, as it turns out, the rumors of it once being a warden's office were true. She had learned that his bedroom had once been a training room for the palace guards and that the secondary bedroom was an armory. The kitchen had always been a kitchen and the foyer a foyer, but the veranda was new. Once it had been a set of temporary holding cells that he had used a spell to blow the walls out of. It was so nicely sculpted now that she never would have guessed it.

Perhaps the biggest surprise the place held for her was how clean it was. When the sorcerer had told her that he had no need for a housekeeper, he was actually serious. The only thing she ever needed to sort were piles of books and the clothes that he left on his bedroom floor. It almost baffled her that he had allowed her to keep her job.

Currently, that job entailed he be dressed appropriately for the celebration starting in a couple of hours. Having arrived in the hallway to the dungeons, she knocked on his door and waited for him to begrudgingly admit her in.

Silence.

She knocked again and was met again by silence.

Uh oh...

She pushed open the door and stepped into the foyer. A quick glance at his desk showed that his apothecary bag was still there, as was his records book. Unless it was something unusual, he was not at work. Kinya then cast her gaze toward his bedroom and saw that the door was shut.

Wait. Is he asleep? She knew he worked erratic hours, but he was cutting it close to an event that demanded his attendance. Pushing gently on one of the two ornate wooden doors to his room, she peeked in to see if he was actually there. Sure enough, she could see his sleeping form lying in the middle of the elaborate canopy bed that she hated to make. *Seriously?*

A need for caution settled in her chest as she stole her way in, making it hard to breathe. The late afternoon sunlight that streamed in through the enormous glass windows on the ravine-side of the room was suddenly too bright and even her near-silent footfalls were too loud. It felt like it took hours to cross the small expanse between the door and his bed because of her stealth and when she finally reach it, she felt ridiculous.

Kinya placed the soft fabric package at the foot of the bed and stepped back to figure out the best way to wake him up. She paced around until she was standing near the headboard, where she found he had buried his face in a pillow. Strands of long silver hair were scattered everywhere, glowing against the deep burgundy sheets. Unconsciously she compared the radiant locks to the only other person she knew with a similar hair color and had to fight to contain her laughter. She loved her mother's friend Eric, but imagining the old fart attempting to brush his hair into anything more than a dingy gray mess was preposterous.

She shook her head to clear it of the hilarious images it conjured and sought to wake the sorcerer by touching the hand that he had draped over the pillow closest to her. She barely extended her own hand when he shifted in his sleep and pulled his away. The moment caused her to jump backward and nearly trip over her own feet. *Calm down, Kinya! He's just another person!* To affirm this statement, she stole a glance at his now-visible face and had to catch her breath.

She had prepared herself to see him as he was when he was awake – stressed to the point of breaking and trying to rein in his frustration with a neutral mask. In his slumber, the stress was gone and he had a shockingly youthful appearance. It was a pleasant scene and she hated to bring it to an end. *But I must…*

She reached out and gently placed a hand on the sorcerer's shoulder to wake him. She had barely even touched him when a powerful hand grabbed her fragile wrist and threw her to the bed. Within seconds, the Scourge was over her, pinning her to the bed with his knee while he pressed a knife to her throat. They locked eyes, and after a moment he let her go to return the knife to its hiding spot under his pillow. "What do you want?"

"I uhhh. I…" She found it difficult to recover from the tussle and she sat up to regain her composure and failed as her eyes landed on his nude form. His scarred, lanky, and yet athletic figure displayed before her caught her off guard and she momentarily forgot how to speak.

He rolled his eyes as he covered himself. "What do you want?" he repeated with a deeper frustration in his tone.

Somehow his comfort in her seeing him as he was, forced her to fight off heavy levels of snark. Of all the things she suddenly wanted to say, she relayed the one thing that she was supposed to. "The royals sent down your attire for the evening's festivities. I'm supposed to help you get ready, but we're starting to run late in that regard."

The annoyance that he had with her shifted into an unreadable expression that sent chills down her spine. A combination of deep loathing, resignation, and a violent rage emanated from the man and Kinya cautiously withdrew from the bed. She reached over and handed him the package, hoping that it would be enough to distract him from whatever violent thoughts were running through his mind.

It worked. As he pulled the old military uniform out of the package, he leveled out and settled into his usual state of apathy. As he laid out the outfit on the bed, she noted the rank on the sash and was surprised to see the bud of a long-stemmed rose embroidered on it. She had heard he had been a part of the Lieron army long ago, but she had no idea he was such a highly ranked specialist.

"What does…" She wanted to ask him about the insignia and tried to speak just as he stood up to dress. She forgot that he had no clothes on and choked on her words. It was all she could do to avert her eyes. Kinya turned her back to him in time to overhear his annoyance with her come out as a loud exhale, followed by a rustling of fabric. More sounds of frustration followed, but she was able to discern that they were the result of making sure he put the uniform on properly.

After several minutes, he addressed her. "Will you braid my hair?"

Kinya turned slowly to face him and saw that he was holding a comb out for her. She took it and raised an eyebrow at him. Traditionally, men in uniform either wore their hair short, or wrapped. Julian had broken this tradition, but those who imitated him still either wore it down or back with a simple ribbon. "Why a braid?"

"It's an order," he mumbled under his breath at her and offered no further explanation as he led her to the armoire on the other side of the room. Even as she started combing out the tangles in his silky-smooth hair, she couldn't figure out if he meant it was an order for her or for him. A heavy silence fell as she worked and her initial unease with the man returned, despite the jealousy she had for the silver strands she was weaving together. She just wanted to go home.

"Um…"

The sound was so subtle that she wouldn't have heard it if not for the quiet it shattered and she leaned around the sorcerer to check to see if he really was trying to catch her attention. "Sir?"

He had obviously been lost in thought and was still calculating something when he made another face that she couldn't read. "Do you want to go?"

Is he a mind reader as well? Kinya gawked at him for moment before returning and completing her task. "If you wouldn't mind."

"Okay." He nodded and stood to gesture toward the bedroom

door. "There are dresses in the room across the hall. You can wear any one that you like."

"Oh! You meant… Oh!" Kinya stared out the door and then shot a glance back at him. She still wanted to go home, but being a guest at a royal event of this magnitude was something she couldn't turn down. "I will not be long."

She skipped out of Flag's room and into the smaller room and stopped as she realized that until recently, it had belonged to his daughter. *Will I be wearing her clothes?* There was something extremely unnerving at the thought, but she couldn't place what that was exactly.

The housemaid inspected the items in the closet and determined that while they were all lovely dresses, they weren't of a quality fit for a ball. She then noticed a chest tucked under the bed at the other end of room and decided to give that a try.

The trunk was filled with all manner of odds and ends, but she did luck out and found several bundles of fabric that turned into formal attire when she laid it out. Picking the dress to wear from them was easy, for one just happened to have ornate beading that formed a design similar to her mother's family crest on it.

The shimmering fabric cascaded off of her like a waterfall and the blue set off her eyes in a way that made her grin from ear to ear. The whole effect was cinched together with a heavily beaded bodice that she knew would catch everyone's attention as much as it caught hers. *And if anyone asks, I can tell them it's from my tribe!* Kinya honestly didn't know if that was the truth, but it made sense considering the kingdom's history.

Once she had finished polishing off her appearance in the tiny mirror propped against the wall, she ran back out into the foyer to join the sorcerer and from there they started their trek back to the surface world. Flag was tense the entire time, but as usual, he kept silent.

It wasn't until they reached the doors of the grand hall that he spoke again. "Take my arm."

She nodded eagerly in agreement and happily locked her arm around his. Together, they approached the silver and gold doors and stopped. He chanted a small incantation and they were suddenly standing in the middle of the grand hall on the other side, a fine cloud of what smelled like smoke wafted away from them. *Did we just teleport?*

Flag stole a chuckle and muttered "nobles" under his breath as he led her into the crowd that was applauding the effect as loudly as they were gawking at them. She was just as spellbound as their onlookers, for it was the first time she had ever heard the sorcerer laugh. She hoped it wasn't the last.

Following a protocol of some sort, they lined up against the wall in a specific formation. Other people, dressed in uniforms similar to Flag's, lined up behind them as they faced the doors to the dining hall. Despite being late and their "grand" entrance, they were not the last to arrive.

"What was with the smoke?" Kinya whispered to her escort as she watched even more people file in.

"Another order," he whispered back.

The conversation dropped again and Kinya became aware that music was drifting in from the balconies above them. It was light-hearted and whimsical, but changed tempo into loud and boisterous when the court caller shouted to announce that the royal family was about to enter. That was when Kinya realized what was bothering her. "Aren't you supposed to be with them?"

"No," he answered curtly as he looked above her and over the crowd as the doors from the royal suites burst opened and the Siameran entourage paraded past them. As his daughter walked past, they exchanged a glance that felt a bit like strained pleasantries to Kinya and she didn't know what to make of the situation.

"But–" Before she could finish her question, he silenced her with a finger on her lips. Following an unseen cue, he interlocked his arm in hers again and they fell in step behind the procession. Even though they were not walking directly behind the royals, they sat next to them once they were in the dining hall.

That was strange, Kinya commented to herself as she nodded graciously to the nobles around her. She mildly pondered on if any of them remembered her from her service to them, or perhaps from when she sat as the prince's guest, but she doubted it. She knew she wasn't memorable as either a housemaid or another of Pavlova's dinner annoyances, but as the sorcerer's guest… that was different.

She smiled and nodded to her gawkers but stopped when she locked eyes with the person who sat directly across from her. Sitting in one of the extended family seats was a disguised freak she'd recognize in the pitch dark.

TOM! Kinya almost shouted his name when she spotted him, but caught herself before she gave him away. She remembered that his disguise was supposed to have been of the king's nephew, but was it really so well done that it fooled them? If that was the case, then was this actually Tom sitting across from her? The panic in his eyes when she met his gaze suggested it was so.

"I see you've met young Sir Milmorda from Lieron." The sorcerer spoke softly in her ear and she had to tear her eyes from her friend.

"Master, I have worked in the palace my entire life. It is only natural that I have served him a time or two." She lied, but hoped that it was enough to dissuade any attention that the sorcerer would pay Tom. If there was anyone in the kingdom who could see through the illusion her mom had cast, it would be him.

"Is that so?" Flag laughed softly for the second time that evening and gently placed his hand on her back. "Glad that is all that it is. He's a known womanizer and you are *my* guest tonight."

He shot Tom a possessive gaze that Kinya followed with a frightened look of her own. It was both completely unnerving and somewhat exhilarating to suddenly be claimed by someone as notorious as the Silver-Haired Scourge in such a manner, but she wished that it had been as it seemed on the surface.

The attention that she enjoyed a few minutes before had turned on her and she found herself avoiding gazes everywhere she could. It wasn't until an unnatural pair of green eyes caught hers that she gave the owner any attention. The soon-to-be princess had recognized her and what she read in her stare was not the same morbid curiosity that the other's had, but a strong sense of concern.

The silent interrogation was thankfully interrupted by the sound of a gong announcing the arrival of the first course. Kinya found herself trying to guess what was on the covered plates as they were set in front of them. *Pan-cooked ovagourd. Skewered beast. Marinated legumes.* She guessed them all wrong and laughed at herself as she figured out they were doing a special menu tonight.

At the end of the first course, she spotted Vika helping to clear plates and shot her a cynical smile worthy of the sorcerer's guest before she started on her first glass of wine. Her fellow kitchen wench scrunched her face up in anger and stormed out of the hall and she stifled a laugh. Perhaps this night would be fun after all.

* * *

Dragonira was really beginning to hate the royal dinners she had to share with her father. The fake way in which he endearingly addressed her was enough to make her go insane. Now he brought a guest with him and allowed her to wear her mother's dress. If it weren't for Pavlova continually gripping her hand under the table, she was certain she'd have blown up at the odd couple.

Those were her surface thoughts on the subject.

Deep down Dragonira held an even more foreboding concern. She knew her father was a power-hungry maniac, and that his doing off-the-wall things like this usually stemmed from that fact. From what she could remember of Kinya, the girl was nothing more than optimism personified. Optimism that would have normally annoyed her father to the point of violence. *Does she have some well of power that I didn't notice before? Wait... since when was I able to detect magic in others?*

Her line of thought derailed and she sat in silence. Eventually, she realized that she had always had the ability to sense magic, but only ever had used it to determine her father's mood – more than his words or body language. As she sat at the table, she could clearly sense different energies coming from other people who sat around her. Next to her father, a man wearing a Siamera military uniform a table over had the most refined energy, while Arminius (of all people) had the strongest. *That's interesting.* She slipped into wondering if he was aware of his potential when he caught her staring at him.

Immediately she diverted her eyes and found herself, once more, gawking at the house maiden who sat only a few seats down from her. Again, she sensed nothing from the girl. No magic. No malice. Nothing that should have warranted her father's attention. She glanced at him and found that he had been watching her. When they met eyes, he smirked and looked away.

WHAT IS WRONG WITH HIM?!

Dragonira slammed back into her chair and huffed just loud enough to garner the attention of her fiancé and his cousin across the table. She then looked down at yet another serving of food and poked at it with her fork even though she had no intention of eating it.

"Are you okay?" came a cool voice to her left.

"Yeah... I'm fine. Perhaps a little confused." She gestured slightly toward her other side.

Pavlova looked past her, but was careful not to make his action obvious. "I can honestly say that I did not expect that." He returned his wide-eyed focus of attention to her. "You think that anything is going to come of it?"

Dragonira shrugged. She honestly had absolutely no idea what her father was up to, nor did she know why the girl he was with hadn't cowered away as she should. "I wish I could say. I don't think that he's ever done anything like this before."

Pavlova's eyebrows raised up one at a time and she could almost see a bad joke climb down from his brain to his mouth. "You mean aside from with your mother, of course."

Dragonira gently punched his leg under the table. "Well of course. Quiet, you."

Terrible as it was, the crack shattered the wall of tension she had built around herself. While the current situation was awkward, she could find solace in the fact that she wasn't completely under her father's command anymore.

The soon-to-be princess almost dropped her fork as a new realization dawned on her and she spun in her seat to observe the housemaid who had first introduced her to the palace absurdity. *Is he... replacing me, with her?* Obscenities flung, beatings accrued, and horrible rituals survived, all flashed through her mind as she darted her eyes back and forth to her father and his guest. *I have to warn her!*

Once again, she was brought to the events at hand by her fiancé, who whispered quietly in her ear. "Eat for now. We'll be able to better address it after dessert."

Dinner dragged on for an eternity and she did her best to take her attention off of the couple to her immediate right, but every escalation in their conversation – every laugh – grated on her until she was barely able to hold her glass. She turned to Pavlova and whispered, "I can't do this anymore."

"Let me see what I can do." The prince had to wave a hand in front of his father's face to divert his attention off of the sorcerer and guest. Once he had it there was a quick exchange of nods and the king stood.

"Your attention, please. Honored guests, today we celebrate the end of my son's reign as kingdom bachelor. As you are all aware, he's held the position for far too long. Many of you have tried to help him out, and the efforts have been greatly appreciated, but you may now relax for he has finally chosen his queen. To commemorate this once in a lifetime occasion, my son has commissioned a lovely gift for his bride-to-be." Julian paused to call over a servant who had been standing off to the side until now. "Go ahead, son. Give it to her."

Pavlova stood to receive a box with gold filigree inlay, which he then presented to her. She gasped at its exquisite craftsmanship and turned it over and over again in her hands. She went to thank him for the wonderful gift when he whispered "open it" and she realized the box was simply the casing for whatever was actually meant for her. Embarrassed, she followed the instructions and nearly dropped the whole thing when she saw what was inside.

Five golden chains wove in and out of each other as tiny, glittering, multi-colored gems sat where they intersected. The necklace paths dipped lower and lower as they approached the center, where a flawlessly crafted pendant of the Siamera family crest sat. Stunning as it was, it had the wrong effect on her.

It was impossible to go through the palace without running into the royal combination of circles and lines. The royals had emblazoned it on practically everything in order to remind anyone with eyes that they were the rulers of Libris Del Sol. They were also completely unaware that the design was the same diagram her father had painted in blood on the floor of his secret ritual chamber and forced her to suffer over time and time again.

"I…" Dragonira realized she was just shy of humiliating Pavlova, which was something she didn't want to do. It was all that she could do to play off her moment of horror as one of awe. Reaching into the box to lift the pendant for everyone to see, she politely exclaimed, "I love it… and you." She then leaned forward to meet Pavlova with a kiss.

Satisfied with her presentation, the king broke out into another, vaguely insulting, drunken speech and Pavlova sat down to help her put her gift on. "Did that work?"

She nodded as she remembered that she wanted a distraction from her father's odd behavior. "A little." Now was not the time to mention the fit of terror the trinket had caused.

The gift-giving was the signal for dessert and a gigantic spread of confectioneries was laid out before them. Dragonira failed to recognize anything that was being served, but she could smell how sweet it was. It was almost as overwhelming as the whole dinner had been thus far. As she scanned the table for something that looked edible, she sensed that her father was agitated and glanced at him just in time to see him look away from the box that she had been given.

What was that about? She looked the box up and down and saw nothing but the hypnotic pattern under the smooth surface of a perfectly aligned inlay. Nothing about it warranted a negative reaction, unless what was in it was not what he expected – a notion that furthered her suspicions about his actions tonight being a front for something more.

When the king stopped talking, people left their tables to mill about the hall. Dragonira and her prince stood up at the same time as the sorcerer and his guest, but they went separate directions. *Oh, come on!* While she understood the importance of speaking with her soon-to-be family, she needed to issue a word of warning to the young housemaid her father was taking out to the veranda.

Pavlova noted her distress and cupped her chin in his hand to bring her attention back to him. "Don't worry so much. My father just went out there. He won't let him do anything to her and we'll be able to keep track of them as soon as we answer a few questions."

Dragonira nodded and turned to formally greet the king's mother and her guests with a poise and grace that she had been forced to master over the last week. However, while she was reciting practiced answers, her mind kept wandering outside. *Calm down. You'll be out there shortly.*

This self-assurance became strained as a line of people who wished to meet her formed and stretched down the hall. She and

Pavlova took turns answering the basic questions: When is the wedding, where it is going to be held, how many kids do you want to have? Most of the actual greeting fell on her. Appearance aside, she was a bit of an anomaly to the nobles who lived outside of the palace walls, for they had little to no idea where she came from.

A break finally came in the form of a loud declaration that a drinking contest had started outside between the king and one of his councilmen. This obviously was more interesting than waiting in line for them and the crowd migrated toward the large glass windows on the other side of the hall. Pavlova caught her elbow and steered her through the nearest set of doors. "It would seem I was wrong about my father. We better use this time to go check on yours."

The veranda wrapped itself along the exterior walls of the great hall and was dotted with small gardens of cacti and succulents. Closer to the windows were palms and low scrubs that sat in planters that served to section off small sitting areas. It was on the cushions in one of these that they found the sorcerer's companion, but not the sorcerer himself.

Dragonira was both shocked to find the housemaid by herself and pleased that she would be able to talk to her without having to censor her words. Neither of these emotions were conveyed when she finally spoke. "Where is my father?"

Kinya's big blue eyes stared out at her in bewilderment for a long moment before the girl's mouth was able to work. "I... I don't... I'm not sure... Your eyes... they actually glow!"

"Oh. Uh. Yeah." Dragonira had forgotten that the last time she had spent any time with the housemaid, it had been in the late afternoon, while the suns were still bright. Now it was dark outside and the only source of illumination came from the moons and what little light the small hearths and torches provided, so her strange birth defect was on full display. "Mind if I sit down?"

Although her body language suggested that this was the last thing she wanted, the small, tan woman nodded her head and moved aside for her. "I don't know where he went, but he said that he would be right back."

"Okay." Dragonira took a seat on a cushion in front of Kinya and grabbed the poor girl's hand in worry. "What are you doing here with him in the first place? Don't you know that he's dangerous?!"

Kinya snatched her hand back and placed it defiantly on the ground beside her. "I hear that, but I haven't seen it. I'm here because he didn't want to come alone. That's reasonable, isn't it?"

It was Dragonira's turn to stammer and after a moment of failing to find the right words to explain all of the things that he had done and could do, she gave up. The best that she could do was offer a vague word of caution. "Just be careful. I spent my whole life with him and have not seen him be truly kind to anyone. This," she waved her hand in the air to indicate the situation as a whole, "is abnormal."

The housemaid nodded and then spotted something over her shoulder that caused her to jump up excitedly and run past her. Dragonira didn't turn to see what it had been. She knew it was a person and the girl's excitement to see him was baffling. Pavlova sat down on the now-vacant cushion and wrapped an arm around her. "Hey. You tried. That counts, right?"

"I don't know." She shrugged and leaned into him. "This whole thing is starting to make me feel like I might be crazy. Like maybe he's not the monster I know him to be... or..." She drifted off, suddenly finding herself fighting back tears.

The prince leaned forward to look at her in concern. "Or?"

Dragonira sniffled and buried her face into his chest. "Or maybe he only hates me."

* * *

Tom must have had the worst seat in the entire kingdom that night. Not only was he seated near the head of the table, with the royal family he was aiding a rebellion against, but he was seated across from the freakiest sets of eyes he had ever had the displeasure of seeing.

What made matters worse was that the owner of the fiery eyes had brought the one person that he cared for more than anyone else in the world as his guest. *For fuck's sake, Kinya, what were you thinking?!*

When she had arrived with the sorcerer, it was all that he could do to keep on pretending that he was a member of the royal family. All that he wanted to do was grab her by the arm, flee the palace, and take her safely home. *But the palace guard would slaughter us before we even left the hall.*

He and Kinya locked eyes only once throughout the evening's events and that immediately garnered the attention of the monster sitting next to her. Thankfully she managed an excuse that took the sorcerer's attention off of him and he sat at the table in silence for the rest of the dinner.

When the sorcerer took Kinya outside, he nearly panicked and chased after them. This urge became even stronger when the king followed them, but this was when he would be able to get the information that Ka'say asked for.

Pavlova was scary for a completely different reason than his fiancé and her father were. Tom, as Arminius, was already in trouble with him and he knew it would not take much for the observant prince to see through his disguise. Hopefully the sorcerer's daughter would keep the prince as distracted for this encounter as she had for the last.

"Way to ruin my reputation. Now everyone's going to know it's me," he said playfully as he approached the couple. He already established his character, may as well keep it up.

The prince scoffed and raised an eyebrow. "You know we're honeymooning in your kingdom, right? I'll ruin your reputation there too."

Tom chuckled and shook his head. "Well then..." He placed a hand on his double's shoulder and smiled. "Congratulations. How long do I have?"

"Thirty days," the soon-to-be princess answered. "From tomorrow, specifically."

Tom nodded and stepped aside. "I better go set things straight before you arrive then," he said through a sly smile and used the opportunity to slink away, leaving the affianced bewildered yet again.

As he made his way across the hall he realized that he kind of felt bad for the real Arminius. It was going to be so awkward when they show up in his kingdom and chastise him for fraternizing in their kingdom again.

Tom stopped cold in his tracks as a realization kicked in, and he turned to watch the happy-looking couple greet the next people in line. *They're never going to make it to Lieron.*

Tom suddenly felt sick and instead of heading toward the veranda, he sidetracked himself to the service hallway by the kitchen. He needed to get out of there. He needed to find either Ta'mika or go back to the twins and try to convince someone to spare the prince and princess from their plans.

Something else reminded him that the whole family had to go. In order for the kingdom to be ruled properly, there could not be anyone left of the Siameras to lay claim to the throne or else they would likely have their own rebellion to deal with.

Tom pressed a hand against the wall to keep balance. "I can't do this."

"Can't do what?"

No... The voice sent a chill through Tom and he froze as he tried to reclaim his breath. The disguised calico turned around and came face to face with the sorcerer.

"What are you doing here?"

"I..." Tom stammered as he tried to remember who he was supposed to be and how he was supposed to act. "I just... couldn't handle the crowd. I'll go back in in a moment."

The sorcerer let loose a frustrated sigh and stepped forward. "You're lying."

Tom took a step backward, feeling the wall to his left for one of those hidden passageways that Eric always talked about. He then noticed that the Scourge was looking at something beyond him and before he could turn to see what it was, he felt a sharp pain on the back of his head and everything went black.

CHAPTER TWENTY-ONE

There were flames everywhere, but they did not burn. They spiraled out in front of her until they reached a starry void that swallowed them whole.

What is this?

Dragonira felt a pressure on her back and realized that she was lying down. As she sat up, she found that she had been placed on an altar of sorts. Her mind flashed through a number of her father's rituals and she curled into herself to brace for what they might bring.

When nothing happened, she straightened out and looked around. The heatless flames danced all around her perch and prevented her from looking out, so she looked down. She was wearing the same dress that she had worn to dinner, but now it was charred and blackened. At first she blamed the fire, but reconsidered when she stuck her hand out and felt nothing.

She reached her other hand through the flames and made a gesture reminiscent of pulling drapes aside to test a theory. She was almost shocked when the flames parted and showed her a view of the throne room. As she stepped down from the altar, she noticed the grand hall of the king was decrepit and empty, save for another burning pedestal.

As she moved toward it, someone attacked and she brought her hands up to protect herself. There was a gurgled cry and the figure fell to the ground, its blood trickling onto her hand from a dagger that she didn't remember having. As she brought it up for inspection, recognition kicked in and she threw the knife across the room. How had she ended up with her father's ritual dagger?

Dragonira lowered her eyes to the body at her feet and she

recoiled backward. She must have stolen the dagger from her father as he attacked, for that was who was now lying dead at her feet. The sight sent a panic through her and she turned to run when a pair of hands came around from behind her and closed around her throat. She lurched forward to throw her attacker to the side and twisted to stab them in the stomach. When they fell to the floor, she realized that she was holding the dagger again and the new body on the floor matched the other one.

This is impossible...

A shout sounded off behind her and she whirled around to see numerous copies of the sorcerer stampeding through the grand hall toward her. Something deep within reminded her of the other altar and advised her to run toward it. She took off like a shot and nearly made it when the mass caught up and began pulling her apart.

She closed her eyes and screamed only to find that she never felt the pain of all those daggers digging into her flesh. As she cracked an eye open, she found that she was sitting in her bed. Through heavy breaths, she realized the horrible experience she just suffered was nothing more than a dream.

Thank the stars. Dragonira flopped backward into her pillows and sighed in relief. The dream had felt so real – well at least aspects of it did. Drowning in a mob that wanted to kill her had been a numb sensation, while the textures were electric. The gauzy cloth of her dress tickled her skin. The altar and the knife were uncomfortably cold, and the blood was warm and sticky.

In fact, she still felt it.

She held her hand out, palm up, and produced a small ball of fire that she caged within her fingers. As she passed the light closer to the sheets, she saw they were a deep red and shimmering. She then noticed that her hand was glistening as well and screamed, vanquishing the flame.

A pair of guards, who must have been assigned to watch her room overnight, burst in through the doors and ran over to her. They came to a halt at the foot of the bed and held up a torch to better illuminate the situation. From the puzzled looks on their faces, she thought that perhaps she had dreamed the whole scene, but then one of them spoke.

"Is this yours?"

Dragonira shook her head and found herself shaking, unable to say anything more.

An awkward moment passed as the guards made it obvious that they were at a loss as to what they should do next. They were saved from having to make any decisions on the matter by the arrival of her handmaidens, who pulled her out of the bed and immediately led her to a washtub elsewhere in her room. Once the guards had been dismissed, she was stripped and scrubbed down.

"My lady, what happened?"

Dragonira was still shaking, but this time it was due to the temperature of the water and the night air. "I don't really know."

The handmaiden wrung a cloth out over a pitcher and plunged it into the basin at her feet. "I must admit that I was going to make a quip about you not knowing your cycle, but this was obviously a vulgar joke someone played on you."

Cycle? The princess-to-be looked down at the pink water and threw her gaze back up to the bed. "Why would someone do this?"

"I don't know, my lady, but we will make sure that we find whoever did it."

The conversation ended there as a concentrated effort to clean her hair demanded every bit of their attention and water. Twice she had to step out and stand on a towel while one of the girls ran to fetch fresh water from the prince's washroom in order to rinse it out. When she was finally clean, she was dressed in a robe and escorted to the balcony while the rest of the room was cleansed.

Even though she was covered, she felt exposed. The first sun was just breaching the horizon and illuminated the endless sea of dunes that lay beyond the city walls. It was beautiful, but disheveled as she was, it felt like it was staring back at her.

She heard the sound of a door opening and turned to see that Pavlova had left his room to join her. "Are you all right? What happened?"

"I really don't know. They said it was a prank." The look of confusion on his face caused her heart to sink as she realized that the handmaidens hadn't told him the details that she wanted to forget. "I had a bad dream and when I woke up I was... covered... in blood."

Even though she mumbled that last part, the prince latched onto it and went wide eyed in concern. He then grabbed her by the shoulders and looked her over. "Are you hurt?"

She shook her head and sighed. "No. It wasn't mine."

The prince raised an eyebrow and glanced into her room. Dragonira followed his gaze for a moment but redirected when she realized that she was still disquieted by the events that took place there. That was when she noticed the prince was not dressed for sleep.

"I posted the guards too late then. Thank the suns you were not hurt."

"You posted guards outside my door?" She couldn't make sense of this. The suite only had the one entrance and that was already guarded.

Pavlova's mouth formed a thin line and he pulled her away from the balcony and into his room so as not to be overheard. "Your father found a rebel spy trying to sneak out of the celebration last night."

Dragonira gawked at him as she realized the in-depth meaning of his words. Not only did they find one of the people who wanted her new family dead, they found one who had been amongst them the whole evening. Even though they had not acted in such a manner, they could have killed them outright at any point in the evening and that was terrifying.

"By the stars..." *If that person got in, then there could be others.* Suddenly the supposed prank from before felt more like a threat.

Pavlova pulled her in and wrapped her up in a comforting hug. Through his embrace, she could feel how tired he was. The sound of his breath and the way he leaned indicated he had stayed up all night. "Even if it's just a little bit, you should get some sleep." She reached up and returned his embrace.

The prince pondered on this for a few minutes before he pulled away from her and turned toward the main door of his room. "I need to speak to my father."

* * *

Julian sat outside of the palace kitchens, staring down the long stairwell that descended deep underground. He spent hours watching the empty hallway at the bottom as he pondered the events from the night before. Certainly the active members of his council were looking for him, but they could wait. It was the most aloof councilman who was bothering him now.

How long had he let the sorcerer's actions go unchecked? Five, six years? Julian frowned as he realized that it was closer to a decade since he had any idea what the man did outside of his palace work. Even longer since he had people keep tabs on him. Perhaps it was time for that again.

He hadn't known about the return of the sorcerer's daughter until she was sitting at the dinner table with his son. Then this thing with the servant girl – how long had that been going on?

A part of him knew that he shouldn't be bothered by such a simple girl, but her presence irritated him on many levels. First, she was a surprise. He hated surprises. Next was that she was providing his once-concubine a service that he himself currently lacked and the irony of it was almost more than he could bear.

Julian picked up the weathered red book that sat next to him and stood to descend the stairs to the old warden offices that the sorcerer called home. He continued down the hallway and stalled at Flag's door. *This isn't my business...*

He stood at the doorway and was about to give up on his planned confrontation when he heard movement inside. All of a sudden his frustration with their affair became clear. *How dare he tarnish Ta'nia's memory this way?*

Julian clenched his jaw and reached up to pound on the door when it suddenly pulled away from him. In the frame stood the petite source of his annoyance.

"Oh! Your highness! I uh... I didn't know you were here. Shall I fetch Sir Flag?"

Julian stared her down. She reeked of sex and had redressed herself in the uniform of her position as though she were going to work. Disgusted, he shook his head and stepped back to let her pass. He then changed his mind and grabbed her wrist once the door was shut. She panicked in his grasp and spun around to gawk at him with her big blue eyes. That was when he made the connection. "You're a Cafra, aren't you?"

The housemaid blinked at him a couple of times before nodding. "Yes, of the Sassin family. My father was a soldier in your army."

Julian didn't care about the clan details, but he could see the faint resemblance that would have drawn the sorcerer to her. "Did you know the lady Ta'nia?"

The girl darted her eyes toward the door and informed him that she knew the strange boundary she crossed. "Aye, my lord. She was my mother's cousin."

He let go of her and frowned as she ran down the hall and out of sight, freshly aware that Flag's choice in her was intentional. *He's getting out of hand.* Julian spun on his heel and made way to go see the other magician on his council. *I really do need a way to keep him in check.* The king allowed himself to get so lost in thought that he almost didn't notice his son in the ground-level hallway heading toward the kitchens.

"You were in the dungeons?" Pavlova inquired.

Julian blinked at the question and then nodded. "I was."

"Good." The prince let out a sigh of relief. "I take it you were checking on the status of our prisoner. That'll make... my..." Pavlova's words evaporated as he read the look of confusion on his father's face. "You don't know about the prisoner, do you?"

The king shook his head, both to answer the question and in reaction to his son's acute perception. Julian prided himself on being able to keep a somewhat joyous face of neutrality, but the prince was always able to see right through it. "I don't."

"Then why were you in the dungeons?"

Julian pointed his thumb over his shoulder. "To see the sorcerer, but he's asleep. Who told you anything about a prisoner?"

The prince shot him half a smile and half a laugh. "Tenoch. He sought me out after finding you passed out in the cactus garden."

That wasn't where I woke up, Julian mused as his son filled him in. When Pavlova finally stated who had been the stranger in their midst he had to do a double-take. "Wait. You're telling me that wasn't Arminius?"

The prince nodded.

"Fuck. He had me fooled. He looked, sounded, and even acted just like him. Who discovered him?"

Pavlova nodded toward the kitchens. "The sorcerer."

And when did he have time to do that? Julian turned to look back the way he had come as if he would see Flag there. "That's... interesting."

"We need to talk about keeping our family safe from threats like this. This was way too close. I'm getting married in a month and–"

"I absolutely agree." Julian held a hand up to silence him. "I have to address the council now anyway. Why don't you join me and we'll work out a course of action."

The prince flashed him the biggest smile he had seen in a long time and Julian couldn't help but smile back. His son apparently had inherited his taste for battle.

* * *

Tom's head was throbbing, the pain emanating from the point on the back of his head where he had been hit. He reached up to touch the knot and flinched, both at its tenderness and size.

On the plus side, the floor was cool and felt good against his face and he tried to come to terms with his situation. He remembered the dinner and a brief reunion with the prince and princess. He recalled the hallway and the sorcerer...

"Oh, that's right," he murmured as he pieced together what happened.

"What's right?" a small voice inquired above him.

Startled by having a cellmate, Tom looked up and saw a small girl with impossibly long pink hair standing before him. She was sitting on an overly elaborate railing that up until this point was just part of the decor of the library.

The library! Tom forced himself into a sitting position and glanced around. Sure enough, he was sitting on the glass floor on the uppermost part of the spire. He shot the girl a look. "Who are you?"

Ignoring his answer, she gazed at him with infinitely deep eyes and cocked her head to the side. "Are you a girl? You look funny."

I look funny? Tom looked down at himself and saw nothing out of place. He was wearing the suit from the night before, but had lost the disguise. "Oh! Right. I'm a calico, but I'm definitely not a female."

The girl hopped down from the railing and continued to stare into him as though he were an open book. It made him uneasy and he turned his attention to her hair, which snaked along the invisible ground until it merged with the railing and stretched into infinity below.

What the fuck?! Tom found himself suddenly afraid of the girl and tried to scoot along the floor to get away from her. Instead, he ended up pressing himself against a bookshelf.

The little librarian held her hands out in front of her. "Don't be afraid. I won't hurt you."

"Who are you?"

The girl looked sad and distant, almost ghost-like in appearance. "Forgotten."

"Forgotten?" Tom had forgotten his previous fear of the girl as something inside him opened up. "Who would forget you?"

She faded out completely and much to Tom's surprise she was suddenly standing next to him. "Everyone."

Now he was lost. "What do you mean?"

She turned and pointed to the grand library in which they were now somehow floating in the middle of. Tom would have normally freaked out by such a sight, but he still felt the ground under him and decided to hold onto that sensation as he tried to decipher her gesture. After a minute he shook his head. "I don't understand."

The girl's frustration showed in her eyes and spilled onto her cheeks.

Tom had no idea why she was crying, but before he could ask, she whirled around and looked upward with a terrified expression on her face. She then grabbed him and forced him to meet her eye to eye. "Do not tell him anything!"

The next thing Tom knew, he was lying on the floor again, but this time it was on the cold dungeon tile he had expected. There was the sound of metal sliding on metal and when he looked up, he saw the familiar silhouette of the rebel's mapmaker. "Eric?"

"Shhh." He reached down and helped Tom up onto the rickety wooden bench on the far end of the cell. Eric then shoved a plate of something supposedly edible onto his lap. "Whisper. What happened?"

With the vision of the girl so freshly in his mind, it took a second to realize that his friend meant his imprisonment. "I ran into the sorcerer. I didn't even stand a chance. He saw right through everything."

Eric nodded and ran a hand through his dingy gray hair. "But what were you doing there in the first place? That was a high-profile dinner. Of course you were going to get caught!"

"I really didn't have a choice. They demanded that Arminius attend or be exiled again."

"You didn't have to attend. So what if that shit from Lieron got in trouble?" The older Sivoan leveled at him. "He was banished before and yet they accepted him willingly enough when they thought he showed up again. You didn't need to preserve his reputation."

"I know, but... that wasn't all." Tom shook his head. "Ka'say had heard about the wedding and wanted to know when it was scheduled for. Said it would be better time to attack."

Eric opened his mouth to say something, but reconsidered and closed it. After a moment of contemplation, he nodded. "Yeah, actually, he's right."

"Okay, so… are you going to get me outta here?"

"I wish I could," Eric answered. "I feed the people who get stuck down here, but they monitor my comings and goings as I do so."

Tom suddenly found it hard to remain upright as that bit of news hit him harder than he thought. He handed the plate back to Eric, no longer wanting to attempt figuring out what it was. "Damn."

"Don't give up yet." Eric pushed the plate back into his hand. "I overheard that the prince wants to interrogate you, which has procedures that buy us time to figure something out. Think you can hold out?"

Tom shrugged. "I should be able to, unless that dream comes back."

Eric raised an eyebrow at him. "What dream?"

Don't tell him! The warning exploded across his thoughts and he had to fight to remain casual. "It's just something stupid. Uncomfortable but stupid. I'll be fine."

The tactician frowned. "You sure? You wouldn't have said anything unless it was bothering you."

Is he probing for an answer? Tom looked his friend over and couldn't find anything but genuine concern in his features. Even so, he still couldn't bring himself to describe it. "You forget that I talk too much. Seriously though, it was nothing. I can't even really remember it now."

"Right. Okay. Well, eat that. I know it looks bad, but it's really not." Eric stood up and reached through the gate to signal for the guard to open it up. He then turned to shoot Tom a weak smile. "Try to hold out for a little while. I'll be back for the plate later."

When the cell door shut, Tom released breath that he hadn't been aware of holding. While it was nice to have a visitor, he was relieved when he left. It felt strange and not quite like him.

Thank you for keeping me a secret, the small voice echoed in his head and he realized then that he was not quite alone.

CHAPTER TWENTY-TWO

Ragnar had walked the vastness of space for eons before he no longer felt his creator chasing him, and that was when he first got his chance to relax. In order to do so, he sat on a rocky path that had an air of comfortable familiarity.

As he looked down the path with the void on each side, he noted it curved downward to a location out of view. Since he had nothing better to do, this piqued his curiosity and he made a decision to explore it once he was rested.

He felt an itch at his flanks and went to address it when he noticed another path stretched out in the direction from which he came. *How strange*, he thought as he stood up to investigate. *There wasn't a path there before.*

As he stood up, he heard the soft crackling sound that had first started to accompany him on his flight from his creator. As he looked down, he saw fire-filled holes with the void at their bottom fill up with rock and seal themselves shut.

This confused Ragnar greatly and he jumped off of the path, only to land on a similar type of ground. That was when everything clicked, and he smiled to himself at the new discovery.

He had created the path as he ran and, unlike the straight line that he had originally thought was his course, he had been running on an astral sphere of some sort, which had led him back to where he had started. This gave him an idea and to celebrate he built a unique landmark consisting of three equidistant spires and continued on his way.

Once he was done with that, he ran, full of life and freedom, alongside the first path he created. While doing so he kept an eye on the landmark he made and when he found that it was directly under him, on the other side of the sphere, he carefully crossed over the original path and continued in a forward direction.

He repeated this action over and over again, forcing the path to become wider and wider until it would overlap itself and form a giant ball that he could play with. This idea was working, but about halfway through it, he noticed something strange was happening.

Each time he made a full circle it appeared as though the pillars he built grew larger and larger in height and mass. Something else that he noticed was that his jogs around the sphere were becoming longer and longer.

Being the stubborn creature that he was though, he continued his quest and after many long and tiring trips he finally found himself approaching the pillars for the last time. Panting and tired, he collapsed against the base of one and went to sleep.

An incredibly long amount of time had passed before he opened his weary eyes and stretched himself into consciousness.

The view that greeted him was alien and he jumped upon seeing it. Then he remembered where he was and what he had done and practically leapt for joy. His project had been completed! Now he had a giant ball that he could play with! All he would have to do is break off the pillars and...

... And that was when he got a good look at the pillar he had spent a millennium sleeping against. The thing was humongous and appeared to stretch upward into infinity. From where he was standing, he couldn't see the other spires.

He turned around and stared at the horizon and saw that it went beyond his range of vision. Upon seeing it, he collapsed to the ground in dismay. He had made the orb too big somehow. There was no way he would be able to bat it around and chase it like he had hoped to. To make matters worse, he was now stuck on it.

Just as he was about to curse his stupidity, a new thought dawned on him. He didn't make the sphere too big, he himself had become smaller! He pondered on the idea and realized that it was while he was running that it happened. Each time his paws landed on his invisible route, parts of him had broken off, causing him to shrink and the paths to form. Now he felt stupid. He was merely a speck on his own body, and he wasn't able to do anything about it.

Annoyed, frustrated, and depressed all at the same time, he imagined his creator laughing at him. He wanted to curl up and die then and there but was interrupted by the sight of another being standing on his body.

This creature was fascinating.

In many ways, it looked like him but didn't. Like him, her hair was dark and her skin was white. Unlike him, her eyes were dark and solid, her skin did not glow, and her hair wasn't lined with stars. She was the simplest, most straight-forward creature he had ever seen and it took his breath away.

After seeing how lost he was with his newfound situation, she took him in and introduced him to others like her. Much to Ragnar's surprise, these people had been living on his body for slightly longer than he had been asleep.

They referred to his body as "Sivoa" and stated that they didn't know how it was that they arrived there, for none had lived long enough to witness their arrival. Ragnar was about to tell them when they cut him off with theories of their own and he found himself so dazzled by their imagination that he didn't have the heart to let them know the truth.

Over time, Ragnar grew to understand the ways of the Sivoans and eventually married Raemona, the woman who found him at the pillar. She taught him how to communicate in the ways that they invented. Fascinated by their creativity, he used his newfound skills and wrote down everything he learned from them, even if he knew their legends weren't accurate. He wanted to remember everything, but in order to preserve what he wrote he needed a place to store it.

He thought long and hard about a good place to store things and decided that his head was as good as any. It took years for him and

Raemona to travel to where he felt it was and while he didn't age, she did. When they finally reached their destination, he was surprised to find her worn, tired, and on the verge of fading away. This threw Ragnar into a panic and he started thinking up ways to preserve her, but she shook her head and told him to calm down.

She then explained to him that this was how the Sivoans were. They didn't last forever, but their stories did, which was why she wanted him to build a place to keep them safe. Considering this was why Ragnar loved the creatures so, he could only nod his agreement. They, along with the family who traveled with them, started work and after many more years were about to finish when Raemona died.

A fiery bolt from the heavens had destroyed the people Ragnar had come to cherish and it seared a deep gash into his body a short distance away from where they had almost completed the library.

As he stood amongst the ruins of the camp, holding the body of the one he loved most, he heard Orianna's voice mocking him in revenge for his leaving her. "You will never be happy, Ragnar."

Stricken with grief, he built a pyramid on top of the library as a shrine to his wife and placed her inside. He then went underground and worked on forging a blade to match his grief. One year later, he returned to the surface with a knife as sharp as the contrast between the light and dark and stood next to the pedestal that held his beloved, vowing one day he would return to her. He then plunged the blade into his chest and severed his connection with his creations.

With his sacrifice, Raemona's body healed itself of burns and scars; of age and wrinkles. It became an intangible thing that filled the library with life and love as well as patience.

The library itself was left unfinished and needing to be filled, but without Ragnar around to write, and Raemona unable to leave, all it could do was sit and wait for others to find it and contribute their tale.

CHAPTER TWENTY-THREE

Elainia had awoken with a start and tried to sit up, forgetting about the physical condition that she was in. The pressure in her legs screamed up her thighs and she vocalize it as she fell back onto the bed.

Her guardians dashed in as the pain subsided and she made an attempt to wave them off. She then changed her mind and requested that Ja'kal stay, which appeased Rinsk and Zellyth enough to leave.

The Orianna smiled apologetically at her friend. He was ragged and gaunt – side effects of having a hate-filled deity screaming in your head, affecting your thoughts. She hated herself for inflicting this on him, but it was necessary. "I need you to take her again."

Ja'kal looked like he was torn between screaming at her and quietly refusing. Despite appearances, he nodded and grabbed her hand. "Before that though, I need to know if we're really going to the library kingdom because of the sorcerer."

Elainia smiled at him and nodded as the goddess left her and abused him once again. A visible change overtook him as it did and he smiled at her. "Good," was all he said before he left the tent. He had no idea that she had lied to him as well as the parasitic deity.

Deep down, she felt horrible. No, she was horrible. She was an extraordinarily horrible being and it wracked her with guilt. Her best friend was suffering because of her and before him, she had tortured the sorcerer.

Everything that the current incarnation of the godson suffered was her doing. When he was little and she new to her position, she had purchased the tiny slave from an old woman and gave him to a lumberjack who she foresaw would later sell him to a brothel. She knew what a terrible curse the keeper there would inflict upon him and included an addiction spell to make it all that much worse.

All of that paled in comparison to the horror that she inflicted next.

She found the one person in the entire world who he would find happiness with and brought them together by forcing him into the Siamera army. Even then, Elainia knew the beautiful desert mystic's heritage would force him to remove her from his life on his own volition. *And when he foresaw that in a dream, I pinned the blame on his daughter.*

It was the girl Elainia felt the strongest remorse for. That simple lie she had told the sorcerer ensured that he would never have a happy family life, but years of conditioning from the goddess Orianna had made her unsympathetic to him. The girl was merely a victim.

Something tugged at the back of her mind and she realized that the smallest sun – the evening sun – was present and thought differently. Elainia tried to inquire why, but the young goddess was not as able to communicate as well as her mother and fell silent. The only response the oracle received was a repeat of the dream of fire as she slept.

* * *

Pavlova let the heavy cell door slam behind him and prayed that he could put this torture to an end. For over a week, he, his father, and the warden had tried increasingly severe forms of punishment in hopes they could get the calico to talk, but the stubborn bastard didn't want to play their game.

They had moved him from the plain prison cell that had been his home for the first night of captivity and into a large, round, isolated cell deeper in the dungeons. It had one opening, but two doors; one a metal grate and the other a thin piece of wood. They had initially left the wooden door open so the prisoner would be able to manage himself in the faint light from the hallway, but they closed it once they realized it was going to take more than a lack of food and some silence to make him talk.

When being stuck in absolute darkness for days didn't shake the impostor, the warden bound the man's hand to his feet and forced him to stand hunched over. The prince found him in a similar manner, but he had fallen over.

"Are you going answer our questions today?"

The prisoner didn't move, but his voice was merry. "I suppose that depends on the questions."

Damn it. Please don't make me keep doing this. Pavlova sucked in his breath through his nose and let it out all at once. "Same questions as yesterday."

"Ah. Then no. I don't think that I will."

Pavlova paced around the center of the room until he was able to get a good look at the man's face. He could still see Arminius' smile on his mottled features, but it had weathered under pressure and he wasn't very good at hiding his pain. "Seriously, this can all end if you would just so much as tell us who gave you my clothes."

"Then who would give me more? You? You don't control your wardrobe."

The prince knelt beside the man and looked him in the eye. "How do you know that?"

The prisoner smiled up at him, but remained silent. As much as the prince wanted to smack that smile off of him, it was not his duty. That privilege belong to Tenoch, who he signaled over. They exchanged no words and whatever the constable had planned waited until Pavlova left the cell, though he could still hear the torture as he walked down the hallway.

The calico's fortitude was beyond his understanding and that scared him. Depending on where they engaged them and if they used certain run-and-hide tactics, the rebels would surely trounce his guards if they shared the prisoner's strength. It made Pavlova's head hurt.

I can't waste my time with imaginary battles. His mind was all over the place and he stopped so that he could attempt to focus on what he would report to the council later.

There was a loud clang behind the door closest to him and he realized that he had made it all the way to the ground-level kitchens. Once again he found his father there, watching something at the bottom of the stairs. Pavlova turned and this time saw the sorcerer's handmaiden turn the corner, on the way to his apartment. As she was carrying a delivery basket, this didn't seem out of the ordinary.

"Don't tell my fiancé, but I think that he invited her to the dinner so that he had someone to talk to."

The king narrowed his eyes in thought before shaking his head to clear his thoughts. "Any luck with the prisoner?"

"None. The guy is a fortress. It's insane." Pavlova sighed. "It brings up some concerns I want to address with the council."

"Did you leave Tenoch with him?"

The prince nodded. "Just like I had all week. He isn't cracking, which makes me worry that the other rebels are that tough."

Julian frowned and made a gesture for his son to keep talking as they walked back into the palace proper.

"I'm worried that they'll employ a tactic to exhaust our soldiers if we go on the offensive."

Pavlova watched as his father first dismissed the idea and then allowed it to come crashing into his consciousness. "That's... actually a worrisome thought."

The prince nodded, glad that he didn't have to go out of his way to explain himself. "Whatever we do, we're going to need to strike fast and hard enough to where they can't recover. I mean, if we can even find them—"

"We need the librarians," the king interjected.

Pavlova stopped in his tracks. "But, the library won't consent to that. They're not the ones under attack and they're busy planning their festival."

Julian placed a hand on his son's shoulder. "Just leave that to me."

* * *

"What about this color? Would this color work?"

"My lady, the traditional color is red."

Dragonira huffed and set aside the basket with the fabric scraps in it and stared at the handmaiden. "Is there really any need for me to go through all of this? Everything has already been coordinated for me."

The middle-aged, orange-striped woman glanced at the basket sadly and then shrugged. "That's true. I was told to have you look it over though."

"By the prince?"

She nodded.

"For my entertainment?"

She nodded again, but then shrugged. "I would assume so, my lady. The Siameras have a strict tradition when it comes to marriages."

Dragonira nodded and feigned a smile as she pushed the basket toward the handmaiden with her foot. "You can go. I'm capable of entertaining myself."

"I was directed to have you visit the queen mother after we were done here."

For the first time that day Dragonira's attention had been roused. She had only seen Pavlova's grandmother in the evening as the family congregated in the dining hall, and she usually sat on the other side of the table, just out of range where conversation was easy. "Will Pavlova be joining us?"

The girl shook her head. "No. He will be away at council all day, which is why the queen mother asked to see you."

She asked for me? Dragonira stared at the handmaiden before standing up and offering her a hand. "We shouldn't keep her waiting then."

They picked up the mess they had created on the floor and left Pavlova's suite.

The royal keep was layered and sorted by age, with the eldest members of the family living on the top floor. This initially confused Dragonira, but as she came to understand the layout of the palace, she realized that this provided Asta with the easiest access to the facilities. She was also placed on the same level as the banquet hall and attached kitchens, so she could go days without having to see a stairwell.

When they reached the top of the stairs, the handmaiden turned to her. "If it is okay with my lady, we will part here." She shifted the basket to her other hip and nodded toward the servants' corridors in the other direction of the queen mother's suite. "I need to return this to the atelier."

Dragonira felt a pang of guilt as she realized that the poor woman had carried all of the fabric up the stairs while she carried nothing. There was no way she would feel right about keeping her. "Oh! My apologies. You may go." She went to offer to help carry the basket, but upon being dismissed, the handmaiden had already taken her leave.

Seeing the woman who was soon to be her grandmother-in-law, without her fiancé, was a daunting task and Dragonira stood timidly outside of her door. After a few moments of wringing her hands, she gathered up the nerve to knock. It was a light knock and she reached up to try again when the door opened and caught her by surprise.

Asta's doorward laughed lightly at her display and pulled the door inward to allow her entrance. "Lady Dragonira. We have been expecting you. Come on in." As she followed these instructions, the large woman whispered, "Don't worry. I won't tell anyone."

The queen mother's suite was vastly different from the others she had seen. This one was smaller and instead of being separated into different rooms, it was one very large room divided by hanging brocades and canvases that were reminiscent of a nomadic lifestyle. The Siamera family crest was everywhere and Dragonira unconsciously reached up to touch the pendant that Pavlova had given her. She was still uncomfortable with the symbol, but she was coming to accept the fact that their clan had it before her father desecrated it.

The doorward had gone out on the balcony to retrieve Asta and they both had returned while she was staring at the large canvas against the far wall. "Is everything okay? You're shaking."

Dragonira jumped and realized that she had still managed to work herself up over what was, in actuality, just a bunch of circles and lines again. "I uhh... I'll be fine."

The older Siamera narrowed her ice-blue eyes at her. "Something your father did?"

She must have gawked because the old woman smiled a sympathetic smile and moved toward a lounge and table positioned close to the balcony doors. She beckoned Dragonira to join her. "To be honest, I never did like him."

Dragonira took a seat on an ottoman across the table from Pavlova's grandmother, but remained silent and vaguely afraid of what she was going to say next. Asta watched her over carefully before cracking a smile. "I did like your mother, and I see more of her in you."

"Thank... you?" Dragonira shifted in her seat, unsure how or if she was supposed to respond to this.

"I apologize for making you uncomfortable. When I saw you standing there, I assumed that your father had forced his predisposition against us on you."

"His what?"

"Perhaps he can do some things right." The queen mother waved her hand to dismiss the topic. "I called you up here because I want to show you something."

A servant who had been hiding in the wings came forward with a box, but unlike the one that Pavlova had presented her, this one was plain wood that was splintering on the edges. It too was branded with the Siamera crest, but it was sloppy and charming, as if a little kid had done it. "My grandson painted that box for me, so I'll be needing the box back after the wedding. It's what's inside I wanted to show you."

Dragonira smiled at Pavlova's haphazard artwork before lifting the lid. Inside sat two small sculptures of what appeared to be armless four-legged Sivoans; feline in shape and stature. Both were made of highly polished marble, but one was black and the other was white. They were positioned in the box as though they were kissing. Her eyes watered at the sight of them. "By the stars... these are beautiful!"

Asta smiled. "Thank you. They took me a long time to make."

"You made these!" Dragonira took in their beauty with a new appreciation. She reached in to pick up the black one and found herself somewhere else entirely; a vast emptiness with two burning energies that were unaware of her presence. Before she could figure out what they were, her fingers let go of the small marble figure and she was once against facing her future grandmother-in-law. Her heart was racing.

The queen mother was eying her warily. "Do you know what those are?"

Dragonira blinked and looked back down at the finely crafted figures and shook her head absently as she tried to figure out what just happened.

"We Siameras have a legend that speaks of a lonely woman who wished for nothing more than a child, but was unable to have one by the men in her village, which was the only village in existence, you see.

"One particularly cloudy day she ventured out into the desert in search of wild moso – a nasty spice. I don't know why anyone would ever use it, but they do – and she came across a sleeping giant.

"Curiosity won her over and she attempt to wake the being by shouting at him, throwing rocks, and even setting a fire near his feet. Eventually, she had the idea to grind the seeds she had collected and she blew the dust in his face. This caused the giant to sneeze and awaken.

"'Who dare wake me!' demanded the giant with his eyes ablaze, causing the woman to hide in a crack in the ground, where he could not reach. He tried for quite some time to pry her out of the ground before calming down enough to reason with her. 'Why did you wake me?' he asked.

"'I apologize, oh giant. I was struck with a curiosity and had to know who you are.'

"The giant laughed and found himself refreshed by her honesty and struck by her simple beauty. He explained that he was the sun – we only had one then – and had been weary over traveling the sky. It was a boring job and he had no one to share it with, so he decided that he would sleep.

"Intrigued by another lonely soul, the woman explain her plight to the giant. When she explained the village, the giant was fascinated. In all this time, he had not known he had been shining his light down on people and he wanted to know more about them.

"The woman answered his every question and when she finished, he told her that he would grant her one wish – to have a child. He took her into the sky, making her our second sun and she grew in size while she was with child, whom then became our third sun when she was born.

"These statues represent their conversation. The black one is Auvier and the white one is Orianna. They also represent a bride and groom, whose job it is to learn to love each other, and pass that love on to their children. I'll give you a statue of Adeen once you have your first child."

Dragonira sat wide-eyed in her seat as she digested the load of information she had received. She eventually turned her gaze down at the box again. "So, these represent Pavlova and me?"

Asta nodded. "I apologize that they are not big enough for the ceremony. My hands are old and carving takes a toll on them. You'll be using mine and my late husband's for the ceremony. They're a good size."

"Please don't apologize. They're wonderful." Dragonira smiled at her future grandmother-in-law. "We'll treasure them forever."

The queen mother nodded and summoned her doorward over with a wave. "I know you will. If you get the chance, please send my grandson up to visit. I need to give him a kick in the ass for leaving you to handle all the preparations while he learns warmongering from his father."

Dragonira laughed at that and the grin stuck to her face as she was escorted out. When she stepped out onto the empty veranda that wrapped around the interior cactus garden, she thought of the story Asta told her and her smile faded.

She walked over to one of the benches that dotted each level of the royal keep and opened the box again. Remembering her vision from when she held the black sculpture, she cautiously placed a finger on the white one. As before, she saw two burning, shapeless beings that paid her no mind.

They flared up as they spoke and only grew brighter and hotter as their argument intensified. Then the one that reminded her of desert heat ripples vanished, causing the other one to explode with rage.

Her finger was still on the white statue when the vision faded and she tried to revisit it by touching the black carving. Apparently, it was a one-time trick, which made even less sense than the misalignment between the vision and Asta's story.

What made things even weirder was that the vision felt familiar, like a story that she heard once, while the queen mother's tale was new. Dragonira tried as hard as she could to remember where she had heard the story before and after a while she realized that it did not feel like something that had been told to her.

It felt like a memory.

* * *

Tom wasn't sure when the banging had started. It was hard to judge time in pitch blackness, but it must have been going on for a while because it was slowing down due to the fatigue of whoever had been assigned the responsibility of slamming a hammer against his door. He wouldn't have noticed that until the small voice that now served as his mental companion told him he would have to revisit the real world because "he" was coming.

Though his reaction to the light was genuine, the calico had to fake surprise at seeing Eric slip through the doorway. "Did you get demoted or something?"

He wasn't able to clearly make out any of Eric's features in the torch light, but he could hear the confusion in his voice. "What? I didn't get demoted. I had to sneak down here to–"

Tom interrupted with a chuckle. "Don't worry about it. I'm just messing with you, but I have to admit that I didn't expect to get any visitors here."

"Ah. Well... about that. I had to pull some serious favors to get here. I couldn't even use food as an excuse."

"What's with the hammering?"

Eric frowned hard enough that Tom was able to see it through the painful light of the torch. "That's an attempt to break you down. Honestly, I'm surprised you're holding out so well."

The way that the tactician trailed his words made him worry. "Something wrong?"

The older Sivoan sighed. "You might sound like yourself, but you look like you've been thrown into the ravine a couple of times. Are you still not sleeping?"

Tom shook his head. "Not well, but I try. There's not a lot you can do without any light."

"The last time we spoke, you said you were having nightmares." Eric sat down on the floor. "Still having those?"

Don't tell him!

The calico flinched as his high-pitched mental companion shouted at him again. He was completely indebted to her for pulling him away from himself when the psychological torture the royals were trying to inflict upon him started to have an effect, but he was too tired to lie. "They're still sticking around, but they aren't so bad anymore. Kind of... distracting, ya know?"

"If you say so." Eric made a face of some sort, but he couldn't see it. "Actually, that makes a level of sense, but it's not good if those distractions are preventing you from being able to rest. If you become delirious, they'll have you. "

"Then get me out of here."

Eric's shoulders dropped. "I would if I could, but it's only the guard right outside that I was able to convince to let me see you. The other guards think I'm in the regular cell block."

Huh? Tom's head had been covered when they moved him from the general holding cells to this deep isolation, but he remembered that it had been quite the walk between the two locations. There had also been a number of stairs, which made it obvious to him that the regular cells were nowhere near where he was now. "I was really hoping you were going to say otherwise."

Eric sighed and Tom realized that he could see him clearly. The light still hurt, but it wasn't nearly as bad as it had been when they started this conversation. His friend looked like he hadn't slept much either and he felt a pang of guilt at that. They sat in silence as the weight of the prison settled in on them, which Eric broke with a sigh. "Want to talk about it?"

Don't!

Again the loud voice sounded off in his head, but when he stopped to think about it, he wanted nothing more than to share some of his burden with someone he trusted. "Yeah." He would just leave out most of the details.

"There's some differences, but they all take place in the library."

Eric snorted and Tom punched him in the shoulder. "Shut up! I can appreciate books!"

The older Sivoan flailed and yelled at him in a hushed whisper. "Keep it down!"

Tom skulked his way down to the floor so that he was sitting next to Eric and let a small laugh escape him. "Sorry."

"It's okay. Continue." Eric snickered.

"I'll punch you again."

"Sorry, but it is funny that your nightmares would involve books."

The calico had to stop again and laugh at himself. Books were always more Eric's thing and now that he thought about it, it was ironic that a denizen of the library would be sharing his head space. "Heh. Yeah."

"Anyway. I'm usually floating through the library. Really high up. Maybe near the domed area and I know that I should be falling, but I'm not." Tom stopped as he watched his friend's face. "What?"

"That doesn't sound very scary."

"Have you ever been that high?! It's terrifying."

Eric nodded. "I've been in the library. Are you afraid of heights? How did you survive the trips down the ravine?"

"I'm not afraid... actually, maybe I am in the dream. Doesn't that make sense?"

"Not really."

"Okay, fine! It's not the height that's the problem. It's the girl."

"Well, that makes more sense." Eric deadpanned at him. "You did manage to piss off all the women at the reception desk that one day."

"No!" Tom could feel himself getting flustered. "It wasn't one of them. It was another girl. A weird one who can merge with the floor and the railings and such. She's creepy as shit."

Am I really? A small voice filled with disappointment rang in his ears. He started to nod, but caught himself. *Yes, actually. We'll discuss that later.*

Eric was staring at him with an eyebrow raised. "I can see how that would be a bit... unnerving. Does she do anything?"

"Ehhh..." Tom was starting to have his doubts about his conversation, largely because now that he said everything out loud, it seemed stupid. A sentiment that reflected in Eric's expression. "Sort of. She eventually takes me to these three–"

STOP TALKING!

"... weird..."

You're telling him too much!

"... pillars that just kind of disappear into the clouds."

The warnings from the girl stopped and Tom could feel panic settling into his chest. What had he done that was so wrong? He looked at Eric, who was still staring at him in complete confusion. There was nothing to indicate that the calico had done anything that could harm anyone.

"I really don't see how any of that is scary," the older Sivoan said as he stood up.

"Yeah," Tom mumbled. "I guess it feels a lot worse than it actually is. Dream logic, ya know."

Eric shrugged and turned toward the door. "I really can't relate, but I'll take your word for it."

There was something off about Eric's voice and it caused a pit to form in Tom's stomach. "Are you all right?"

"Not really," Eric confessed in a downtrodden voice that wasn't quite his. He turned back around, the high contrast from the torch in front of him made his features sharp. He looked younger somehow and Tom felt that there was a missing truth in that.

"What's wrong?"

The tactician stepped forward. "The last time we spoke, you were hesitant to tell me about your dreams. Why tell me now?"

Are these really that important? Tom could hear the little voice in the back of his mind screaming at him, but it was distant and possibly just a memory. "I... I didn't mean to upset you with that. I was just... kinda... embarrassed."

Eric peered at him over his glasses. "Is that the truth?"

Tom looked his friend over in an attempt to figure out what he was trying to get at. "Well, no." The torch light flickered and played an enchantment on Eric's gray hair, making it almost look silver in the warm light.

Silver... The calico stared at his friend in disbelief as his heart started racing. He worked his mouth, but the words he wanted to say caught in his throat.

Eric pressed his lips together and glanced at the floor. "Damn. You figured it out." As he removed his glasses, the familiar earthy greens of his eyes caught afire and burned into the crimson sunsets from days before.

Had he not already been sitting on the ground, Tom would have certainly stumbled over his feet and fallen there as he tried to put some distance between himself and the sorcerer. "But, but, but…"

Flag stayed in place as he appeared to mull something over in his mind before placing a hand in his pocket. He pulled something out of it as he crouched, a motion that could have been a comforting attempt to bring himself down to his level had Eric done it. "I've always said that you talk too much."

The movement and the sentiment confirmed for Tom that this wasn't a one-time rouse. The Scourge had always been amongst them, aiding them in planning his own demise. None of it made any sense. "Why–"

The sorcerer held up a hand to silence him, but dropped it in defeat. "I had wanted you to live, but you're going to sing like a bird to whatever side in this gets to you first."

"Wait! No. I hadn't said anything to the royals!"

Flag shook his head. "Even so, I can't have you giving my daughter's wedding date to the twins."

"They're going to get that information anyway. Too many people know," Tom blurted out.

The sorcerer cracked a crooked smile at him. "Not if I'm the one controlling the flow of information."

Tom's heart sank as he realized the Scourge was right. The position he held within the rebellion's ranks gave him that kind of control. In fact, from all that he's heard, the position he had on the royal council gave him that kind of control. *What the fuck is he doing?*

As he watched the twin sunsets across the room, Tom remembered the first time he saw them up close and the familiar blue oceans that accompanied them. "What about Kinya?"

Eric's conflicted expression crossed the Scourge's face a second time, but whatever it meant wasn't relayed. "Unfortunately, I have plans for her."

The pit that had formed in Tom's stomach filled with rage and he charged at the sorcerer, with the full intent of killing him. However, the second that he was within range, the sorcerer swiped at him with the knife he had hidden and Tom fell into the iron door behind him.

The strange thing about this action was that he watched it happen from the sidelines. *What the fuck? What just happened?*

Over here. A familiar small voice beaconed from above.

He looked up to see her, but found himself standing, once again, at the base of three pillars. *Where am I?*

No time to explain. The girl appeared next to him, carrying a heavy blue-and-silver book that she shoved into his arms. It squirmed in his hands, but he wasn't sure if that was because it was moving or he was shaking.

What am I supposed to do with this? he asked as he flipped through the infinite number of blank pages he held.

Protect it for me, please. It is the life of that man's daughter… but she… she is something more.

Tom's eyes shot up and he nearly dropped the thing he was just asked to watch over. As if offended, it melted through his fingers and took on the form of a young boy with faded pink hair and starry voids for eyes.

I... I don't understand.

The young girl took his hand in both of hers and stared up at him. *Soon I will have to follow Orianna's lead in this celestial thing. While this will let me protect the stories within my walls, I cannot watch over those who escape.*

Tom remembered his previous visions of her and gawked. *You... you're the library?*

She nodded. *I am Raemona. The story keeper. I regret to inform you that you just died at the hands of my beloved...*

I just what?! Tom turned his attention inward and realized that while he felt his heartbeat, it was extremely weak and fading fast.

That is why we have no time. Will you protect her story?

Tom felt himself being called away elsewhere and he nodded.

Raemona hugged him. *Thank you. This journey will take many lifetimes and you will not remember anything previous to them until you reach an age where you are capable of bearing a weapon. You will then venture out and find the tool of your previous life and remember a little.*

Tom glanced at the book person before he returned his gaze to the library. *Uh... okay.*

I tell you this now, for the weapon will first appear here. Burn it into your eternal memory and live. Tell me what you wish this to be.

He felt his connection with his body drain away and a remembrance of the betrayal that he felt kicked in. *I think that I would like a set of claws.*

With that last thought, Tom left to go experience the world anew.

* * *

The presence of the sorcerer must have startled the late-night visitors of the café, for as soon as he came skipping out across the glass floor, they made way toward the wall chimes that summoned the librarians to take them away. They rang these with more urgency once he stopped his bizarrely cheerful display.

As his eyes scoured the inside of the gold and glass dome, Flag clenched both his fists and his teeth. There was nothing that even remotely resembled what Tom had described. Just glass and more glass, marred by an ornate, but haphazard stand that the kitchens provided with food every day. He tried to visualize the place without any of the royal additions, but found that an empty dome didn't provide him any further insight. This was frustrating because he was certain that the pillars in the calico's dreams tied into the Siamera mythology somehow and he was certain he would find something for them in here.

Flag cast his eyes down in frustration and was greeted with his dust-covered reflection from the floor. That gave him pause. Perhaps, in his haste, he had missed the first clue from Tom's dreams. The calico had mentioned that he had been floating in the middle of the library.

Flag walked toward the center of the now-empty room and looked down through the café's glass floor. From here he could see the familiar twists and turns of the library below; nothing was out of the ordinary. He had seen this sight a million times over the years of living in the palace and joining the royal family on various exclusive parties in the café. The remembrance of some of the more "private" celebrations caused a shiver to run down the sorcerer's spine and he shook the thoughts from his mind.

The sorcerer crossed his legs and sat so that his face was only about an inch from the floor. Looking through it one again he studied the massive book hall below him with an open mind. After looking over the intricate designs of the levels below, he started to notice something that he hadn't before.

The architecture in the library wasn't quite like anything else in the castle. The various levels of endless books were arranged in a unique cascading pattern that suddenly seemed much more ancient than anything else in the kingdom. It wasn't that the castle didn't match at all, but more like it was built onto the library centuries after the spire's erection and only imitated the complex designs that could be found there.

Yes, there was some sort of pattern here. Each level contained three round platforms, which were interconnected via a walkway along the hall's outer wall. The combination of pathways and platforms reminded Flag of something he had gotten to know very well over the last couple of years.

Each level looked like a slightly rotated version of the ritualistic symbol he had stolen years ago and matched the royal branding on the rest of the palace. The problem here was that the library was far older than the rest of the kingdom and the Siameras had not ruled for more than a generation. "Will wonders never cease?" he asked under his breath as he passively traced out a flat perspective of the view in the dust on the floor.

This action in itself proved useful, for it drew his attention to the three strange railing-like structures that spiraled around the library and connected each platform to a counterpart on the level above it. When he traced this out over top of the dust drawing, he noticed that he had drawn a fractal pattern that appeared to spiral outward as though it were trying to eat him whole.

This, combined with the cascading depths below, caused a moment of vertigo and he looked up in an attempt to avoid it. That was when he saw something else of significant importance that he had never noticed before.

The pendentives, which sat just under the ring supporting the bulbous dome of the library, were made of glass like the rest of the spire's topper. However, they were etched with fake clouds meant to catch the colors thrown by the suns throughout the day. Flag had noticed these before, but he had missed that three of them had solid lines going up through the middle of them.

Assuming that these represented the pillars that Tom had

mentioned, he allowed his eyes to trace one down to the jamb of the arches surrounding it. There he found a hole that was unnaturally dark, even considering the night sky beyond it.

"Huh." Flag got up to inspect the hole as best he could from this elevation and made a mental note to come back during the daylight hours to see if it, and its two matching brethren, had the same effect when fully illuminated.

The sorcerer looked around the dome for more clues, but found nothing else stood out in particular. He walked the outer edge of the room, stopping at each hole, feeling like he should be able to make a connection here, but he just couldn't. As he stopped for the third time he looked down through the floor again and saw that one of the spiral railing had ended just below the glass.

Or wait, no.

The railing was actually touching the glass. He looked across the room at the other railings and saw that it was these that were actually holding the whole level up. That was a shock. They didn't look like they were strong enough to handle that kind of pressure, which meant that they had to have some sort of magical property.

"Now we're getting somewhere," he spoke out loud to himself again, not really caring because of the fact that no one else was around. An idea clicked in his mind and he looked back at the pendentives once again. Yes. He could see that, had the railings continued, they would have gone right through the holes in the ceiling. Now the only question was why this was.

The sound of a chair falling over caught his attention. *What now?*

The newcomers to the café were not strangers to Flag, though he wished that they were. In fact, he regretted he had not killed them ages ago.

Gared and Jinto were not the biggest of men, but they definitely relied on their strength more than their brains. They also only showed up when they caught wind that the king was displeased with him.

By displeased, he meant lusting for him to the point where hired muscle was necessary. Almost to add insult to injury, these two knuckleheads were the same two people who had purchased him from the brothel ages ago and dragged him kicking and screaming to the forever-hated military camp to become the king's concubine.

The king had relied on them frequently when they first moved into the castle, for Flag often made it a point to avoid him whenever possible. Once he had purchased his "freedom" from Julian, they were not needed because Flag didn't mind openly opposing the king himself.

Julian seemed to be slipping into a mid-life crisis now, however, and his old lusts and urges were coming back. He wanted everything he had when he was younger and loved by all as the new king who saved Libris Del Sol from the tyrant who lived before him. Funny how things flip-flop when one doesn't pay attention.

Flag glared at the two thugs. "He could have just summoned for me."

Gared and Jinto glanced at each other and shrugged.

"Suppose he could have," Jinto said in that horrible decayed accent he developed after getting kicked hard in the teeth by Flag when they were all more than a few years younger.

"It's been a long time since we've done this," Gared said.

"Almost twenty years," Flag retorted back with acid, "... and we don't need to do this."

Gared raised his eyebrow. "Will you comply then?"

That's a big word for him, Flag thought in slight amusement, while staring him down.

"I'll go see him," Flag said, standing to his full height.

Jinto decided to throw his two cents in. "That's not what he meant."

"I know what he meant and Julian needs to back down. I've got my freedom." Flag growled.

That was apparently too much for Jinto, for he lunged forward in an attempt to tackle Flag to the ground. Gared taking this as his cue to act, ran around behind the sorcerer with intent to catch him in case Jinto missed. Neither expected their target to do what he did.

Flag ducked and grabbed Jinto's arm, pulled down, and stuck his foot out. This action mixed with the speed at which the brute was traveling caused him to trip and tumble headlong into his accomplice, who simply fell over backward.

It didn't take them long to recover but by that point Flag had already put a good amount of distance between himself and them. If they wanted to spring another attack on him, they would have to run across the room to do so, and he had the advantage in that he would be able to watch them as they did so.

He mentally ran through a list of spells that might help, but there were none with a ritual small enough to be performed quickly and his charm was in a sealed box within his room. What he wouldn't give in order to have the opportunity to set the two of them on fire.

The hired goons knew they didn't have much to worry about from the sorcerer as long as they could get him pinned. They've seen his magic in action before, and they knew the consequences he'd suffer if he used it against them. They were actually hoping that he'd attempt a spell so they could grab him while he was incapacitated afterward.

They charged for a second time, playing on a pre-planned formation and deciding to try splitting up again. This time they staggered their attack so Flag wouldn't be able to repeat his little stunt from a few moments earlier.

The Scourge saw the whole thing unfold as they ran toward him, and he was able to sidestep Jinto's attack. What he didn't expect was for Gared to grab his hair and yank on it. It felt like his scalp was on fire and the force of the pull caused him to nearly trip over his own feet.

Jinto had come back around and used this momentary distraction to charge on Flag again. Using the force of his own fall, Flag aimed a kick for Jinto's mouth for the second time in his life. Much like it had the time before, his boot met its target and the brute went reeling backward. He now only had one more to deal with.

Gared had wheeled around after grabbing Flag's hair and snaked his arms up under his own and placed his palms against the back of his head.

"The king didn't like that little stunt you pulled at the gala the other night," Gared whispered into his ear before lightly nibbling a bit on it.

This threw Flag into a blistering rage and he tried to wiggle out of the hold by throwing his body weight backward and dropping his posture, essentially pulling his captor to the ground behind him. Unfortunately, Jinto came back and grabbed his legs before he could take full advantage of the move.

One of Tom's favorite words came to mind then as he attempted to jerk himself free of their rather painful grasp. "Fuck!"

Without thinking, Flag scrunched himself up into as tight a ball as he could and managed to head butt Jinto in his already-bleeding face. The pain must have been severe enough, for the thug dropped his feet immediately. The sudden unbalance flipped Gared forward on top of the sorcerer, who was able to shove and roll his way to freedom. Instead of running, however, Flag stood over Gared and sneered down at him.

There was a pause as though he wanted to say something, but the words just didn't come out. Instead, he raised a foot and brought it screaming down on Gared's skull. The sickening crunch that resounded as the steel heel of his boot met bone brought a smile to Flag's lips and a sense of horror to the goon holding his teeth several feet off.

"This ends now."

With a furious speed that an even completely unharmed individual would have trouble avoiding, Flag charged at Jinto and knocked him to the ground. Before either of them really knew it, the brute was fighting for breath as the sorcerer's grip on his throat tightened.

Though Jinto tried valiantly, he failed at his attempts to pry the sorcerer off of him. After several minutes of gasping blood instead of breathable air, he lost the battle and his life.

Even though he watched the man's face as he died, Flag felt no remorse for him. In fact he was glad that the struggle was over and he stood up and tried to figure out the best way to dispose of the bodies.

What he didn't notice was that during all of this, a figure hidden within the shadows of the doorway had been reciting words from a battered red leather-bound book.

"Impel quiescence!"

Flag had barely had the chance to turn around to see who had shouted such a thing when the horrifyingly familiar sensation of his major motor functions shutting down overwhelmed him, forcing him to collapse on the cold glass floor.

"Wow! That actually worked," came a cool voice that was missing its usual drunken tint. Flag didn't even have to guess at what happened. He knew that Julian had somehow rediscovered the spell from the brothel. The world spun in confirmation as the king rolled him over onto his back.

"Just like old times, isn't it?" Julian knelt beside the sorcerer and gently brushed aside the silver hair covering his face. "Crazy. Now that I see you like this, you don't look like you've aged a single day."

I haven't been binge drinking for over ten years either, ass hat. As he was unable to speak, Tom's insults readily came to mind and a twinge of regret settled in his chest. The king picked up on this, but misinterpreted it to mean something else.

"I know that you've been sneaking about." Julian sat on his legs in a gesture of dominance and began undoing the clasps on Flag's robes, making it obvious that he planned on reminding the sorcerer of his lowly status in other ways. "We can't have that now, can we?"

All Flag could do was glare into the king's sky-blue eyes, which unfortunately held more than a hint of a ravenous hunger in their depths. He tried to relay his anger by growling, but he couldn't even manage that. The subservience spell was simply too complete.

Julian leaned forward and kissed his neck, using the closeness as an excuse to whisper declarations into his ear. "You know, you were quite smart to give your daughter to my son as you did. She's the best of both of you and I would have much liked to have tried this out on her... it looks like I'm stuck with you."

The king uttered the part of the spell that filled his head with whatever fantasy he wanted to see and Flag felt him shudder under its effects. "By the stars. I forgot how intoxicating this is." He then completed the spell with a puppetry command that forced Flag to return his every embrace, which he fought as best as he could by breathing angrily through his nose.

"That's adorable," Julian commented after another stolen kiss and sat up, swaying under the euphoric effects of the illusion sub-spell. Balance wasn't the only thing that the king was having trouble with and Flag could only guess that his majesty was only now wrestling with the morality of the situation. He would have rolled his eyes had he the ability to.

After an irritating amount of time, in which the sorcerer's pants had been undone, the king found justification for his actions. "You know, it upset me when you brought that wench into the hall. I just can't believe that you would bed anyone after losing a goddess like Ta'nia."

Julian caressed his chest as if there was something there for him to hold on to. "I can see the resemblance though, even if I didn't catch it at first. She might not be as pretty, but the wench does possess a sort of charm of her own, doesn't she?"

Flag knew that the question was rhetorical, but that was the line of thought that he had been hoping for. He knew what ultimatum his lord was about to propose and he wasn't going to concede this time.

"I suppose that you can have this fling of yours, but I'll be taking it out on you as you take it out on her." Julian flicked his tongue over Flag's lips and realized that the sorcerer was forcing air through his nose rather vehemently. "Oh. You're… trying to speak."

Julian said the words for the counter-spell that undid the silence portion of the spell and Flag broke into a coughing fit as his vocal cords were released. Eventually, he managed to choke out the words "You can have her."

The king blinked down at him in surprise. "What?"

Flag pressed his eyes shut and shuddered as a suppressed cough took its toll. "You're right. It was the resemblance that drew me in, but you can have her. Put false hair on her, or whatever. Just forgive me my time of weakness."

The euphoria that had overtook the king was completely gone now as he mulled the words over. He had been counting on Flag to do the honorable thing and agree to the king's deal, as he had before. "Well… okay then."

Julian gathered the spell book and stood over Flag, casting his gaze toward the minions he had sent after the sorcerer a short time earlier. "Of course you took out the one person who would allow me to play this trick on someone else. Seems such a waste on you now."

With that, he left the sorcerer alone with his anger, unable to move and exposed on the glass floor.

CHAPTER TWENTY-FOUR

Pavlova had been in the room when his father was advised that it was insane to plan a wedding with only two months' notice, and now that it was two weeks out, he could see that this was no small exaggeration. The basics were easy. The ceremony would happen in the grand hall, where everything happened. The food would be provided by the whole of the kitchen staff, which they did at every event. Clothing was of traditional dress, which should have been easy enough, but was becoming more and more of a problem as they couldn't identify what clan Dragonira would represent.

All of the problems from there were minute in nature, but compounded so quickly that addressing them felt like commanding an army of deaf taratin. *I guess this could be considered leadership practice.* This thought amused him as he traveled up the stairs to meet his fiancé in the grand hall, where they were to meet with a decorator before coordinating with Boris on ceremony etiquette. It was the last thing he wanted to deal with this morning and so he found himself pleasantly surprised when his father greeted him at the landing. "What are you up to?"

The king smiled and nodded his greeting in reply. "I'm heading down to the council chambers for my morning meeting, but I thought that you would appreciate knowing that I solved our little library problem."

The prince was unsure about what his father was referencing at first, but understanding soon washed over him. "You got them to help?! That's... that's amazing! How?"

Julian placed a finger on his lips and shook his head. "Oh, they haven't agreed yet, but after this meeting, they'll be all for it." The king patted his son on the back and started down the stairs Pavlova had just left. "Good luck with the wedding committee."

The prince watched him descend until he was out of sight. Shaking his head, he pushed open the hall doors and found his fiancé in the middle of a throng of people vying for her attention. Dragonira looked exhausted, like she hadn't slept in years. This concerned Pavlova quite a bit because she had been tense over something unspoken the night before.

He waved a hand in front of her face. "Everything okay, my love?"

She nodded, but didn't say anything else. The prince waited a little bit before asking another question. "Want to talk about it?"

Dragonira smiled at him and shrugged. "It… it really isn't a big deal. Just something I will have to take care of by myself later today."

She stood up on tiptoes to give him a kiss on the cheek before turning her attention to a girl with a scroll that might have contained dance instructions. The prospect of practicing choreographed movements so early in the morning didn't appeal to him, so he directed himself toward the kitchens instead.

Breakfast was still being prepared when he entered, so he was advised to wait in the little alcove until the cooks were finished. As this wasn't dancing, he was fine with the prospect. Plus, it let him eavesdrop on the staff.

He learned a couple of things that morning. The first was that there were four new mounts in the stables. The eggs that their breeder taratin had laid a couple of months back had hatched and the babies were already trying to race each other. Pavlova smiled as he remembered the sight of the new nest. It was this that he had been inspecting when he tripped over a dark-haired girl in the dirt outside.

Time flies… He smiled to himself and continued to listen in on the gossip.

The next bit of news pertained to their fathers. Some odd nights back, the sorcerer had disrupted the late-night happenings of the library's café patrons. There was a sort of scuffle afterward and the king himself had checked in on it. Whatever happened had left the sorcerer unconscious and he was brought back to his chambers by the library staff. Pavlova frowned at the odd story and wondered if that was what had his fiancé out of sorts this morning. It was certainly strange.

He tried to listen into more of what was being said about the encounter, but was cut off when Huruga appeared in the doorway with a basket containing fruit and some bread. Pavlova nodded his appreciation and uttered a quick "Thank you" before heading back into the hall.

Space was extremely limited at the head of the dining table, where they usually sat and he had to push aside a number of scrolls to find a place to rest the basket. He had to push aside even more people to get back to Dragonira.

"And where did you go?" Her frustration at having been temporarily abandoned played at her face.

"To get us some food." He glanced at the basket and then outside. "Actually, we should go out there."

Pavlova grabbed the basket and her hand and dragged them both out onto the terrace. They sat down on some cushions that allowed them to gaze upon the desert from the comforting shade of a potted palm. He apologized for his awkward behavior as he sliced up a piece of fruit for them to share. She nodded but remained silent as her thoughts stole her from him again.

"Concerned about your father?"

Dragonira snapped to attention at his words and blinked at him, stunned. "Uh. Yeah. " She brought her hands up to rub at her temples. "I don't want to, but I really need to talk to him."

Pavlova smiled, impressed by her compassion and he reached his arm around her shoulders to lean her against him. He kissed the top of her head and nodded before handing her a piece of the melon that she liked so much. "Want me to come with you?"

"Actually…" She had taken the fruit, but only held it in her hands and she contemplated his words. "I think that, this time, it would be best if I spoke to him alone."

* * *

Flag had been wary of answering the king's summons ever since the night in the library, but this particular call was almost routine. Julian often had Rayya fetch the sorcerer and his bag of potions so he could relieve the hangovers of he and his councilmen.

As he mixed and handed out his medicines, nothing appeared to be amiss. However, when he handed Julian his drink, the king shot him a grin and whispered the simple phrase that activated the spell he had inflicted on him some nights before. Before Flag collapsed, however, the king instructed him to stand. Had anyone been watching, it simply would have looked as if the sorcerer stumbled and caught himself.

"My councilmen, it would appear that one of our own is a traitor," Julian announced as he stood from his seat at the head of the table. "It saddens me to say this, but Gared has been in cahoots with the rebels for some time now."

A murmur had gone through the council chamber and while all eyes had started out on the king, they jumped quickly to the seat of the missing water manager. While everyone was distracted, the king placed a hand on Flag's shoulder and muttered another command spell under his breath before his stride placed the sorcerer between him and the council.

"I can confirm this. Last night I caught him in a meeting with a man who later confessed to being a spy." Flag had said this, but the words were not his. "They plan to strike during the gala."

As the words left his mouth, panic started to settle in Flag's chest. *How could he possibly know that?* The sorcerer and message keeper had done everything in his power to keep that information under wraps. There was no way that he could possibly know.

Julian stepped out from behind him and placed both hands on the table for emphasis. When he spoke, Flag realized that the king's information had been a guess at best. "Yes. They plan on attacking the gala."

"But you're not going to be there," reproached Nuha, the head librarian. "You royals never go, despite the open invitation."

Julian frowned and postured. It was obvious to Flag that Julian was pretending, but the council bought into the charade. As the king passed him again, Flag heard another whispered command and his mouth was again talking without him. "I believe that they are planning to attack the citizens."

Tenoch chortled and Nathara gasped. The others eyed the sorcerer for an explanation, but Caiside spoke. "Why would they do that?"

Julian had spun around to fake shock at Flag's words, but now he addressed Caiside's question with a practiced speculation. "That... huh. Do you think something like that would have the ability to turn the populace against us?"

Everyone eyeballed the king, trying to pick up on his line of thought. Before anyone asked, Julian held out a palm in explanation. "I mean, it would put in doubt our ability to protect everyone. Even worse if it's in the library, which is considered untouchable — right?"

The council murmured again as it considered Julian's question. Nobody bothered to address Flag, who was the only one who could see through the king's awful performance. For the first time ever, he found their aversion to him disturbing.

Julian smiled at him then and walked over. "Time to finish this." He muttered under his breath, reciting the echo command again before pacing back across the room. "Perhaps we should step up our reconnaissance. If we–"

"Forget your reconnaissance," grumbled Nuha. "I'll handle them."

The room went silent and everyone stared at the head librarian. Flag caught a faint smile at the corners of Julian's mouth before it vanished under the same somber mask everyone else in the room wore. "Well, we won't get in your way, but if you need assistance, I advise speaking with my son. He's been heading the charge to collect information on the rebels. He might be of some help."

Nuha nodded as he stood and pushed past his peers. "I'll do that."

The other members of the council followed him out the door. They took no notice of the fact that Flag still had not moved, nor did they care that Julian had shut the door behind them.

Julian grinned as he crossed the room back toward the sorcerer. Once he was in range, he placed a hand on the back of the Flag's and pulled him in for a splenetic kiss he was unable to fight. When the king was satisfied with his physical declaration of possession, he backed off and left through the door on the other end of the hall. "Guess it wasn't such a waste on you after all."

For the second time in a handful of days, the sorcerer found himself trapped, stewing in his hatred for his sovereign. Even with this potential hiccup in plans, he would get his revenge. He would get his revenge on them all.

* * *

Dragonira hadn't been back to the underground lair that the sorcerer called home since he arranged for her to marry the prince. She intended to never return, but after her meeting with Pavlova's grandmother, something that had only bothered her on a subconscious level had burst forth into her full awareness and she needed to address her father about it.

She had suspected that there was something more to his arrangements than her general well-being. He forfeited any and all titles that would have rightfully been his, so he wasn't after the throne, but he was after something. More specifically, she suspected, he was after two somethings.

Even with the resolve to get confirmation, she had difficulty knocking on his door and it was annoying her guard. She could tell from the little huffs he made and the way he shuffled his feet while he fought with himself to stay polite. After several deep breaths, she finally brought her hand to the door.

There was no answer.

Frustrated at having her bravery go unanswered, she knocked again. Again, no answer.

"He's not home?" the guard offered.

"It's unlike him to be out." She tested the handle and found it locked. "But, maybe he is."

"Maybe I'm what?" came a haggard voice behind them.

Dragonira and the guard turned back in the direction that they had come and found the sorcerer finishing his descent of the stairs. He moved stiffly and was carrying his leather medicine bag. He pushed past them and dug into his pocket for the key. "What are you doing here?" he asked coldly.

"Inside." She tried to match his tone, but was unable. Even with how angry she was with him, she couldn't bring herself to hate everyone and everything as he did. When he got the door open, she held a finger up to let her escort know that she wished for him to wait outside.

Dragonira followed her father into the apartment, not expecting him to say anything. She was not disappointed. This conversation was on her. "You're after the statues, aren't you?"

He had begun unpacking his bag but snapped to attention at her words. He didn't need to give voice to an answer. She had it. The arrangement that had saved her from him was born from a selfish desire to obtain the artifacts of her betrothal. *Powerful artifacts*, she admitted to herself, but would follow up on that later.

"You're not going."

"Excuse me?" The tone of his voice was low and unamused. He raised an eyebrow at her, but made no other attempt to move.

"You are forbidden from attending my wedding," she rephrased.

He laughed. "You can't do that. In case you have forgotten, your wedding was arranged by the king and me." He narrowed his eyes at her "I will be there."

"No. You won't." Dragonira's voice resonated with an absolution that she didn't feel beyond the anger she had toward the man in front of her. "If I must, I will answer to Julian, but you will stay away."

Her father glared at her in silence. Dragonira sensed that he was doubting both her authority and his, but he said nothing more. She could have left it at that, but she wanted to make sure he knew that his power over her was gone. "You're not getting the statues either."

He struck her then; an open-handed blow to the side of her face that was nothing compared to what she had expected. It had sent her reeling, but she caught herself quickly and grinned at him as she backed out through the hallway door. She had won this round and he knew it.

* * *

It had been weeks since they heard from Tom and the stream of hope that he would return to the camp had run thin. Ka'ren felt this more than anyone. It had been his idea to send the calico out in disguise and it had been his idea to have Tom heed the call for Arminius. It was so obvious a trap, but the information they could have won was valuable. At the time it had seemed worth the risk.

In his hands he held a note that Tom had slipped him at a meeting some time back. It contained a confession of love for one of the girls in camp and was asking advice on how to approach her. Ka'ren had made fun of him in writing at the bottom of the page, but never returned it. He meant to, but he also meant to correct the rude statement before he did. Now the letter was a reminder of how terrible a friend he had been.

"I'm sorry, Tom," Ka'ren apologized out loud as he stood up from the box he had been using as a stool since they rebuilt the camp. He crossed the glade and stepped past the grass bushes to look out over the ravine, where he was greeted by the last bit of darkness before the suns ushered in the day. "I promise, we'll get you back... somehow."

The early morning still reeked of the cold evening air, and a fine mist from the waterfall floated about the ravine, making it impossible to see through the purples and blues to the ground below. There was a certain, untappable magic to this time of day and Ka'ren felt none of it. Instead, he was allowing his grief to overtake him as his mind drilled the possibility of his friend's demise into his head over and over again. He didn't notice Eric until he damned near plowed into him.

The tactician's clothes were put on hastily, with his shirt being both inside out and buttoned wrong. His normally bound hair had broken free of its string and had collected in a tangled mess around his shoulders. His chest was heaving as though he had been running for hours to get there. "We have to get everyone... to the earth ship... now," he urged between breaths.

Ka'ren watched the man a moment before his words set in. "Why?"

Eric waved his hand out to his side in frustration. "We... The library is going to attack. We gotta go."

"Wait. Why?!"

"No time! Just go!" Eric shouted back.

Both men had already started running to the remnants of the camp and as they got close, Ka'ren waved Eric toward the north end. "You get that side. I'll find Ka'say and get everyone over here."

Eric nodded and was gone. Ka'ren shifted his course toward the tent that he and his brother shared, shouting at everyone he passed to get to the earthen ship. This was their contingency if the library advanced against them and honestly, they weren't sure that it was a good plan. According to the crew that manned it, the vessel was, for the most part, grounded. Getting it ready to fly was a long and arduous process, so it wouldn't be of use as a means of escape. It did however have a means of blending into the environment flawlessly and was just weird enough that perhaps the librarians wouldn't try to teleport into it.

Ka'ren found his brother just outside of the food tent, looking perplexed at the people that were running past. When he spotted his twin brother, he ran over to catch up. "What's going on?"

"Eric says that the library is coming."

Ka'say kept in pace with him, but frowned in thought. "That doesn't make sense. Why?"

Ka'ren shook his head, indicating that he didn't know and the two of them ran up the path toward the ship, shouting to everyone they passed who wasn't already heading that direction. They were just on the outskirts of the camp when a black dot appeared in the sky above them and vanished. The next thing they knew, there was a large woman, dressed head to foot in mailed armor on the path in front of them. They made eye contact with her just long enough for her to disappear completely.

"Oh no."

Eric shoved both twins from behind. "Hurry!"

What happened next was pure chaos. More mailed figures appeared and were grabbing people left and right. Ka'ren found himself running erratically in hopes of making his moves unpredictable enough to keep from getting snatched. At one point, he felt a hand on his shoulder and he dove into a roll on the ground before the connection swept him off to the palace dungeons, or ravine, or wherever the librarians were taking their hostages.

A loud thud to his left made him realize that they were sending people into the sky.

"Suns, help us." Ka'ren breathed a prayer as he got back to his feet and started running, full tilt, up the remainder of the path. Eric was ahead and to the right, then he was not. Panicked, he turned to see if Ka'say was still with him and was pleased to find that his brother had avoided being abducted. When he turned back around, he had to throw himself sideways to avoid an outstretched hand. He repeated his prayer until he dove through the illusion wall around the vessel and hurled himself through the open bay doors of the lower deck.

Entering the ship had been all too easy and he looked up, expecting to see the armored librarians stealing people away, but was met with no such thing. What he did see was an all-too-small group of people huddling around each other. Bik was sitting off to the side, looking defeated and vulnerable for the first time that Ka'ren could recall.

Ka'ren reached back to direct his brother's attention in the way of the archer and grabbed only air. He turned and felt his heart drop. Ka'say wasn't anywhere to be found.

* * *

Ka'say landed hard on a rough brick floor a moment before someone else expertly landed on top of him, pinning him down so that he couldn't move. "Hey! This one on the list?" a voice bellowed out above him and he assumed that it belonged to the weight on his back.

He moved his head so that he was looking up from the corner of his eyes and saw around a dozen mailed figures popping in and out of existence, depositing people he knew on the ground while other heavily armed people dragged them off. Behind them was a sign board with a map featuring a number of black X's and one large circle. *So that's how they found us so fast.*

He always knew that the library was terribly efficient, but because they had worked hard to avoid their ire, he hadn't really considered how fast they could coordinate a search. As he watched them come and go, he found that he also severely underestimated just how quickly they moved people.

Much to his relief, the arrival of friends had stopped and reports about a strange anomaly in the woods started coming in. *Good, they made it to the ship*. In particular, he was glad he didn't see his brother or his tactician in the throng.

"He matches one of the descriptions. Let me go get Flag."

Ka'say's attention was brought back to the brute on his back upon hearing the sorcerer's name. Who matched a description? Were they talking about him? Could it be that the bastard was still searching for him and his brother after all these years?

He tried to wiggle free but was punched in the back of the head by the still-unseen guard who had him pinned. The impact must have knocked him out because they next thing he knew, he was dangling over the shoulder of someone quite large. Someone in black robes was following them and he kept his eyes down, not wanting to confirm his suspicions on who that was.

"Put him in there."

The sound of metal creaked loudly in his ear and the world spun until he was on his back. The way that he landed had him facing the door, where he could see the sorcerer in full. The Scourge made eye contact with him momentarily, but was otherwise preoccupied and left the dungeon without ceremony.

Ka'say wanted to be thankful for that, but somehow it left him even more unsettled. The Scourge had a list with him and his brother's descriptions on it, which meant that he wanted them for something – which could work in his favor in that the guards would go to lengths to make sure he and his brother weren't harmed in their custody. It potentially gave him time to figure out a way to escape.

He got up from the floor and peeked through the small window at the top of the heavy metal door. Even with it barred and locked, a guard was posted outside. *Well, that's a good sign... I think.*

The rebel leader backed away from the door and crossed the room to sit on the stone bench that would serve as his only place of comfort in the tiny cell. The air was a bit cooler here and he found that he was able to better mull over his situation in the slight evening breeze. He could take a page from Tom's antics and make as much noise as possible to keep the guards on edge. Eventually they would have to come in and shut him up or check to make sure that he wasn't inflicting harm on himself. Then he'd attack them and steal the keys. *That's a terrible plan.*

The breeze shifted and he felt a chill run down his spine. The notion that there should not be a breeze in the dungeon hit him then. Ka'say shifted and turned to look at the wall by his elbow. Sure enough, there was a loose brick. *Well, now. Maybe I won't have to hurt myself after all.*

* * *

Kinya's daily routine had changed significantly since the engagement dinner. She'd do whatever normal morning things happened at her house, but before dawn as she needed to make sure that the sorcerer was up and ready for his regular routine.

This could have been a problem because she liked to sleep, but thankfully the sorcerer usually had a means of waking himself when he needed. If she ran late, it wasn't really a big deal. What was a big deal was making sure that the man was fed, for he had a tendency to skip breakfast and she discovered that this would affect his mood greatly when he would return from his midday rounds for lunch.

Today he was missing completely.

When she arrived with breakfast, he was gone. His usual uniform was discarded in a pile on the floor and his apothecary box had been tossed hastily on the floor by his bed. After checking to make sure the bottles inside it were undamaged, she tried to find any clues he may have left that would explain what had happened.

A simple search turned up nothing, so she cleaned the mess in hopes that she would turn up something buried. When that didn't work, she picked up the breakfast tray, locked the apartment door, and returned to the kitchens with the uneaten meal.

She checked with Yaran, the head of the kitchen staff, to see if she knew where the sorcerer had gone and received no useful answer. She was then ordered to go home since her ward was missing.

A day off would have been welcomed news in the days before the prince's engagement, but now she was both worried about Flag's disappearance and if it would affect her income. Even if she didn't secretly enjoy being in his service (and being serviced by him), he was what she was paid to take care of. If she couldn't do that, then she was without a job.

Worry followed her out into the palace courtyard, where a loud commotion interrupted her thoughts. What she saw there didn't make sense until someone in heavy mail popped into existence several feet in front of her, carrying a scrawny woman who looked like someone she had once seen in her mother's company. *Why are the librarians bringing people here? Why are they dressed like that?*

As she watched, she realized that all of the people being delivered had an air of familiarity pertaining to her mother and they were being arrested. It finally hit home when she recognized one of the twins being carried away under the direction of the sorcerer who she thought she had lost.

Unsure of what to do, she spun around and dashed back into the kitchens. From there, she would use the service ways to get to the library and head home. It would be a longer trip than cutting through the courtyard gates, but she needed to distance herself from anyone who would recognize her.

"And where are you going?" came a calm voice from behind her as a living wall of a man jumped in front of her, knocking her down with his beer gut. She looked up from her position on the ground and saw the king and his guard standing over her.

"Wait, you're Flag's little whore," he stated as he paced a little to the side. "What were you doing out there?"

"I..." Kinya cursed her brain for not coming up with a usable answer immediately and she stammered for a bit before she caught that the king had associated her with the sorcerer. "Flag... I–"

"You didn't know he was out there," Julian knelt down to meet her at eye level, "and he certainly wasn't why you ran away." He leaned in close. "You recognized some of the people out there, didn't you?"

Kinya tried to back away from the king, surprised at how intimidating he had become, and couldn't move for the constable behind her. Whatever words she might have used to defend herself got stuck in her throat.

The king smiled. "You're more interesting than I thought you were." He snapped his fingers and pointed at her. "Tenoch. Arrest her, but skip the dungeons. I'd like to interrogate her myself."

Kinya's anger with the situation finally hit and she tried to stand up, only to find herself being grabbed from behind by the captain of the guard. "What? No! Go talk to Flag. He can clear this up."

Julian shook his head and laughed. "My dear, he's the one who sold you out."

She tried to scream then, but a giant hand covered her mouth, muffling her attempts. The king pulled a handkerchief from his pocket and the ribbon from his hair and, with Tenoch's aid, shoved one into her mouth and tied it in place with the other.

"Flag belongs to me. Did you know this?" The king gripped Kinya's chin in his hand and lifted her face so that he could stare into her frightened blue eyes with his own. "What's his, is mine."

She caught his meaning and kicked out in a panic. The guard tightened his hold on her, threatening to break her arms. Julian only shook his head, smiling. "Take her to my chambers, Constable. Make sure she's comfortable."

CHAPTER TWENTY-FIVE

The nights used to be her respite; a time where she could keep to herself and sleep. Now they were filled with a wordless presence that bounced off of the moons and demanded her attention with ferocity. The images it forced into her brain insisted that they were running out of time.

"I know, that's why we left when we did," the exhausted Orianna grumbled to herself, only to be greeted with a blast of urgency from the unseen deity. She shifted in her bed to avoid the pain in her head, only to be harshly reminded of the pain of her missing legs. A pain so sharp that it wasn't until Ja'kal threw the tent flap open that she realized she had cried out.

"Hey, what's wrong? What's happening?"

"I kicked the bed," Elainia whined between sniffles, thankful that Adeen had temporarily faded to a mild buzz at the nape of her neck. Ja'kal ran to her and helped her prop herself up on the folded blankets she had been using as pillows. In the process, she grabbed his arm and he flinched away. Before she could ask why, she saw a number of horizontal slashes on his arms. "By the goddess, Ja'kal! Your arms!"

Her assistant lowered his eyes and tried to cover the scabs with his hands. "Pay them no mind, my lady."

"No, no. Don't tell me that." She reached over and pulled his hand back so she could see his forearm clearly in the moonlight, the little voice in her head ebbing at her consciousness again. "Did you do this?"

He withdrew from her grasp. "It's nothing... just... it's the only thing that tones down the goddess for me. I... I don't know how you do it."

Her heart went out to him. She knew that her patron goddess could overwhelm him, but she had no idea that it would be to that extent. "I apologize. Ja'kal, I didn't mean for it to be such a burden for you." She paused to try to gather her thoughts. "You're the second strongest oracle at the spire, after all, and I assumed you would be able to great her like I did."

He shot her a puzzled look through the moonlight. "I'm afraid that I don't understand what you're saying."

Elainia clicked her teeth together as she thought of a way to reword it. "When I took over as host, it hurt, but I took the pain as a sort of grand confirmation that everything I knew and worked for was right – that it was as it should be. Even though you are male, I thought that it might be like that for you, too."

"In a way it kind of was." He sat on the foot of her bed, careful not to jostle her. "It was honestly a shock that she was willing to come to me at all, and so I expected to be overwhelmed, but this..." he frowned as he tried to figure out what he was talking about, "this entity that hurt her. Her hatred for him is so encompassing and anyone who has anything in common with it – him – is guilty by her association and–"

"All men are terrible?" she interrupted, paraphrasing the feeling that he was unable to describe. "I know what you're talking about, but I don't agree." She sympathized with him.

"You don't? But how can you... how are you able...?"

"I lie," Elainia confessed. "I lie to her, I lie to myself even and I do her bidding. It's not easy, but it works."

A long silence fell between them as Ja'kal processed this new information. "The sorcerer... is he the one? The one who..."

She nodded.

"But how? He's only a little older than we are."

"I suspect you're on the verge of realizing a frightening truth that is probably better left unsaid."

Ja'kal nodded and took in a deep breath to re-orient himself. "Is he the only one?"

Elainia shrugged, but then spoke to correct the silent statement. "Actually, no. I don't think so. You and I for example. We serve as a home to the goddess. I think he's the same way, even if he doesn't know it."

"How would he not know?"

This time she shrugged in earnest at his question.

Ja'kal watched her for a moment before asking, "Is that why we're going to the library kingdom?"

She shook her head. "No."

He frowned. "So you lied the other day, too. Why are we going then?"

The buzzing in her head grew a little louder and she had to fight to ignore it. Her assistant noticed her agitation and leaned back apprehensively. She found it increasingly hard to hide the tiny goddess anymore. "Something terrible is going to happen there and I don't think it can be stopped, but we can save the people from it."

Ja'kal frowned at her again. "Where are you getting that information? Not the goddess. I would've known, wouldn't I?"

"I've been conferring with the evening sun," she finally admitted. The buzzing stopped as soon as the words left her mouth, startling her.

"Adeen?" He paused again in thought. "And she wants us to save everyone?"

Elainia nodded.

"Even the sorcerer?"

It was an honest question which, somehow, had never crossed her mind. While their dominant sun harbored such a loathing for the man, the small sun's only mention of him was the use of his dream to get them to leave the spire. In the dream, he was a victim too – the primary victim considering that it was his point of view, but she couldn't see that Adeen harbored any of her mother's ill-will toward him.

Elainia nodded, but before she could open her mouth to elaborate, Ja'kal's hands were around her throat. A voice that was not his screamed at her. "Traitors!"

As she struggled to draw in air, the buzzing returned and she realized that the urgency and caution she felt earlier was not directed at getting to the library. It was a warning that Elainia had been abandoned by Orianna and Ja'kal had completely taken her place.

Remembering the cuts on his arms, she grabbed them and dug her nails in. He called out and withdrew, giving her a moment to catch her breath, but then what? She couldn't flee from him. She looked around for anything she could use as a weapon and found nothing. He lunged at her again and she grabbed an arm and flung it to the side only to get punched in the face with his other fist.

"HELP ME! Somebody!"

Elainia suffered another blow to the head and everything felt like it was on a moment's delay. She saw Ja'kal's fist returning and tried to put a hand up to block it, but missed by miles. The impact happened, but she didn't notice it until she was on her back with his hands on her neck again. She didn't notice her lack of air at all and instead felt like she was melting into the noise in her head.

There was a commotion at the entrance to the tent as two people she felt she should know burst in and began shouting. Suddenly, they were standing over her and Ja'kal was gone. Whatever pain she had missed returned in full force and she gasped it all in shortly before she threw it up on the floor.

She attempted to apologize for the mess, but Rinsk placed a hand gently on the side of her face to hold her attention. "It's fine, my lady. We can clean that up, but what happened in here?"

The ex-Orianna glanced past him, through the opening of the tent and frowned. "I've just been anathematized."

The sand cat drew in a deep breath and glanced at Zellyth who returned his concern. "What should we do?"

A familiar need to hurry had taken hold of her, but this time there was clarity to it. "We have to get to Libris Del Sol before Ja'kal does."

"I don't think that the caravan can pull that off," Zellyth stated.

"Yeah." Rinsk nodded before focusing on Elainia. "We'd have to leave it behind, but with your condition, I'm not sure that is possible."

Elainia fought back tears of frustration because she knew that he was right, but she was desperate. "We have to try."

* * *

Ka'say sat with his back against the door of his cell, listening to the sounds of the hallway beyond. The echo of keys and distant murmurs indicated that a change in shift was happening, which provided him a brief moment to relay a message to his men. "Au'de, You there?"

"Where else would I be?" came the faint, sarcastic whisper from the cell next door.

"Right." The rebel leader smiled at that, glad that even after a week of imprisonment, the man had managed to keep his wits about him. "Hey, I'm leaving tonight."

"Okay."

"Remember what I said to tell the guard?"

"Yeah. The sorcerer got ya. I know, I know. Anything else?"

"Tell the others to remain vigil. I'll be back for them soon."

Footsteps in the hallway ceased their conversation, but Ka'say had faith that Au'de would carry out his command.

The new guard came into the hall and banged on the dungeon's main gate to announce his arrival to the wardens in the other wing, so that they could make their shift change. Next he was supposed to check through the view hole of the cell doors to make sure the prisoners were where they were supposed to be. After that, Ka'say had no idea what the guards did, but they were always present if someone acted out.

Between the attentiveness of the guards and the daily group interrogations, it had become quite the challenge to loose the bricks at the back of his cell. It took several days, using the brick he discovered on his first day, to quietly free a hole just big enough for him to wiggle through. Now was his chance to see what the tunnel on the other side would lead him to.

Pulling the bricks out as fast as quiet would allow, he stacked them to the side of the opening and crawled through. He then pulled them in and replaced them in what he hoped would be an unnoticeable piece of wall.

Feeling around to find his way through the tunnel, he followed the soft breeze until a faint blue light showed that the space was large enough to stand in. In fact the passage could accommodate two people with ease, which indicated whoever dug it out had help. If he ever met these fugitives, he would have to thank them.

His need for thanks vanished when he turned the corner and nearly found himself falling into the ravine. *Suns and stars!*

He clung to the wall and crouched low to keep oriented. After a moment, the vertigo passed and he was able to access his situation without worry of his legs giving out.

The excavators must have had some idea of what they were doing for the tunnel opened up right at the edge of the opening of the grand cavern, under the palace. Had they dug any more to their right, they would have fallen out and into the void like Ka'say nearly did.

But where would they go from here?

This cavern was impossible to miss when one looked at the library spire from the rebel camp. They had inspected this opening many times using Terran surveillance equipment and found that it didn't connect to anything anymore (if it ever had). It was just a big mysterious hole in the cliff... right?

He stepped on the berm and paced so that he could look down into the channel that ran down the middle of the cavern. The moonlight illuminated it just enough to where he could keep track of it as he followed it to the back wall. There it met a smaller channel that went up the wall and into the ceiling. He stuck his head into this out of curiosity and saw only blackness. *Great.*

As he pulled himself back to gain footing on the berm again, a glint of light caught his eye. He leaned out into the gap in the wall again to try to spot its source and after a little bit of swaying, spied it. A little ways up, past the cavern ceiling, a metal rod hovered about a hand's width away from the wall. At first Ka'say didn't know what to make of it, but as he stared, he spotted the faint reflection of metal beyond it.

A ladder! Excited by this new discovery, Ka'say pulled himself back onto the berm and stood to survey where the channel in the floor met the one in the wall. He noted the one in the wall continued all the way to the bottom of the trench in the floor. The ladder rungs were on the opposite side of the shaft and didn't continue past the ceiling, so if he were to make use of them, he would have to climb. This was a problem because, in the low light, he couldn't see anything to hold onto.

This meant that he'd have to run. Ka'say wasn't nearly as good at scaling walls in this manner as his brother was, but the distance he'd have to climb from the berm wasn't too much. If he launched and landed just right, he might be able to make it. With this in mind, he jogged down the cavern a ways and gauged the distance. Then he was off.

One. Two. He hit the wall with his left foot and pushed up as hard as he could, throwing himself forward to push his momentum upward while his right foot hit the wall and followed through. His reach overshot the lowest rung, but he was able to catch it on his descent. He made it, but now he was just hanging next to the wall. He pulled with his arms as he used his feet to walk up the wall, but it took a few tries to push off so that he could grab the next rung. Once he had it though, the climb was simple.

The ladder ended at the mouth of another tunnel. That was all he could see. The reflected moonlight of the cavern didn't carry up the shaft well and it was nonexistent at the new opening. Even after all of that effort, he wasn't sure that he wanted to venture into the depths of the cliff blindly, but he had a promise to keep.

Ka'say found out that the tunnel wasn't tall enough to stand in comfortably when he hit his head on its ceiling. He could have continued down it while walking stooped, but he decided that crawling was best. Feeling the ground in front of him as he went, he made his way through slowly. Very slowly.

On and on, the tunnel went as the thrill of escape left him. He was tired. His body was heavy on his knees and hands. He had no idea what time it was anymore and he couldn't see anything. It was the longest crawl of his life and it kept going until his face hit a protrusion jutting out of the wall.

"DAMN IT! OW!"

His heart stopped as his exclamation resonated all around him and echoed off into oblivion. Once it faded, he rolled back so that he was sitting and rubbed his forehead, checking to make sure that there was no sign of blood. As sharp as the blow felt, it didn't break the skin and, at that, he felt some relief. *What was that?*

He waved his hands around in the air in front of him until he connected with whatever it was that he hit. It was made of wood. His fingers could feel the splinters below the surface, waiting to break free. As he ran his hand along its length, he discovered it was nothing remarkable. Just a large beam. A beam that intersected with another large beam.

No. The second beam sat on top of the first beam, but at an odd angle he couldn't understand the practicality of, until his hands came across another beam. *Are these stairs?*

He allowed his hands to continue their climb as he raised himself to standing. As they ascended, he felt himself turn to keep track. It certainly felt like he found a spiral staircase. He backtracked a little and climbed onto the stack. There was a wall on one side and he decided to hug it with his shoulder as he felt forward in the same manner as he had in the tunnel. The distance he traveled before he hit his head again was nowhere near as long. *Okay, Ka'say. You keep running into objects like this and you won't have a head to get back to camp with.*

His hand told him that he hit a ceiling made of wood, with an extremely large metal ring hanging from it. When this felt off to him he thought about the stairs and how it didn't make sense to build them so that they dead-ended in such a manner. It was a door.

The door was heavy and it took him bunching himself underneath to push against it with all his weight to get it to move, but he succeeded in shoving it up and over. For the first time in an eternity, he was able to see the faint hint of light coming in from what he assumed was the other side of the room.

There was something about that light; the way that it framed the doorway and stopped about three hands down from the ceiling was familiar. It made his heart race and the blood in his veins felt hot as he looked at it. *It can't be…*

He fought the panic in his breath as he felt along the wall behind him for a sconce that he prayed wasn't there. When he found it, he also found that he was crying. There was no way this could be *that* room. No way because it didn't have a door in the floor. It couldn't have had one.

Contrary to this logic, he found the torch in its perch and pulled it out. He could smell the oil on it and he knelt to find a rock to spark against it. Now he needed to know, to confirm, that this was not the room that he had lost his other brother in.

Instead of a rock, he found what felt to be a scrap of metal. He hit it against the wall to see if it would spark, but had no such luck. He threw it at the door frame and reached down again, this time finding a chunk of a material he couldn't identify by touch. This however did spark and within moments he was able to see – until he let the torch fall.

There was no mistaking it. This was the sorcerer's ritual chamber. For the few seconds that he was able to see it, he knew. The diagram of blood on the floor was new and the wooden pillars that he and his brothers had been chained to were gone, but the holes in the floor where they had been was evidence enough.

Ka'say's entire body shuddered and he fell to the floor, gasping as he fought back tears and tried to gain a semblance of composure, but all he could see was the memory of Ka'lee's corpse. Other memories flooded in then, drowning him in his anguish.

It had only been a couple of months since the tyrant had been overthrown that the teenage triplets happened upon the sorcerer outside of the dark portion of the town's market. At the time, he looked concerned and upset about something that the boys never figured out. He seemed like an easy target.

All that they had intended was a harmless prank, maybe steal a couple of coins from him, but he was a noble and the guards they hadn't seen snatched them up before they could even lay a hand on him. They were thrown in a ground-level cell for the attempt, but they expected to be freed come morning. They usually were. Not this time.

In the middle of the night, the sorcerer and a terrifyingly huge man, who later became the constable, put bags over their heads and ushered them to a room where they were chained. They were tortured and experimented on, all in the name of the suns – because there were three of them. They were an anomaly and, unfortunately, they yielded results. Ka'say could vividly remember him and his brothers being cut with that evil curved dagger and the burning, needling sensation of energy being forced through them. None of it ever made sense. All of it hurt.

One day the sorcerer unchained a weakened Ka'lee and laid him in the middle of the then-chalk circle. He used a spell to paralyze him before cutting him open to place an amulet into his chest. Undoubtedly, they would have shared this fate had the king's voice not floated in from somewhere. In a fit of rage, the sorcerer left to dismiss the king, but never came back to repair the gaping hole he left in his victim.

Despite the fact that he was bleeding to death, Ka'lee managed to lift the paralysis curse (he always was the most observant and had learned the words) and grab the shackle key from the table the sorcerer left it on. He freed his brothers before giving in to the all-encompassing darkness.

It was pure chance that Ka'say and Ka'ren were able to shove their way into the old warden's office and out into the halls that eventually dumped them out into the palace courtyard. From there they were able to run to freedom through the open bath hall gates.

Ka'say remembered the open gates and focused on them to try to calm himself down. They were closed and heavily guarded now because he and his brother's punitive attempts at avenging Ka'lee. The stealth and speed at which they were able to dodge the guards and the proximity they would get to the royals won them the respect of the tyrant's sympathizers, but they lacked the skill or focus to do anything more than haphazardly throw daggers.

Eventually, Shoa supporters approached them and offered weapons training, but by that point the gates were sealed and a hefty bounty was placed on their heads. They moved in with the nomads across the ravine and from there began making efforts to recruit and build their forces.

Breathing deeply, Ka'say stood and replaced the extinguished torch in the sconce. He then felt around for the secret door and lowered himself back onto the staircase below it. He resigned himself to the fact that he would have to wait until morning to scale the cliff face and ride the waterworks down to the other side. He didn't have any other way out of the palace, but now he knew of a way in.

* * *

"A prisoner is missing," Pavlova said as he slid a shoe onto his foot. "According to the guards, your father took him."

Dragonira hadn't bothered to move out from under the covers of the bed she shared with the prince, but this statement caused her to sit up. "Is that normal for him?"

"That's what I was going to ask you." Pavlova turned on the bed to face her. "He lives in the old warden's office. Did he ever bring people there?"

Dragonira shook her head. "Not outside of the occasional member of staff." She wanted to go into more detail, but if there was ever such an occurrence, she was usually locked in her room or the ritual chamber. Sound carried though, so if he was out to torment someone other than her, she was sure she would have heard.

Pavlova sighed. "It could be that he was following orders, but I would have been informed if that were the case."

"Orders for what?" Dragonira raised an eyebrow and leaned forward to hug her pillow.

Pavlova sat in silence for a long moment before he caved into the want of answering her question. "My father has been known to have your father torture prisoners for information.

Dragonira wanted to be surprised at the news that her father was used in such a way, but she wasn't. What did upset her was that the royals would employ such measures. "Do you think that's what happened?"

"No." The prince shook his head before standing. "Like I said, I would have known."

He leaned in and gave Dragonira a long, passionate kiss before turning to leave. "I don't know when I'll be back, so don't wait on me to eat."

Dragonira sighed as she watched the door shut behind him. They had spent less and less time together since he took up this mission to protect her. She appreciated the sentiment, but she honestly would rather he spent that effort with her.

She flopped back into the pillows and tried to convince herself to go back to sleep. Nothing she thought helped. In fact, the act of thinking made sleep impossible. Giving up, she dragged herself out of bed, dressed, and went out onto the balcony.

The morning air from the ravine mingled with the smells from the desert and cast an enchantment over the world, while the early light played tricks with the dunes. Dragonira wished that she could share this moment with her beloved, but duty called.

She leaned over the railing and closed her eyes to listen to the sounds the wind would bring and nearly fell over when she heard an anguished cry on it. She darted her eyes to the perimeter wall beyond the palace and saw nothing unusual there. Looking upward, she spied the oasis on the other side of the ravine, thinking for just a moment that the sound came from there before writing it off as preposterous.

She was beginning to think that she had made it up when she heard it again, this time from below. She moved to a part of the balcony that allowed her to brace her foot against the wall for support and leaned over the railing to see the palace ground below. Nothing.

The wind shifted again, moving the sound with it. This time it came from the air above and remained. Pulling herself back onto her feet, she turned and looked upward, seeing only the bottom of the king's balcony. Suddenly worried for her future father-in-law's safety, she shifted her gaze to the sky above and mimicked the trick that introduced her to the family in the first place.

She had aimed high in order to give herself time to observe the palace's structure as she fell, but the distance from the ground was frightening. She had to fight to remember why she had done something as insane as teleporting in the sky in the first place and focused her attention on seeking out the king's mezzanine. The view was unfamiliar and spotting became more difficult. The longer she took, the more her heart thumped in her chest, but she was finally able to find it. In a blink, she was there – stumbling as she had forgotten to take her prior momentum into account as she materialized.

The sounds had direction now. Consistently they emanated from the door at her far left. Approaching it, she realized they were the cries of a female voice who could not possibly be the king.

Peering through the heavy glass, she saw a figure rampaging in tightly restricted circles; mostly just jumping in place. As her eyes adjusted to the low light, Dragonira could see that this was because the girl had been chained to the wall. "What…?"

Before she could stop herself, Dragonira knocked on the door. The girl whirled around and by her eyes alone she recognized her father's escort from weeks before. Dragonira held up her hands in a gesture of patience that she also hoped indicated the need for calm. A moment later, she was standing in the room beside the girl.

"You!" Kinya screamed as she tackled Dragonira and grabbed her hair. "He wants you! You should be in here! Not me!"

Dragonira wheeled backward and fell with the kitchen wench on top of her. "Damn it! Stop hitting me! I'm trying to help!"

After a few more assaults, the girl backed off and sat at Dragonira's feet, glaring at her through tear-stained eyes. She was dressed in a simple green frock that laced up the front and had been torn. While this was strange, it had nothing on the girl's hair, which had been haphazardly dyed black.

"What happened?" Dragonira inquired gently as she sat up.

Kinya's lip trembled and she shook her head. "Just get me out of here."

The list of places Dragonira knew was very short and as she ran them through her mind, the only location she felt might help was the library. "Okay. Hold still."

Careful not to startle the girl into another frenzy, Dragonira placed her hand on Kinya's shoulder and closed her eyes; both to concentrate and out of remembrance of how they unsettled the girl at the engagement dinner. She had never transported another person through the void before and had to be careful and deliberate about it.

The sensation of moving from one place to another felt different this time. Like she had melted through herself, to a dark world where everything was cold and crisp. Her companion was radiant and warm, but Dragonira knew she would fade if they didn't return to the world in that very instant, which they did.

Dragonira opened her eyes and found that she was standing next to the desk on the library's first floor. Kinya had obviously regained her senses faster, for by the time Dragonira had come around, she was running out through the public entrance. She started to chase after her, but decided against it at the last moment. Kinya made it clear that she found her presence unnerving and pursuit certainly wouldn't help with that.

Not knowing what else to do, Dragonira returned to the royal suite she called home and sat on the bed. "I hope she'll be okay," she said aloud to an empty room.

* * *

Kinya ran as hard as she could through the market, the village, and the streets; until she reached the locked door of her own home. "Mom!" she bellowed as she banged on the wooden slab, unable to open it on her own without a key.

She kept this up until her fists were sore and bruised. Then she collapsed against the door to let the tears of disappointment and anguish run their course. Getting in the house wasn't the problem. Everyone knows how to break into their own home. No, it was the fact that nobody was inside. Her mother was across the ravine, helping with the tribe. Tom… Tom was…

Kinya couldn't bring herself to fully address the memories of him hanging around the house, or waiting in the garden for her to come home. Thanks to a particularly condescending assault from the king, she knew that she would never see the quirky calico again. She couldn't face his ghosts. Not on top of what happened to her. She needed comfort – her mother's comfort.

I should have asked that demon child to take me to the oasis. Kinya entertained the thought just long enough to make herself angry all over again. She knew that the sorcerer's daughter had not done anything directly to her, but she was the reason that she had been targeted. Had the girl not presented herself to the prince, Kinya would have never ended up in Flag's service and she would not have attended the dinner with him. In turn, she would never have caught the attention of the king, who so desperately wanted to bed his son's fiancé.

She shook her head. She knew that she shouldn't be mad at the future princess for the king's lust or the sorcerer's dealings. The girl even tried to warn her, but she couldn't shake her rage. The more she thought about everything, the more she agreed with her mother; the nobility of Libris Del Sol needed to go.

Having given into the fact that she would find no comfort at home, she paced the streets until she was back at the library. Much to her relief the sorcerer's daughter had left. Sure, she had taken her abilities with her, but there were plenty of people here that…

Kinya stopped as she remembered a detail from the day she had been captured. The rebels – dear family friends – who had been detained were teleported into the palace courtyard. This meant that the library had allied itself with the royals.

She wanted to cry all over again.

Her sulking presence had attracted the attention of one of the librarians who, despite her haggard appearance, greeted her warmly.

Unable to ask for what she really wanted, Kinya simply held up three fingers. In less than a heartbeat, she was on the third floor and wishing she was anywhere but.

Why did I do that? She wondered as she drifted around the circular balcony. Eventually she landed in a plush couch at the end of a row of shelves, where she allowed more tears to escape her. She was free, but she still felt trapped.

Small, bare feet stepped into view and she looked into the face of a pink-haired librarian, who smiled warmly at her. "Can I help?"

"Not unless you can deliver me far away from here," Kinya blurted out mirthlessly.

The girl tilted her head, but kept smiling. "I can do that."

Kinya gawked at her. "What do you mean?"

"Exactly as I said."

Kinya's mother once told her that she could go to the library for help if she ever needed it. This was, of course, before the alliance. "How far?"

The girl looked around the floor cautiously before leaning in to whisper, "Across the chasm?"

Could it be? Was there a secret group of librarians who had sided with the rebellion even though they were sworn to their institute? "Yes!" Kinya vocalized a little too loudly before slapping her hands over her mouth.

For the second time that day, the world around her shifted and she found that she was sitting on a path. The little girl was gone, but she called out after her anyway. "Thank you!"

Kinya followed the faint sounds of activity up the path until she saw the almost-floral emblem of the true Cafra clan. Excited by the sight of the nomad tents that belonged to her aunts, uncles, and cousins, she ran into the heart of the camp. Before long, she was pointed in the direction of the tent where her mother was located.

Ta'mika's joy at seeing her daughter was rapidly replaced with concern when she took in her ruined appearance. "By the stars! What happened?"

Kinya explained what she had seen in the courtyard and the horrors she had endured afterward. She told of how the king forced her to change her hair and wear the dresses of whores. How she was chained until the sorcerer's daughter set her free. Kinya hadn't been able to finish the tale before her mother pulled her into a near-suffocating embrace, but she kept talking.

"Oh, my sweet child! I'm so sorry I have been a way for so long! I thought you would be safe in the village. I... I don't... I could have protected..."

Kinya pushed back so that she could pull her mother into a hug of her own. "Don't apologize, Amma. You couldn't have known." Try as she might, she couldn't find fault with her mother being on this side of the ravine for such long stretches of time. There was a lot of work to be done here. Between serving as a liaison for the tribe and the rebellion and taking care of the clan elders, it was little wonder that the woman was never home. "But I'm not going back."

Ta'mika nodded and Kinya could see that, for all that the small house had provided them, it was written off. It was no longer their home. "Does this mean we're nomads now?"

Kinya watched as her mother pondered the question before nodding. "Yes. If we can ever get this stubborn bunch to leave."

That's a strange statement. "What do you mean?"

Ta'mika moved back on the pile of folded blankets they had been sitting upon. "The twins have advised that we get moving well before they attack the palace. Our family here has decided they would stick to tradition and not leave until the day the suns line up — when the library throws its party. This is when the council plans to attack, but they want to attack sooner.

"The tribe agreed to leave earlier if an attack date is provided, but," Ta'mika sighed, "we would need to know when the prince's wedding is for that."

"Uh…" Kinya blinked back at her mother as she processed her words. "I know when it is."

CHAPTER TWENTY-SIX

The spires of Libris Del Sol were a much more welcome sight than she ever could have asked for. The marathon through the desert was a terrible trip filled with many stops because she was still healing. Even with a custom modified saddle meant to hold her in place, with as little pressure on her legs as possible, her wounds kept opening and needed to be redressed. Zellyth was proficient, but they were running low on supplies.

All of this was compounded with the fact that Ja'kal had completely lost himself. He would appear at the worst times to attack them and steal whatever he could get his hands on. At times it was like he had been following them instead of the other way around, but he definitely left a trail for them on the road to the kingdom.

He's probably already here. Elainia sighed as they approached the kingdom.

There was a crowd forming at the gates, which must have struck Rinsk as odd because he grimaced when he saw it. "Something is going on, but I don't know what it could possibly be. It's too early for the Gala of the Suns," he paused and smiled back at her, "which I'm sure you'd love if not for our current circumstances."

Elainia smirked and watched as the walls grew in perspective of their approach. Of course she had been invited to attend the event many times since becoming the Orianna, but it was a taxing endeavor for many reasons. First was because it wasn't supposed to be a festival honoring the suns at all. It was supposed to be in remembrance of the lovers who built the accursed house of stories in the first place.

It had taken generations for the sun-blessed to suppress that knowledge and her being there (or any Orianna for that matter) ran the risk of that information coming to light. This made worse recently by the fact that both lovers lived there now, though one didn't know his status in the celestial story.

Raemona is going to kill me, was Elainia's initial thought on the matter, but she then corrected herself by remembering that Ja'kal was actually the current Orianna. Still, it was she who put the incarnation of her ex-goddess's son there.

"What's going on?" she heard Rinsk ask. As she was lost in her thoughts, they had worked their way through the line for the gate.

"The prince is getting married today," the gatekeeper explained.

"It is a public affair? Why have such security all the way out here?" Zellyth inquired.

"There has been an uptick in rebel activity. It's just a precaution."

Rinsk blinked at that and shot Zellyth a look that Elainia didn't understand. "Is there to be any admittance into the city today?"

The guard, obviously bored, shrugged and gestured toward another officer a bit beyond him. "By his approval. So far, no. Nobody's been allowed in."

Elainia had unknowingly held her breath as the man spoke, but she released it now in relief. If nobody had yet been allowed in, that meant that Ja'kal couldn't be inside. "May we seek entry?" she asked, leaning around her rider.

The guard looked at her first in slight annoyance, but then in vague recognition. She had not been to Libris Del Sol in ages, but it was hard to forget the aura of a highly ranked oracle. Without anything more than a nod, the gatekeeper went to get his superior, leaving them with the throng of soldiers watching the outer walls.

It wasn't long before the captain greeted them. "My lady, we weren't expecting you."

Elainia smiled. Evidently, she had been recognized. *Thank the suns that they don't know I no longer hold that office.* "That's unfortunate. It has been quite the trip."

The captain eyeballed her lack of legs and Cafra escorts. "Yes, I can see that." He paused as something crossed his mind. "You're not here for the wedding, are you?"

She shook her head, impressed by his intuition.

"What is the visit–"

"We need to evacuate the city," she interrupted, "now." The buzzing and the visions in her head had been intense all day, but it doubled upon hearing mention of the wedding.

The captain stared at her, perplexed, before stepping to the side to speak with another officer. They both returned with more than an air of skepticism between them. "An evacuation of that scale is not easy, nor plausible without the aid of the royal family and the library. The entire guard is at the ready though. What's going on?"

Elainia knew the next thing she was going to say would sound insane had it not been her saying it. "I'm not sure why or how, but the whole city will be destroyed. Today. We need to get everyone out."

The two officers shared a look and then discussed quietly amongst themselves again. The captain then ran off and left them with his subordinate. "You can go in. Talk to the head of the guard on the inner wall. We'll evacuate when he orders it."

Elainia let her frustration at this show on her face, but she thanked the man and they moved on. An understanding came over her as they passed through the wall though.

The fields that sat in the shade of the great wall were quiet. The tiny homes on the outskirts of the town were quaint and filled with content families that waved at them as they passed by. The city proper was bustling in all of the expected ways. There was no sign that anything was going on. The people even were oblivious to the fact that the royals were hosting a wedding.

"Are you sure something is going to happen?" Rinsk mirrored her thoughts aloud.

As much as she wanted to voice her doubt, the visions from the smallest sun wouldn't let her.

"Oh, something is definitely going to happen," a voice seethed behind them just before their taratin bucked and fell onto its side. Once again, Elainia found herself pinned underneath something she could not lift. Rinsk had managed to jump off and stood over her with his sword drawn, his eyes locked on Ja'kal, who was extracting a pole arm from their mount.

"Goddess please listen! We've got to save the people of this kingdom! We can skip the sorcerer if it pleases you, but we–"

"Save them from what? From themselves and their petty wars? That's not something we do. From us? You know we had no plans for this pathetic house of lies. If anything happens now, I'm going to blame it on you."

It was strange to hear the goddess's mirthless taunts through Ja'kal's voice. It was also sad because there was nothing of her once best friend in it. Elainia wanted to apologize, but was stopped by Rinsk rushing forward to once again thwart an attempt on her life. "Zellyth! Get the sun-blessed and run! I'll hold him off!"

Hearing the title that rightfully belonged to the avatar of Orianna applied to someone else angered Ja'kal enough to focus his attention on the sand cat. This gave Zellyth enough time to push the dead taratin to the side, pick up Elainia and hoist her up in the saddle on her mount.

Rinsk was a skilled fighter but he didn't have the fury of a deity behind his attacks and as they made their escape, she saw him fall under a blow from Ja'kal. *Oh smallest sun, Adeen, please protect them both.*

* * *

This was only the second time that Ka'say had used the water lifts as transport, but as he tumbled into the water basin at the top of the cliff, he vowed it would be his last. "That was terrible."

Bik laughed as he pulled his commander out of the water. "Yeah. It sounds like fun before you try it. Then it's nothing but desperately clinging to slippery ropes."

"I apologize for ever making you guys do that."

"Ready to go cling to more ropes?"

"Sure."

The banter with Bik was a welcome lightheartedness considering how stressful the last handful of days had been. Upon his return to the rebel camp, they finally had the information needed to infiltrate the palace. The only thing that was missing was when, which just happened to be provided by Ta'mika's daughter. As he lowered himself over the side of the cliff and took hold of the ropes that his comrades hammered into the rock, he allowed the story of what happened to Kinya invade his thoughts.

It had been an effort to keep her out of their silent war. Ta'mika had made it a point to keep all rebel activities out of earshot of the girl once she had turned old enough to pay attention. With the small home that they lived in, this was difficult and eventually they had to move such meetings to the nomad camp, then to their own camp. The move meant that Kinya needed to take care of their home, which required money and for that, she had to get a job somewhere.

Unfortunately that somewhere wound up being in the palace. This was a double-edged sword. As much as they wanted to use her as a resource, they also wanted to get her out of there. Ka'say didn't even want to guess what would have happened to her had Eric not stepped in to make sure that she stayed out of harm's way, no matter how close she got to the royals.

Of course this excluded recent events. Ka'say wanted to pin Eric's recent lack of protection on the attack from the library, but whenever he did the math, it didn't add up. From what Kinya had said on the night that he returned to the camp, she had been invited to the engagement dinner, which had taken place well before the library got involved.

Eric should have been able to keep her from being sent to serve the sorcerer, but had slacked on his watch and Ka'say couldn't help but feel that it was somewhat his fault. He had been working the man hard regarding the maps that, for the most part, laid out the course for their actions tonight.

It still should never have been allowed to happen. The terrible collaboration between the sorcerer and the king to isolate the handmaiden as the drunkard's personal sex slave was unthinkable and only strengthened Ka'say's resolve to end their reign.

He finished rappelling along the cliff face and reached out into the maw of the massive cavern below the library. Ka'ren grabbed his hand and pulled him onto the berm, where the remaining rebels had gathered slowly over the last three days. "It looks like Kinya was right. The guards are out in full force today."

Ka'say nodded, not surprised at his brother's news, but still a little frustrated by it. "We'll have to take extra care not to get bottlenecked in the kitchens then." He glanced at the people in the cavern and frowned. "Do we have enough men to take the towers?"

Ka'ren's face mirrored his in every way and he sighed. "Not really. They can take them by surprise, but keeping them will likely be short-lived."

"So we really will have to take the kitchens and the dungeons at the same time then. Great."

The layout of Libris Del Sol was largely symmetrical, with the bulk of its access ways buried within the curtain walls, but when it came to the underground, it was significantly less so. Underneath the southern wall dead waterways that had been converted into dungeons on the western side, while secret tunnels for use by the warden were on the eastern side. *Of course now that the Scourge lives in the warden's lair, they're exclusively his.*

The waterways in the levels above them were largely a mystery, but if Ka'say had to guess, they were likely used for their intended purpose but fed from the large cistern at the top of the wall. His only basis for this was that the bathhouses and public fountains were located within the arches of the eastern wall. It was safe to assume that they didn't have to worry about guards using those channels to surprise them.

The initial plan was to split up and conquer the dungeons and the ground level of the noble towers, which accented the joints of the curtain walls. The problem here was that they would wind up running across the open courtyard to get to the royal keep, making them easy targets for the archers on the walls. It was decided then that they would have to overrun the multi-level kitchens that were built into the halfway point of the southern wall so they could use the service entrance to raid the grand ballroom.

In order for their small force to not be slaughtered in the kitchens, they would have to prevent the royal guard from trapping them within. This meant taking over every single level of the joint towers and holding them until their advanced force made it into the palace proper.

"Have we found a way to signal between the groups?" Ka'say asked. It had been one of the biggest issues for them to work around and remained an unsolved problem all the way up to when they started sending people over.

Ka'ren smiled. "Yes, actually. We were able to acquire some whisper papers from the sorcerer's study."

Ka'say leveled his gaze at his brother. "You went into the Scourge's study?"

"Well, yeah. How else were we going to find something to make that work?"

Ka'say nodded. His brother had a point, but considering how freaked out he himself had been when he climbed into the ritual chamber, he was surprised to hear that his brother had such resolve. "How bad is the recoil?"

"Not bad. We did two tests, but only lost the ability to speak or hear for a few hours. We can work around that easily."

He nodded again. "Good. Did we lose anything on the ride up?"

Ka'ren shrugged. "Just a handful of miscellaneous things. It was a good idea to delegate everything individually beforehand."

"So we're ready?"

"We're ready."

"Good. Let's go."

* * *

It was a contained chaos that greeted them at the palace walls. The townsfolk who occupied the marketplace and bathhouse were definitely not used to being nearly run down by a taratin, nor were they particularly pleased at having beams of light tear through their stuff. By the time that Elainia and Zellyth plowed through an archway and into the fountain area of the inner wall, people were beginning to act on their complaints against them.

"Can't they see that you're not the one shooting light?" Zellyth shouted over her shoulder at her disabled passenger.

"Doubtful. Whoever heard of a male Orianna?" Elainia retorted. "Even it if appears backward, they are assuming I am the one casting it. Come on. We have to get through this gate before they give us away."

According to the captain they had spoken with earlier, there should have been guards posted at each of the heavy archway gates that led to the palace grounds, but here they were missing. This was particularly strange because of the commotion going on just outside of them. "Why aren't they here?"

Elainia shook her head at Zellyth's question. "I don't know. Think that you can break down the gate?"

The Cafra nomad shook her head. "Too thick. Hang on!"

A quick kick to the beast's side and they vaulted back out the way that they had come, clearing the heads of the villagers who had tried to form a mob at the mouth of the archway tunnel. From there, they followed the palace wall, dodging both the occasional overgrown merchant booth and searing lights of their main pursuant. They had just made it to the next archway when their mount bucked forward, launching them into a pottery booth.

Through a haze, Elainia saw Zellyth jump to her feet and begin... dancing? No. Not dancing. She was signaling a contract through her movements. Within moments, she was grabbing shards of plates and vases to release into the wind that came to her call. The strong air currents flung these down the road at Ja'kal, who incinerated most of them before they got anywhere near him. A few stray pieces of pottery clarified who was attacking who and the mob finally realized that, somehow, the crazed man walking down the street was the one who had burned their livelihoods.

The villagers panicked and ran in all directions. The few unlucky ones who passed too near the Orianna were obliterated in the heat that radiated off of him. Others attacked him from a distance and were able to buy the girls some time to get away. Instead of the poor half-cooked taratin, Elainia rode on Zellyth's back as she darted through the rows of market stalls. They lost sight of Ja'kal again by dashing into a pub full of confused day drinkers.

"Suns... what now?" Elainia asked as she stole a glance out the window before being dropped to the ground by her exhausted escort.

"I have no idea." Zellyth exhaled.

"What's going on?" A patron of the bar inquired before staring out the window in confusion. Catching onto what he could be looking at, Zellyth dropped to her knees and gestured wildly for him to keep silent. The man didn't register any of it, which was to their benefit as the source of his bewilderment moved on.

"Thank you." Elainia sighed before looking helplessly at her companion. "It won't be long before she relays to him where we went. If only we could teleport so she wouldn't be able to see our movements."

"I can teleport," interrupted a smallish man with spotted fur and wide ears.

Both Elainia and Zellyth ogled at him in a combination of awe and disbelief at their good fortune. "Oh, please sir, if you can get us in the palace gates, you would be doing the whole city a favor."

The man shook his head. "I can't do that, but I can get you to the library."

Elainia's heart sank. There was no way she would be accepted into the library; not with all of the heartache she and her former patron had inflicted on it in the past. "Zellyth..."

The tribeswoman nodded and stood up to speak, somehow catching onto her ward's disdain for the tower of learning. "Take me. Take me to the head librarian."

The man blinked back at them for a moment and then both he and Zellyth were gone. By now the no-legged, ex-Orianna had caught the attention of everyone in the room. The bartender spoke first. "Everything okay?"

Elainia shook her head. "We need to evacuate the city, but we can't get to the palace guard to warn them."

"Why do we need to evacuate?" inquired another patron.

The former sun-blessed sighed. No one in here recognized her, which took away the only credence she had toward looking sane. "I'm from the Sun Spire. I have been cursed with very specific visions of the razing of Libris Del Sol and I know it will happen today. I just hope that we can get you all out in time."

There were looks of concern coming at her from all directions, but none of the faces she saw were worried for anything other than her mental state. *They don't believe me*, she thought as a few patrons rolled their eyes and almost all looked away. Only the bartender continued any sort of interaction with her. "This anything to do with the scary guy outside?"

Elainia's eyed went wide as her heart jumped into her throat. "Is he out there now?" she whispered.

The man shook his head and she let out a sigh of relief before addressing his question. "He's more a side effect of my journey than the cause. No, a catastrophic force will suddenly appear and that will bring about the end–"

She was interrupted again by the sudden reappearance of Zellyth and the librarian. A third man, dressed in a combination of Siameran and librarian robes appeared immediately after. "This her?" he asked of the Cafran who nodded.

"I am Nuha and we'll keep this short. If you are who she claims, answer me this; my daughter, Damia sought you out four years ago. What was her problem and what was her solution?"

Elainia had to think on this. She never forgot a private session, but sometimes the details got muddled. To try to remember the girl, she sought her out in the man's face. It was unfamiliar aside from where his eyes sat closest to his nose. She focused on this part of his face and was granted the vision of a beautifully striped woman with golden eyes and curled ears. "She was unable to sleep because of the noise bouncing off of the moons. We knit a hat for her to wear at night."

A smile crossed Nuha's face. "I must thank you for that. It worked wonderfully."

The former Orianna was pleased for both having proven herself and at finding out that the strange, and relatable, solution worked so well. *If only that would've solved my problems.*

"This one here," Nuha said, gesturing to Zellyth, "said that you're wanting to evacuate the kingdom. Is this correct?"

Elainia nodded.

"You know this from visions?"

Elainia nodded again.

"Answer truthfully, have your visions ever been wrong?"

This time Elainia shook her head. "Not since I became a midtowerer. Otherwise, I would not have become the Orianna."

"Can you share these visions?"

She shook her head solemnly. "No. Not anymore."

"I hope you know that what you're asking for is an impossible task."

Elainia nodded.

"Good." Nuha turned to the barkeeper. "I will send out whispers, but you should get the word out as well. Start gathering people here and my staff will bring them to the oasis." He glanced back at Elainia. "Will the other side of the ravine suffice?"

She recounted the visions that the smallest sun fed her and nodded. Elainia had not seen anything specifically regarding the oasis – neither good nor bad – but she wasn't going to tell him that. The ambiguity was a gamble, but one she was comfortable with.

Upon receiving his answer, Nuha vanished. The shorter librarian stepped forward in his place. "I have it on good authority that there is a structure near the river that is indestructible. Would you like me to ask the inhabitants if they can house people there?"

Elainia's mind went blank at this question. For the most part, she had known everything there was to Libris Del Sol and its outlying structures. While she might not have ever visited the place personally, her patron goddess had allowed her a sun's perspective of it on occasion and it always amazed her that Orianna could see so much of the tiny blue marble that floated around her. It was also somewhat alarming that something so close to a place of interest had gone unnoticed. "Is there really such a structure? How large is it?"

"Quite large, but it's hidden from view using a strange magic I can't explain."

She still couldn't wrap her head around this and finally decided to take the man's word on faith. "Then yes. Let's go pay them a visit."

* * *

Storming the palace turned out to be a slow and anxiety-inducing process.

Ka'say had allowed his brother to lead the group through the old warden's lair since his aversion to the place faded over time while his own had only grown. There was also little doubt that the second party would run into less trouble than those raiding the dungeon, or so he hoped.

There was less reason for the sorcerer's domain to be guarded like the dungeons would be, especially since the Scourge should be away at the wedding. A lingering doubt settled in the back of the rebel leader's mind though and it took every bit of effort to not waste a whisper on tracking his brother's progress.

In the long run, they were all moving single-file through small dark spaces. Ka'say had misunderstood the width of the chiseled tunnel during his escape and they had to sneak through it, one by one, until they reached the cell at the end and broke through its door. This they wouldn't be able to do until they got word from Ka'ren that their side was secured and they'd be able to help fight off any guards who would otherwise simply pick them off as they traveled the hallways to the kitchens.

The light vanished by the time they reached the fake wall that lined the back of the cell and Ka'say shushed Bik, who was directly behind him. Bik in turn passed the command down the line until there was no sound other than their collective breaths. The rebel leader removed the first brick and peeked through the hole in the dark.

A pair of bespectacled green eyes greeted him and he jumped backward into the archer behind him. His tactician's familiar voice followed him into the darkness. "About time you got here. I unlocked the door but it won't be long 'til the guard decides to check on me."

Ka'say and Eric removed the bricks in tandem and began ushering people through until the cell was filled. Eric handed his leader a set of keys and explained that he had to check in upstairs and that they should follow him soon after. Then he was off.

Thank the stars! Ka'say released his breath. With the doors unlocked and the dungeon vaguely unattended, they would be able to move in synchrony with his brother's group. This was a worthy excuse to send off a whisper.

Au'de volunteered to sacrifice his ability to speak for this, explaining that Ka'say would need to whisper what he wanted written, while he repeated it aloud as he wrote on the summoning paper. A strange ritual, but it worked as the words caught fire and took the parchment and Au'de's voice with it. A short time later a purple flame appeared above his head and a voice that Ka'say couldn't place simply said, "Give us few minutes. We're still amassing."

An understandable response as they were still filling up the lower level of the dungeon themselves. Ka'say pulled a soldier aside and instructed him to stand by the cave entrance to relay what was going on to those who came through later and then waited anxiously for his brother to send word that they were ready.

Another purple flame and they were off.

Ka'say allowed Bik to lead the charge up the stairs where they met their first guard, a roundish man who was completely shocked to see them and failed to reach for the horn at his side before a sword took his head. They weren't as lucky with the second guard who had seen the fate of his comrade and managed to pull the ropes for the bells of his station before he met his end.

Hitting the palace's basement level, the group split. Ka'say sent a party to raid up the stairs of the southwestern tower while he led the rest of the group down the long hallway toward the kitchens.

They burst through the narrow doorway next to the window where the dungeon dwellers picked up food, and ran into a surprised kitchen staff and more guards, who were responding to the bells. Bik met one with an upward slash of his sword and stumbled out of view behind a brick oven while Ka'say parried an attack with his own saber.

Another guard tried to take him from behind, but the now-silent Au'de caught him under the arm and allowed Ka'say to focus on his opponent, who feinted left and nearly caught him in the hip with a low-flying thrust. The eldest Wiltafoir spun out of the way and accidentally put himself up against a rack, limiting his movement.

The guard immediately took notice of this and attempted another feint, but Ka'say mimicked the trick himself and went low while the guard swung high. A quick thrust and his saber found a brief home in the man's groin, causing him to drop low enough for a well-placed kick that toppled him to the floor. The tip of Ka'say's sword dipped into the soft spot between armor and helmet, and ended the fight between them.

Bik was already on the move ahead of him with some of their compatriots, running up the square staircase in the middle of the kitchen. The kitchen staff was hiding in the space under the landing, save for one woman who was waving him hurriedly on. *She must be one of our spies*, he realized as he followed her instruction.

He met Ka'ren on the next level and simultaneously they sent more raiding parties, down the hallways toward the tower to aid the first groups dispatched. While they were at this, Bik had a few men shove a heavy shelf up against the main ground-level door to the courtyard and barrels against the secondary doors. A single palace guard had made it through one such door, but was shot down by a well-placed arrow to the eye.

Only three more levels to go.

They left a sizable group to hold the ground level of the kitchen and moved upward, repeating their dispersal of soldiers down each intersection of hallways as they went. For the most part, they were unopposed until they reached the top level, where the kitchens opened up to the top of the wall, which had no shortage of palace guards.

Expecting this, the twins allowed their more heavily armed swordsmen, followed by crossbowmen to clear the uppermost room of the kitchen. Once the sounds of skirmish died down, they sent up their archers and then led the rest of their raiding crew through.

Their plans to take the towers were a success and those who weren't needed to hold them were sent along the top of the wall to aid in taking out the guards who were unfortunately caught between the different groups. Now it was a battle of archery between the different factions on the wall.

So close… Unlike the lower levels of the kitchens, this level opened up into a large, empty room. The eastern and western walls of it featured glass doorways that led to the wall outside, next to ornate troughs that contained water from the cistern above. Not wasting the opportunity, Ka'ren drank from them and advised that the rest of them do as well.

Where the other walls should be, were covered sky bridges, both featuring ornate glass and gold walls that allowed them to view the battle outside in relative safety. The northern hall was the one they wanted.

Sensing eyes, Ka'say turned around and found two armored librarians staring at him from the other end of the southern sky bridge. They had their pikes drawn forward, but otherwise were as still as statues. Swallowing the knot in his throat, he held a hand up in a gesture he hoped they would interpret as his meaning the ancient institution no harm. One nodded, but they still remained at the ready.

"Whatever you do, do not go down this hallway!" he commanded the men in the room as well as those below. "In fact," he turned to his brother, "Ka'ren, could you stand guard here and make sure nobody bothers the library?"

His younger sibling went wide-eyed and worked his mouth to complain, but understood the importance of such a suggestion. The raid they had received on their camp only a week ago was a devastating reminder of the library's power. Whatever the reason for attacking then, they were being neutral now. They needed to make sure they stayed that way. "Will do."

Ka'say turned and pointed with his saber down the northern sky bridge, toward the set of double-doors that led to the grand hall where the reception would be; the wedding taking place in the smaller hall on the other side. "Okay, men! Onward to the royal keep!"

* * *

Dragonira could hardy breathe. In front of her was the door that led from the antechamber where she had been bathed, dressed, painted, adorned, and otherwise prepared for her union with Pavlova. As soon as it opened, she would be forever chained to the library kingdom, but under the best conditions possible.

In reality, she never wanted something more than she wanted this wedding now, but the permanence of it made her nervous. *Why?* She'd be free from the tortured life she had lived up until this point, and she liked Pavlova enough. His family more than accepted her. There was nothing to worry about…

… Except her own father.

She hadn't seen him since the day she forbade him from attending the ceremony, but she was certain he'd somehow find his way in. Of course, she had expressed her concerns regarding him and her soon-to-be husband had posted guards outside his door, but she knew they would not be an obstacle for him.

The sound of strained hinges startled her and she struggled to swallow her heartbeat. She could see into the gathering hall that would lead them to the throne room. Across it, another large door was opening in time with hers, signaling the start of the long ceremony. In its frame, she spied Pavlova and fought very hard to keep from laughing.

Dragonira's dress, while elegant, wasn't much more than a red sheer lace flowing out from her hips. It obscured the view of anything underneath with countless beads made of glass and gold, but she had pushed for a smaller skirt underneath all the same. Her top was a cropped, fitted blouse that stopped above her ribs, leaving her entire midsection exposed. The handmaidens had glued gems to painted lines here and she had not even the faintest clue to what it all symbolized. She wore a circlet on her head, and attached to it was a matching red veil that hung down to her ankles; the only bit of the outfit that she had gotten to pick.

She was dressed as though she were a gift to the prince and after seeing him she was almost thankful to be his complement instead of his equal here. Generations of pomp and circumstance buried the prince from head to foot in the red and gold robes of tradition. They looked suffocating and unbearably formal even though their cut was clean and highlighted his physique. Pavlova was adorned with a strange cloth and a gold crown that was not unlike her circlet and veil, except in that where hers flowed behind her, his sat as a bubble on his head. That was perhaps the simplest piece of jewelry he wore as the rest of him was decked out in necklaces, pendants, rings, and other accents. He jingled as he walked and that was what finally caused Dragonira to loose a bit of the laughter she had been holding back.

"I'm cooking in this thing," he whispered as the joined hands.

"You look like one of the banquet tables at dinner," she rebutted in an attempt to play on his words.

"If I'm dinner, you're dessert."

Dragonira's bright eyes went wide and she tucked into herself, flustered. *Damn it. That was good.*

Marboe, the chancellor, stepped forward to greet them. Intertwined in his fingers was the chain that held the Siamera pendant Pavlova had given her all those nights ago. When the time came, it would be pulled from the altar fire and placed between their pressed palms, branding them husband and wife for eternity. "Come. It's time to start."

The betrothed took a deep breath and nodded in unison. They then followed Marboe through the throne room doors and into the next phase of their lives.

The throne room was much like everything else in the desert palace; massive and overwhelmingly ornate. The vaulted ceilings featured large glass chandeliers that dangled on thick cords made of hand-woven gold and steel wires. Not designed for fire, they caught the light that poured in from the upper arches. Supporting these arches were delicately carved columns that dipped down into the fancy crowd that had gathered to witness the making of a princess.

Some of these people Dragonira recognized from the engagement dinner and other banquets. The others she assumed were from outside the kingdom until she noticed they were appropriately dressed for the desert heat.

The couple slowly followed the chancellor as he walked them through the great hall, speaking stories that eventually launched the Siameran legend of the story collectors that Asta had told her. As he spoke, the queen mother's large statues were brought forth to the altar and waited for her and Pavlova's arrival.

"I feel like I'm going to die in this garb," the prince complained under his breath as he stepped into the shadows of the great statues.

Dragonira shot him an apologetic smile and grabbed his hand. Although she was practically naked in comparison, she was feeling a bit overheated herself. She might have commented then, but she felt eyes on her and turned her head ever so slightly to catch sight of the king staring at her.

After what she learned from the servant girl the day she rescued her from his bed chambers, Dragonira felt uneasy in his presence. Now it seemed that the half-drunken lord was feeling her up with his eyes and she quickly averted her gaze to focus once again on his son.

Pavlova didn't notice the tension that his bride felt, but he melted it anyway, smiling in the way that showed his dimples and warmed her heart.

Marboe droned on, with the couple before him and the audience beyond. As his words left his mouth and floated past everyone's ears, sounds of restlessness started creeping through the room. At one point a loud bang made everyone jump, but as no source could be located, it was quickly dismissed.

Another bang resounded through the room just as the chancellor finished the speech that allow him to drop the branding pendant into the flames between Dragonira and her prince. Everyone stopped and looked around, murmuring about the rudeness of such sounds. There was another and then another and people stood up in response. Dragonira thought she saw her father for half a second, but when she sought him out with her eyes, he was nowhere to be found. A long pause between concussions allowed them to resume, though Dragonira noted that the king was now missing as well.

They listened to Marboe carry on, with somewhat less enthusiasm than before, until he got to the part of the ceremony that Dragonira was most eager for. In rehearsed unison, she and Pavlova turned to face each other with the flames still separating them. They then side-stepped so they were between the audience and the altar. She no longer heard the chancellor's words. In fact, she was no longer aware of anything outside of the quickly shrinking space between herself and Pavlova. She only knew the rhythm she had to step in until she was clasping hands with her husband. One more shared smile between them and they closed their eyes to kiss.

The kiss was unexpectedly awkward. His breath was ragged and he was twitching, as if the heat were really affecting him. She must have also greeted him at an odd angle for she felt a sharp pain in her neck. She opened her eyes and met Pavlova's, which carried a look of panic mixed with sorrow. Suddenly afraid, she tried to pull away to ask him what was wrong, but she was unable. She also found breathing impossible and as the steel blade in her throat slowly made its way back out, she understood why.

The pandemonium around them was evident now. People dressed for function were chasing and easily cutting down those dressed for form. The chancellor had died on the flame where her pendant continued to burn; the pungent stench of his hair filling the room.

Dragonira fell with her prince to the floor, where they convulsed in each other's arms as their life drained from their pierced throats. She tried to call out, comfort, or say any damned thing to him and was unable to do anything but cough up blood. She could see he was trying to do the same and failing similarly. He gave her an apologetic look as a final shudder overcame him and he closed his eyes. Pavlova was gone.

Her vision blurred and after an eternity of pain, she joined him.

* * *

Returning to the library was strange. Everything was operating like normal. Librarians, casual readers, and scholars alike were going about their usual business – totally unaware that something cataclysmic was on the verge of befalling them.

In theory.

Nuha was not sure how to feel about the legless woman's words, but she had passed his test flawlessly. His youngest daughter had claimed that she had only spoken to the Orianna when she visited so, as much as he wished that he could claim that the woman just happened to be in attendance on that particular meeting, he could not. She had to be the genuine article, which also meant that her worries were too.

He watched from the balcony a moment longer before the view shimmered out of existence and blended into a soft light that rapidly faded into the picture of the royal council's meeting chamber. As he paced along the stone table it dawned on him that he could have teleported to the sorcerer's seat instead of his own. He laughed at the display of habit.

The council table was riddled with markings that meant and did various things. Right at the edge of the respected places to sit, were glyphs assigned to each council member. When activated, these would send a summons of sorts to the member it represented. He grabbed the tinderbox and candle from the center of the table and ignited the small wax column. He then dripped the wax onto Flag's glyph and waited.

Nuha knew the sorcerer could teleport, though the means of how were beyond him. The man was not a librarian, so it should have been impossible for him to use the magic of one. What he didn't know was if the man would utilize that means of transport to answer the call or if he would make him wait. *If he shows up at all.*

The head librarian was fully aware the sorcerer's only family member was getting married, but he also knew he had been banished from her wedding. The thought brought a smile to Nuha's face. Whatever it was that Flag had done, he was certain that he deserved that. The man deserved whatever punishment he got, but right now, he needed him to alert the town.

More time than Nuha was comfortable with had passed before he concluded that the sorcerer would not show. Even though he did not know how to write/send whispers, the librarian searched the council chambers for the necessary papers. He found none. Had he known where the sorcerer resided in the palace, he'd go visit, but the secretive man had made it a point to avoid the council whenever possible and Nuha lost track of his residence after he had left the tower. Additionally, the only people he knew would know, were participating in the ceremony...

The wedding! Nuha's heart leapt up into his throat as his current quest and the family festivities lined up in his mind. Aside from himself, the most important people in the kingdom were gathered in the keep and they would need to be evacuated with the townsfolk. The council chamber morphed into a room full of smoke and unfamiliar shapes and Nuha tripped over a lump on the floor, causing him to fall hard against another bundle of fabric and...

The head librarian screamed as he recognized the charred face of Gillot, another member of Julian's council, and he threw himself off of her. The figure he had tumbled over was that of Rayya, another peer. In a moment of panic, he teleported himself back to the library and stood in shock over the scene he had just left.

A small, pink-haired figure dressed in librarian garb tugged at his robes, pulling him out of his stupor. She hadn't said anything, but he felt he needed to tell her. "Everyone. The king, the prince and princess, the council. They're dead."

She nodded solemnly and then pointed downstairs, to the cobblestone floor of the public entrance level. Nuha realized then that he had never seen the girl before, which was weird since she was dressed as someone that should answer to his office. Instead of questioning her arrival though, he took in what her simple gesture was trying to tell him. "Yes. The people. We need to get the people to the oasis."

He grabbed the nearest library patron and together they vanished from the library. Unaware of the princess's tactic from a week earlier, he imitated her use of the sky to survey the unfamiliar ground that made up the other side of the ravine. Just as the girl whose hand he held started to scream, he brought them to a grassy area nearby the river. There a few other villagers who had been deposited by librarians ran to greet them.

"It's true," he found himself saying. "The nobles are already gone. We'll save as many people as we can. If there are any magicians here, please send whispers however you can. The more prepared everyone is, the better that we can..." His voice trailed as he spotted the oracle sitting across the field. In a blink, he was at her side. "Did you hear?"

She nodded and grabbed his arm. "Your colleague, Leith, informed me of an invisible structure over there." She pointed. "Get as many people as you can inside, but bring me back to the pub. Zellyth and I — I left a big problem back there and I need to take care of it before it makes things worse."

Nuha frowned at her, but was still too stunned about the wedding hall images that continually clarified in his mind to ask about it. He didn't see the woman's companion and assumed she must be back at the bar. Reaching down to grab the Orianna's hand, he verbally confirmed this before taking the both of them back there.

The Cafra tribeswoman had been expecting them and wasted no time in hoisting her ward up on her back. Before they ran out the door, she had turned to Nuha. "Did you get the whispers out?"

The librarian shook his head. "No papers or sorcerer to send them. I asked some people across the ravine to –" He cut himself off at a look from the amputee whose name he realized he had never caught. "What?"

"No sorcerer?" she asked in an annoyed tone that felt somewhat out of character for her.

He shook his head. "No. I don't know where he went, but I couldn't find him."

She closed her eyes and took a deep breath, cursing silently as she let it out. "Thank you," she told him genuinely before speaking softly to her escort. Zellyth simply nodded at him before they both took off out the front door. Nuha watched them for a moment before realizing he was being watched.

Despite popping in and out of the pub, Leith had been unable to clear it of its occupants. With more coming in, this was understandable and Nuha found himself impressed at the power of the word of mouth. It was something he would have to use.

For the third time in what accounted for a handful of moments, he was back at the library. This time he was focused on his tasks and arrived at the service desk, where he rang a bell that resonated all the way up through the vertebrae of the large spire. Within seconds the floor was covered in its staff.

"I'll be brief because time is short. We have a crisis within the city. Don't ask me for details, but be aware that the royal family is dead. We have to rescue as many citizens as possible by bringing them to the oasis across the ravine." He turned to dismiss them and get back to work, but remembered something last moment. "And by the suns, if anyone has a means of coordinating this, please step forward."

* * *

Dragonira pulled air into her lungs, but it was filled with tiny gravely flecks that scratched her throat and forced her into spasms as she coughed them out again. Once out, she'd breathe in again to the same result.

Everything was black and indiscernible. There was a pressure on the entirety of her right side that made no sense and the smell...

She opened her eyes and found that she was on a floor. It was unfamiliar in texture, but the red color was right. Another bout of coughs caused her to roll slightly onto her back and she was able to see pillars and a beautiful ceiling that faded into obscurity through a heavy gray cloud.

She stared at the cloud for a while, noting that it appeared to be fed from a flow just outside of her range of vision. Directly above her, there was a black protrusion with a sparkling aura that blurred and then clarified as she watched it. After a while of watching this strange display, she blinked and finally focused on the chandelier she had been observing. *Since when did Father get that?*

Dragonira turned her head to follow one of the arches down to the nearest column, which she then tracked downward until she saw a figure dressed in elaborate reds and golds. His hand was extended out toward her and stained red from the pool of blood that was always present when she woke up feeling like this. It perplexed her. There was never another person in the ritual chamber before. Upon comparing this experience with her last, she realized that was not where she was.

With more energy than she had, she sat up and pressed her palms to her eyes. The mental fog lingered, but the action was a childish reflex to get rid of the nightmare forming with her consciousness. "No, please no..." she said before tentatively moving a hand down so that she could peer out from between her fingers.

Her husband – no, her betrothed as they never finished the ceremony – lay on the ground before her, transformed by the absence of life in his once-bright features. The cry that emanated from her pierced the air and forced another series of coughing spasms. These dropped her back to the ground where she curled up into herself and sobbed; every wracking pain brought back a vision of the ceremony that ended so abruptly.

She pushed herself up and found she too was covered in blood. This time she was absolutely certain that it was her own as the drying stain around her was separate than the pool around Pavlova. But how? She reached up to her throat, where the blade had exited as it entered Pavlova and felt a rise. There was one on the back of her neck as well, but both were completely dry. Healed as if they were old scars.

Fighting to look the prince over through a watery blur, she saw that his identical wound had been the end of him. *So why am I still alive?* Something in her brain was trying to scream to her an obvious connection that she had missed and she wound up thinking about her father again. Then onto the clothes he wore during his brief appearance, back to the scars, and then Pavlova's hand, repeating until she dropped the thought on the clothes to focus on how she felt when she had awoken. That feeling was familiar.

Years of waking up on the ritual floor came back to her then, taking the wind from her lungs. All that blood, had been hers. Every single time. It was hers. He had been using her a sacrifice to appease the recoil – or something else. He, her father, had murdered her.

And he knew that I would awaken here this time.

A tingling formed in her chest and rapidly grew to burn as her breaths became rapid and shallow. She pressed her lips together and dug her nails into the floor beside her. Her jaw hurt as she clenched her teeth and her eyes burned as she stared through her memories. He had cut her tail off when she was little. Used it as a macabre paint brush for the circles that forever stained the floor of his ritual chamber. She watched this from the floor where she bled until she passed out. She had assumed he had somehow healed her after he was done, but now she was certain he had left her to die.

Later, she had had a terrible dream where he had sliced her open and shoved three new and pure gemstones into her heart before she passed out. Now it was clear that had not been a dream for, after that, he had the accursed pendant he made he wear at rituals. She tried to count how many times she had put that thing on and was unable. The numbers were too high, but she was certain now she had died every time she wore it.

He murdered me. Over and over. My own father...

Heat radiated off of her as she stood up, unaware of anything but the continuous flicker of rituals – deaths – he had put her through. She didn't notice the graceful step she took around the prince, nor the ones down the stairs from the altar, or any of the ones after that. The world had become black, leaving her alone with her enmity as she paced the halls, level by level.

* * *

Ka'ren actually had hated seeing his brother and group running down the corridor, away from him, while he simply stood there to watch. For the first minute or so, it was absolutely necessary. Those who had missed the fight in the kitchens, or the initial exchange in the hall, all had to be pointed in the direction they had to go. However, once the tail end of the raiding party had vanished from view, it was just him and the two librarians.

It was awkward.

They stood watching him silently, fully aware that he was there. He had tested this by taking a step across a line on the floor, which immediately resulted in them pointing their spears at him. When he crossed back, they lifted them and stood sentry once more. He did it twice more out of an attempt to amuse himself, but found the effort didn't pay off. Next, he figured he'd try some light conversation. "How come you attacked us? I thought your institution was neutral, as you are now."

The guards said nothing until one caved into her boredom with the situation and spoke. "We had been informed that your group was going to attack our gala." She glanced down the hallway. "It seems that we were misinformed."

Ka'ren stared at the women in shock. While the detail of who was to be attacked was off, the date had been true up until a few days ago. "Yeah."

He paced to the glass door on the eastern side of the hall. A sparse row of dead archers greeted him, broken up by the rebels who had looted them of their weapons and took over their watch. One such compatriot spotted him and nodded while Ka'ren surveyed the wall beyond.

They had only taken the southern wall. There was not a western one to worry about thanks to the way the ravine swung north, cradling the kingdom on its cliff. The northern wall was quite a distance off and it, along with their immediate problem – the eastern wall – were still held by the nobility.

The rebels had barricaded the tower entrances which prevented the eastern archers from being able to overrun them easily. Their only option to fend off the rebels was to file down the narrow triangle of stairs that protruded from the side of the wall, which made them easy targets for his own men. Ka'ren hated watching them fall. A childish part of him assumed they would have surrendered as soon as the royal family was removed from power, but they either didn't get the memo when the horns had sounded, or they were choosing to ignore it. He could see it on his men's faces as well. It was over. Why were they still fighting?

Any and all thought was interrupted by the peculiar sound of air being sucked through a million straws and rapidly followed by a low rumbling that grew until his knees threatened to give out. "By the suns! What is that?!" he shouted as he turned toward the librarians, who had dropped their spears and were staring at him with the same question in their eyes.

A fluttering sound, followed by a high-pitched chime, somehow caught his attention over the noise and he glanced up to see a glowing purple puff of smoke. *A whisper!* He steadied his legs against the rumble as best as he could and waved his hand through the smoke to get the message:

"Everything's gone wrong!" came his brother's panicked voice. "A… woman? A thing… Another sorcerer is imploding everything! Return to camp! Get out of here!"

As the smoke cleared, Ka'ren shot another look at the librarians just as a third appeared in their midst. "We're evacuating the city. Everyone is going to the oasis. Help anyone and everyone you can." With that said, she was gone.

There was the slightest hesitation as the sentries exchanged glances and that was enough to nearly suck them out into the ravine as the library entrance behind them fell away. They dove forward and Ka'ren caught one just as she started to teleport.

The landing in the marsh was rough and he cut himself on a grass stick that had been poking out of the mud around the oasis in just the wrong way. The pain it caused was nothing compared to what could have been. He brushed it off to stand as he looked at the sky over the kingdom and prayed that his brother made it out as well.

* * *

Elainia and Zellyth had barely stepped foot outside of the pub before a wave of heat alerted them to a blast of incinerating light. They dropped behind a cart of succulents in time to avoid a direct hit, but the temporary shelter caught fire and nearly collapsed on them.

"We have to fight back," Elainia shouted to Zellyth, who was tossing debris up for the wind to fling at the real Orianna. "We need something more than this though."

Before Elainia could do anything, she was being hoisted back up onto Zellyth's back and they were running through the alleys and streets again. "Looks like I managed to get him near the eye."

Elainia released a breath just as she realized that it was her once best friend that had gotten hurt and she felt guilty about finding comfort in his pain. The sorrowful feeling persisted even as they heard his enraged pursuit behind them.

After the reports from Nuha, the palace of Libris Del Sol was no longer where they needed to go. They were too late to save the residents there, but its walled-off courtyards would serve to wrangle Ja'kal into a space where they could prevent him from harming the citizens. Taking a chance, Zellyth ran out into the open street and made a mad dash toward one of the palace wall archways, taking refuge in the bathhouse entrance just as searing light filled the breezeway outside.

When the light died down, they darted out into the breezeway and toward the gate to the palace courtyard. It was still glowing red hot from the heat and a few well-placed kicks from Zellyth sent it flying open. They ran through and found themselves without direction. It didn't make sense to scout out places to hide since their pursuant was being fed updates on their location by a sun that was more than a little interested in their demise.

Elainia had considered the notion of giving up, afraid that this race would bring about the outcome whose dread had caused her to come all the way out here, but the little voice trying to speak to her through her mother's screaming was saying otherwise. Actually, now that she was thinking on that voice again, she realized that Adeen was actually freaking out. *What is wron–*

The silent inquiry was cut short by a deep rumbling that originated from the near south, but reverberated through everything. It stole the air from her lungs and Zellyth, who still had a pact with the wind, collapsed in its effect. Even Ja'kal was unable to withstand it and stumbled, holding his hands to his chest.

A resonating crack tore through the air next, but this sound was unrelated to the first, sharper and more easily tracked. Elainia cast her eyes in the direction of the library spire, just in time to see it teeter and fail to collapse in on itself. Three golden metal rails shot up through the dome from within, miraculously without shattering the glass, which melted and then slid back over the smooth metal surfaces in even planes that would taper to a point if the rest of the spire had not been in the way. The strange form lifted from the ground and began to crumble, but not straight down. The porcelain white bricks from the spire dropped downward, one at a time and swirled in the air until they positioned themselves uniformly along the rails. Bricks from elsewhere joined in the ruckus, flying in from all directions.

At first, Elainia thought this strange form was absorbing the kingdom around it, but she slowly began to realize that these were not bricks. They were books, enclosed for protection in cases of solid white stone. Before her eyes, the largest store of knowledge the world had ever seen was sealing itself off in the form of a massive floating pyramid.

The rumbles persisted through this and the inability to breathe or think was taking its toll on her. Reflexively, Elainia reached up and caught one of the book-bricks as it flew past, whipping her into the air and very nearly ripping her arms off. How it was that she hung on, she didn't know, but any chance that she had to marvel at it was stolen by what she saw next.

At the heart of the palace – the keep where the royal family lived – the building was being devoured by a lightless, formless thing. Tendrils streamed out from it, permeating into everything they touched and making it simply cease to exist. The air around it rippled as it, and the light it shared atmosphere with, fought the incredible gravity of the sprawling void, and failed.

This is what she was warning about… Elainia thought as she recalled her first glimpse of this prophecy. Just like the sorcerer had claimed in his dreams, a monster with tendrils would take away everything he loved.

* * *

A crunch under his boot told Flag he had stepped on his glasses and he swore under his breath, but there was nothing he could do about it while Julian continued to flail. A few quick kicks to the gut and the king was doubled over on the floor, allowing the sorcerer a few moments of time to remember what it was that he needed to do here.

The statues.

It hadn't escaped Flag's notice that they had used Asta's sculptures at the ceremony. He knew this could not have been a precautionary measure taken against him, for everyone thought he was locked in his apartment the whole time. He also knew that while the gargantuan carvings were visible, the statues gifted to his daughter had to be present as well. Since he was excluded from the ceremony, the only one left to hand them off was Julian, his dear old "friend."

For good measure, he kicked the king again, rolling him onto his back so he momentarily choked on the blood that flowed from the hole where his tongue had been. Flag then crossed the chamber and made sure the locks on the trap door were secured and would no longer allow his rebel comrades entry. Julian had made it to his knees by the time he returned and was gawking at him in horrified disbelief.

The sight annoyed Flag, who just grabbed the man by his hair and slammed his face into the blood-stained brick at his feet. Even with the massive blood loss and the repeated concussions, the man would not lose consciousness. It wasn't fortitude. It was a spell. "Being manipulated by magic feels wonderful, doesn't it?"

Julian let out a gurgling sort of hoot in reply to Flag's seething sarcasm, but was interrupted again by the sorcerer rolling him back onto his back. This time to search the king for a small wooden box he knew had to be tucked into his robes somewhere. His victim spasmed and kicked, a foot hitting the ground with more force than made sense. As the rumbling echoed through the chamber, the sorcerer realized that it was something going on elsewhere.

He grabbed his knife and cut into the king's sash, being particularly careless so that the blade entered the soft flesh of Julian's stomach as he sawed the fabric away. The box he sought fell out as the threads unraveled and he wasted no time in snatching it up. Mimicking his death blow to Gared from a few weeks before, he stomped down on the drunken tyrant's face and used his purchase there to spin on his heel to leave, finally allowing the man to die.

A second later he was standing in his ritual chamber. Another second later, he was still standing in his ritual chamber. Another second later, still there. He attempted to teleport again and again, but found that despite flickering out and back into the material realm, he was unable to go anywhere.

Just as he was about to question it, the air on the opposite side of the chamber began to distort. It shimmered and rippled as though it were trying to melt in the same way that the walls were. Fire ate away at and seeped through the grout that held the bricks in place and as the flames grew, so did the darkness around them. The contrast between the smoke and flames was so acute that when a figure stepped out from the shadows, Flag failed to register it until its green eyes fixed on him. The ongoing nightmare that plagued him since he first set foot in Libris Del Sol was coming to life before his eyes, except something was missing.

While keeping his attention on his daughter, he stole glances around the chamber in hopes that he would catch a waking vision of Ta'nia and was granted no such luck. Frustrated, he finally addressed the monster before him. "You should have stayed down."

"You knew...." Dragonira's pained and anguished voice was barely a whisper in the dark and she stepped forward before fully taking in the sight before her. "King Julian. You killed him too." She breathed out her disbelief and glared at him. "You bastard! You killed them all!"

Reflexively, he raised his hand as if to slap her, but was stopped short by an unseen force that sent him staggering backward. Tears were streaming down her face, glistening golden in the reflection of the fire against her shadowy form. "You knew! You knew I wouldn't die... Why!"

Flag said nothing to defend himself. He had known about her immortality for years. Relied on it time after time so he could avoid arousing the suspicions of the townsfolk, who had (correctly) believed that he was stealing their loved ones. A renewable sacrifice was valuable and he couldn't have been more fortunate in that one fell into his lap. This was a problem for him now, but he also knew if he could take her out again, he would have enough time to vanish before she recovered.

Lightning flashed throughout the chamber as Flag – moving almost just as fast – reached into his pocket and withdrew the pendant that he relied on for rituals and quick castings. Rather than use it to perform a spell, however, he uttered a phrase that caused it to act on fulfilling many years' worth of recoil contracts. He then threw it at her.

His aim was true and the amulet struck her in the chest and stuck, recognizing her as a source to draw power from. She screamed as it attempted to pull her life source into its heart and she reached up to try to pry it off with her hands. A deafening silence fell as she enclosed it in her grip, followed immediately by a thunderous boom that resonated throughout the kingdom.

Where the amulet touched her, she solidified from the smoky ghost that she was, only to crack and collapse into the endless void that became her silhouette. This expanded to engulf her completely before reaching out to pull on her surroundings. The loud knocking of massive bricks hitting other bricks reverberated down on them from above, followed by an atmospheric tearing sound that muted everything else. Brilliant, scorching sunlight poured in as the ground and the building above them buckled and fell into the living abyss that was now Dragonira.

Flag finally started to feel the gravity of his demise pulling on him and he attempted to teleport once more and failed. Stepping backward over the dead king, he stood and threw the statues on the ground in front of her. The answers to both of their questions lie there, in legend, but they would never know them. He grinned defiantly, aware that his lack of knowledge would offer her no closure either.

That was all she could take from him and she just screamed. She closed her eyes, threw her hands out in frustration, and was greeted with a strange electrical hum. Remembering that he could manipulate lightning, she opened her eyes and damned near fell from surprise. Her father was gone, but in his place was an allusion to a creature so massive she could not see it in its entirety. While nothing about it was particularly distinct, its eyes were his.

A combination of rage and terror made her scream and throw her hands out again in an attempt to keep the monster away. As fire flew from her finger tips, she dropped to the ground to cower.

It was gone.

She sat in silence for a moment, surrounded by nothing but black with sunlight pouring down on her. Her heart thudded against her chest and before she could figure out where she was, a horrified cry tore through the atmosphere and pierced her skull.

"What did you do?!"

Dragonira cast her gaze skyward and was greeted by four massive eyes, three golden and equidistant from each other, with a green one similar to her own in the middle. The top golden one was blazing, its gaze scorching the air around her and burned her skin. It had been the one screaming.

Even more frightened, she raised a hand to ward it off and found it grasped in the ghost-like hands of a small, pink-haired girl who whispered, "Calm down."

Dragonira tried, but the girl's grip burned, or the sun burned, or the eyes burned, and she felt the panic rise up in her. She shoved the girl to the side and was greeted by an identical ghost boy, who also tried to restrain her. She pushed him aside as well and threw both of her hands toward the green eye in the middle of it all. The boy and girl jumped on her and she felt a loud pop at the base of her skull. All at once, the black walls that surrounded her became one with her vision and she collapsed.

She awoke to the hot air gently caressing her cheek. It tugged at the fine strands of hair that had fallen in front of her face and tickled her nose. She sat up and found herself on a brick floor amongst a pile of rubble, in the sun.

Remembering the eyes, she jeered her face skyward and found herself staring down the gently glowing green glass point of a giant brick pyramid that could not be in the sky as it was. Its other three points barely blotted out the Sivoan suns behind it.

That was it for her. Overcome by fear and anxiety, Dragonira finally left Libris Del Sol.

CHAPTER TWENTY-SEVEN

Kinya was almost afraid to set foot on the blood-stained, circular patch of bricks that served as the only ground in a sea of nothing. Literally nothing. All around her was what could only be described as a hole, or perhaps more accurately, a bottomless pit that went in all directions. It climbed up the cliff face where the library and southern wall had been. It traveled north and east to devour well over half of the outlying town. It even reached up into the sky in some places.

Ka'ren, who had been the real reason that the librarians carried them here, was pacing the circle endlessly. Throwing bricks at the anomaly and pausing when the skyward protrusions swallowed them in the same manner as their ground-based counterparts. It was as if gravity was the same for it anywhere. After a moment of contemplation, he fell to his butt and grabbed the back of his head with both hands.

Kinya ran to him and had him in her arms before his cries of anguish broke the silence. She barely knew the man, but she did know that his sibling trio had dwindled down to a solo act of survival. *Poor guy...*

Unable to do anything else as he sobbed into her shoulder, she cast her gaze upward to the mysterious pyramid that had devoured the library. The whole thing was cockeyed. Tilted awkwardly so that the glowing emerald tip was now pointing off in a vaguely northeastern direction. The fact that it was floating was enough to creep her out.

"What's this?" asked the librarian who had delivered her as he bent down and picked up a faded gold thing.

Kinya craned her neck to see it, but the woman had turned away to show the object to the legless woman who had been brought over before she and her mother had. The oracle took it and flipped it over a few times and shrugged before handing it back. This second exchange allowed for the golden chain it was attached to fall into view and Kinya frowned. "Hey, let me see that."

Her elevated voice naturally summoned her mother, who she nominated to take her place as Ka'ren's crying post as she ventured over to the librarian. Elainia eyeballed her as she took the pendant out of her hand and looked it over. After a moment she handed it to the oracle. "I think that belonged to the sorcerer. He kept something like that on him if I remember correctly."

Elainia dropped it as if it had suddenly caught fire and she fanned her hand at it. "Well, I don't want it then."

The librarian shrugged and went to pick it up before the oracle shouted, "Stop!"

Elainia then turned to Kinya with a strange look on her face. "Perhaps you should take it. It's valuable and should buy you safe passage for you and your child."

Kinya had imitated the librarian's actions all the way down to the awkward pause just before her fingers touched the pendant, which then led to her standing up straight to stare the oracle down. "Me and my what?"

The legless woman became flustered and blinked up at her, the conflict of whether or not to speak her thoughts played across her face. After a moment, she bit her lip and spoke. "I apologize. My sun is quiet now, but she has informed me that you are with child. I assumed you knew."

It was Kinya's turn to allow her emotions to force her to the ground. While she was not a virgin by a long shot, the only man who could have impregnated her was her captor, the newly deceased king. *And also the man who set me up for him*, she reminded herself sharply. "Please say there's a chance you are wrong."

The oracle cast her gaze downward in apology and Kinya could feel her eyes welling up with tears. "But... no. That's not fair,"

Kinya stammered, trying to find the words for her feelings and failing. "I… What should I do?"

Elainia leaned forward and picked up the dead amulet and held it out for her. "Take this to Lieron and tell the Milmordas what happened here. All of it. They'll take you in since…" she paused, trying to be tactful, but gave up, "they'll feel an obligation to. Make sure you present the necklace to Chiarina. She'll recognize it."

Kinya took the pendant and stared at the woman coldly. Before she could say anything, the oracle had cupped her hand with her own. "Don't do anything that could put you in harm. I know the situation is undesirable, but the royal family of Lieron is a noble one and they won't let the atrocities you've faced degrade your status. They'll see you as one of their own. It would be a good life."

The ex-handmaiden yanked her arm back and wept into her hands, causing her mother to abandon one crying individual for another. Kinya divulged everything that Elainia had told her and the elder Sassin glared at the oracle from over her daughter's shoulder. The look eventually softened as she glanced around at the destruction around them. They had already determined there was nothing left in Libris Del Sol for them, but they hadn't even had a chance to prepare for the nomadic life they settled on. "We'll talk," she said as she led her daughter back toward Ka'ren and waved his librarian over.

"That was unpleasant. Do you think they'll go?" The librarian who had found the pendant turned toward Elainia after watching her associate take the others back to the oasis.

Elainia shrugged. "I can't see the future anymore. Just the hidden truths of the present. I think I might give this up though."

The librarian nodded and looked up at the pyramid longingly. "What about all of this? You said that the sorcerer's daughter did this. Where did she go?"

The oracle of Adeen shifted her gaze in the direction that the former library was pointing in. "Far away, across the desert. She's in trouble."

The librarian looked down, then across the void, and then back at the oracle skeptically. "What makes you say that?"

Elainia sighed. "There are a lot of forces after her."

GLOSSARY

PLACES

Arlogate:
Lieron province known for exporting lumber. Where Flag was born.

Karnindishar:
A village on the northern edge of the Ogait Desert. Located in the Mizzaltolte province. Where Flag was sold to Reddlion and later purchased by Gared and Jinto. Leveled by Flag later on.

Libris Del Sol:
A giant library in the eastern region of the Ogait desert. Also the name of the kingdom surrounding it.

Lieron:
Northern Kingdom that encompasses Arlogate and Mizzaltolte. Also the name of the capital city where the Milmordas live. Patron kingdom to Libris Del Sol.

Mizzaltolte:
Lieron province. Where Rinsk is from.

Nathcaroto:
Sivoa's largest continent. Where the Kingdom of Lieron and Ogait desert are located.

Ogait Desert:
Extremely large desert that dominates most of the Nathcaroto continent.

Orianna Spire:
Home of the influential cult of Orianna. Home of seers. Located in the southeastern region of the Ogait Desert.

Sun Spire:
Another name for the Orianna Spire.

PEOPLE

Adeen:
Smallest of Sivoa's three suns. Sometimes referred to as the "evening sun" as it is the last to set. Deity.

Auvier:
Second largest of Sivoa's three suns. Sometimes referred to as the "morning sun" or "morning star" as it is the first to rise. Deity. Creator of Sivoa, husband of Orianna, and father of Adeen in Asta's story.

Au'de:
Member of the rebellion.

Arminius Milmorda:
A prince of Lieron. Pavlova's look-alike cousin.

Asta Siamera:
Queen mother of Libris Del Sol. Julian's mother.

Bik:
Master archer for the rebellion.

Boris:
Chamberlain on Julian's council.

Caiside:
Cofferer on Julian's council.

Chiarina Siamera:
Queen of Libris Del Sol. A princess of Lieron. Julian's wife and Pavlova's mother.

Dragonira:
Daughter of Flag and Ta'nia.

Dodihuatu Naftali:
Boy who appears in Dragonira's dream.

Elainia:
The Orianna. Born and raised at the Orianna Spire.

Elcin:
Steward on Julian's council.

Flag:
Magician on Julian's council.

Gared:
Water manager on Julian's council.

Gillot:
Harem servant on Julian's council.

Huruga:
Overseer of the royal kitchens in Libris Del Sol.

Julian Siamera:
King of Libris Del Sol. Pavlova's father.

Ja'kal:
Assistant to the Orianna and Elainia's closest friend.

Jinto:
Doorward on Julian's council.

Ka'lee Wiltafoir:
Ka'say and Ka'ren's brother. Killed by Flag.

Ka'ren Wiltafoir:
Acting leader of the rebellion started by Ta'mika. Youngest brother of Ka'say and Ka'lee.

Ka'say Wiltafoir:
Acting leader of the rebellion started by Ta'mika. Eldest brother of Ka'lee and Ka'ren.

Kinya Sassin:
Serving wench in the palace of Libris Del Sol. Ta'mika's daughter.

Marboe:
Chancellor on Julian's council.

Raemona:
The smallest librarian. Appears in Tom's delusions and Asta's story.

Nathara:
Beast master on Julian's council.

Nuha:
Chaplain on Julian's council.

Orianna:
Largest of Sivoa's three suns. Primary deity of the cult of Orianna, which rules over the Orianna spire.

Pavlova:
Prince of Libris Del Sol. Julian and Chiarina's son.

Rayya:
Cup bearer on Julian's council.

Ragnar:
The son of Orianna and creator of Sivoa as presented in Dragonira, Flag, and Elainia's shared dreams.

Reddlion:
Slave trader, brothel owner, and sorcerer from Karnindishar. Sold Flag to Gared and Jinto who, in turn, gave him to Julian.

Rinsk:
Cafra nomad from Mizzaltolte.

Silieae Milmorda:
Queen of Lieron. Chiarina's mother.

Shoa:
The former "tyrant" king of Libris Del Sol. Went insane.

Ta'mika Sassin:
Daughter of the Cafra tribe and key founder of the rebellion against the Siamera reign of Libris Del Sol. Retired servant of the palace of Libris Del Sol. Kinya's mother and cousin by marriage to Flag.

Ta'nia:
Cafra tribe chief's adopted daughter. Julian's war magician. Flag's wife and Dragonira's mother. Died in childbirth.

Tenoch:
Constable on Julian's council.

Thomas Majicou:
Ex-circus freak. Adopted son of the Earthers.

Vika:
Serving wench in the palace of Libris Del Sol. Kinya's work rival.

TERMS

Amma:
Short term for mother. Like momma or mommy.

Earther:
A hairless, tailless, Sivoan-like being with round ears and eyes. Not from Sivoa. Traveled from another realms by the name of Earth.

Moso:
A spice for cooking.

Nargazoth:
I fictional monster made up to scare children or play pranks. Like a snipe.

Nyanyranall:
Language with high and low dialects.

Surla:
Language

Usan:
A dialect of Surla.

PREVIEW OF BOOK TWO

Otnas Ognum was little more than a few wooden docks and handful of fishing huts back then, but it still had served as a major port of trade. It was also where she first laid eyes on the ocean.

She had been a fugitive already by that point, so her travels often led her to take paths less traveled. The desert wasn't so bad in that sense as nobody dared cross it on their own, but the woods contained camps and other wayward travelers – most who thought it to be in their best interest to kill her and claim their reward for her head. The woods were also confusing for she couldn't see the sky readily. When she crashed out of them and onto a tiny strip of beach, she was thoroughly taken by surprise.

It's like a desert of water. She had thought upon seeing it and it took a long while to build up the nerve to stick her feet into the cool, salty water. The second that she did, she needed to be completely submerged. She jumped in fully clothed and kicked around in the shallows that way until she realized that she seriously needed to bathe. She had been alone on the beach when she stripped down, but as she started washing her desert robes a voice cut through the serene ocean winds.

"I didn't think you desert folk knew how to swim."

She had turned toward the voices origin and spied the first of the three brothers that had haunted her since… since when? Where had she first crossed paths with them? She couldn't remember, but at the moment she knew he had her at a disadvantage.

They wore uniforms of a militaristic sort, but had trim in colors that indicated their specialty. This one wore red, so he was the one who could manipulate fire and was her most even match. The fact she couldn't spot the green or blue brothers had her worried.

She and the red brother threw red hot air at each other at the same time, but she made sure to include water with her attack. The steam from the collision blasted Red in the face and he reeled backward.

It was the perfect opportunity to land a maiming blow, but as she marched up through the shallows something caught her ankle and sent her face first into the water. As soon as she set her hands down on the shore to push herself back into the air, she was ensnared by all manner of plant life. *The green brother.*

It took all her effort to breach the surface of the water so she could gasp for air. When she did, her face met with an explosion of heat and pain.

"Wonderful feeling, isn't it?!" Red replied as he stepped into the sea. When he unleashed more fire at her, she turned in an effort to use his flames to release her binds. It was an effective trick outside of the water, but with the vines soaked all the fire did was heat them up.

Dragonira called out as the plants around her constricted and pulled her downward. She rolled backward so that she was sitting on her feet, gaining the leverage she needed and jumped to a standing position.

The air had turned different and before she could make sense of it the green brother shouted. "Vojin! She's doing it again! Hit her now!"

The red brother unleashed a torrent of fire at her feet, melting the sand and shifting her focus from conjuring the darkness to keeping her feet from being encased in glass. As she jumped sideways, the green brother yanked the vines backward, pulling her into the ocean's depths.

Enough of this! she thought as she turned to address the plants that ensnared her, dragging her beyond where she could stand. Not caring about the air that escaped her, she bit into a vine and tore it with her teeth. With one hand free, she reached around and ripped the others off her arms and legs. It was then that Red's taunt echoed through her mind.

"I didn't think you desert folk knew how to swim."

He was right. She had no clue and she kicked and squirmed in an attempt to breach the surface just above her head.

She didn't remember much after that. Just an explosion of pain everywhere followed by extreme cold and darkness – an eternity of it. It wasn't until nine months ago that she learned she had been impaled by and encased in ice.

ACKNOWLEDGEMENTS

The amount of work that goes into a piece of writing amazes me. When I started this venture, I had the mentality that a writer works alone until they emerged from the word cave with a completed book for the world to read. I was so incredibly wrong about that. From brainstorming, to editing, to reading, it takes a team. In the case of this story, it's a fairly large team that has had to deal with my obsession over it for many years.

First of all, thank you to Chris, Lynn, Tabatha, Travis, and my brother Kevin for staying up late with me to populate an imaginary bar with made-up characters until Dad yelled at us to go to bed. Also, thank you Mom and Dad for letting a bunch of pre-teens pretend the kitchen was a bar, as if we knew anything about one.

Thank you Sarah for digging out my old sketchbooks and harassing me about the characters you found within them. If you hadn't, I never would have drawn the Sivoa comics to answer your never-ending stream of questions.

Thank you Stephanie for agreeing to read for me and forcing me back into online role-playing. Thank you Liz and Chailen for making me take that so many steps further so that I could be a better writer. Pru, thank you for polishing up those flights of fancy so that I could see what my writing looked like with effort.

Thank you Lesi, April, and Anie, for allowing me to brainstorm and hash out the pieces that made it all fit.

Thank you to Patti, for patiently sitting through a sob story over text and agreeing to take my beat up manuscript to the next level. I knew I needed an editor and I could not have found a better one.

Thank you Arlene for helping me understand query letters, which literally brought me to tears trying to figure out on my own.

Thank you to everyone who bought the original, self-published, hand-bound, awkwardly labeled issues of the comic (and my apologies for the mess that those actually were). Thank you to everyone who purchased this book. More are coming.

Finally, thank you Justin, my amazing husband, for putting up with my annoying ramblings about this story for twenty years. Not once did you tell me to stop and for that, I am eternally grateful.

Without all of your support and feedback over the many years, I might not have ever done anything with this story. It's a part of my life on par with family. I can't even imagine what l would be without it.

You are all amazing.

H. Gorlitz Scott was born somewhere between orange groves and raised amongst the alligator people of America's most phallic of states – Australia Lite. There, she and her sentient hair have taken to drawing a land of make believe to live in so that she did not become one of the zombie hoard.

This hobby turned fully-professional after she and her husband spawned a swamp elf that constantly needs to be fed. In addition to publishing her own line of comics, Scott has provided illustrations for gaming companies such as Aldorlea Games, Rose Portal Games, and The Historical Game Company.

Not wanting to leave the make-believe adventures of her early life behind, she turned to writing them down; a process that was significantly faster, and more effective, than interpretive dance (which she is terrible at).

Scott continues to write, draw, and stare at spaceships from her home in Orlando, Florida to this day. "Hey, somebody has to live here.

To follow all of Heather's adventures online (including more things Sivoa), check out her website at http://dragonmun.com